CW01432083

G. B. Rubin is the *Sunday Times* bestselling author of *The Turnglass*, written under the name Gareth Rubin. His other books include *The Waterfall*, a companion novel to *The Turnglass*; *Holmes and Moriarty*, a new official Sherlock Holmes novel endorsed by the Conan Doyle Estate; *Liberation Square*, a thriller set in Soviet-occupied London; and *The Winter Agent*, a thriller set in Paris in 1944. He lives in London and writes about social affairs, travel and the arts for British newspapers.

Also by G. B. Rubin, writing as Gareth Rubin

Holmes and Moriarty
The Turnglass
The Waterfall

MURDER AT CHRISTMAS

You Solve the Crime

G.B. RUBIN

SIMON &
SCHUSTER

London · New York · Amsterdam/Antwerp · Sydney/Melbourne · Toronto · New Delhi

First published in Great Britain by Simon & Schuster UK Ltd, 2025

1 3 5 7 9 10 8 6 4 2

Simon & Schuster UK Ltd, 1st Floor
222 Gray's Inn Road, London WC1X 8HB

Simon & Schuster Australia, Sydney
Simon & Schuster India, New Delhi

www.simonandschuster.co.uk
www.simonandschuster.com.au
www.simonandschuster.co.in

The authorised representative in the EEA is Simon & Schuster Netherlands BV, Herculesplein 96, 3584 AA Utrecht, Netherlands. info@simonandschuster.nl

A CIP catalogue record for this book is available from the British Library

Hardback ISBN: 978-1-3985-4348-5
Trade Paperback ISBN: 978-1-3985-4349-2
eBook ISBN: 978-1-3985-4350-8

Typeset in Sabon by M Rules
Printed and Bound in the UK using 100% Renewable Electricity at CPI Group (UK) Ltd

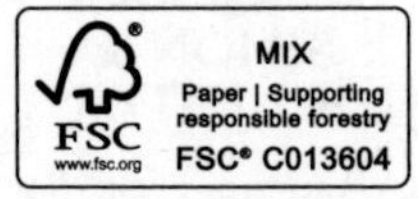

INTRODUCTION

It's Christmas 1932, and the perfect time to solve a murder. In this book you are Dr Kinn Tenor, police pathologist and brilliant amateur sleuth who often shows up the boys in blue. You will follow the clues, interrogate the suspects and finally accuse the killer.

Throughout the story you will be presented with options: will you pursue this thread? Chase the mysterious stranger? Lay a trap for the guilty party? The choices you make will take you on your own path to the final unmasking of the villain – or failure. Good luck.

DRAMATIS PERSONAE

Dr Kinn Tenor, police pathologist and celebrated detective
Johnny McAlister, nightclub owner and friend of Kinn's

York

Melissa Thresh, co-owner of a pharmaceutical business in Harrogate
Freddie Thresh, Melissa's husband
Tim Fortiswood, Melissa's cousin and a senior executive at her business
Eve Tiggworth, Melissa's childhood nanny
Pererin Yarrow, Tim's personal assistant
Simon Yarrow, Pererin's husband, an ex-footballer
Julia Georgiou, a childhood friend of Melissa's
Constantinos Georgiou, her Greek husband
Inspector William Reeves, Special Branch, Metropolitan Police
Detective Inspector Wilkes, Yorkshire Police

Hurley Court

Algy Hurley, Kinn's friend, younger son of a wealthy Kent family
John Finney, butler at Hurley Court
Colonel Harrison Hurley, Algy's father, master of Hurley Court
Mina Hurley, Algy's mother
Gervaise Hurley, Algy's elder brother, proprietor of a gossip newspaper
William Leaner, one of Gervaise's journalists
Major Wilfred Tun-Hurley, Colonel Hurley's cousin
Mickey Plank, a bookmaker
Mrs Blenkins, a kindly postmistress
Rebecca, a maid at Hurley Court
Sally, a maid at Hurley Court
Inspector Rollinson, Kent Police

1

'Oh, Dr Tenor!'

Miss Haverstock, your secretary, calls from the office. You're gazing out of the frosty window at the London traffic drifting past on a December evening. Piccadilly Circus is lit up with a thousand coloured lights advertising everything from tooth powder to the latest Noël Coward play. It's two days before Christmas and you can sense the thrill in the air – kids are jumping up and down, pointing to potential gifts in the shop windows, adults are dropping pennies in buskers' hats, even the dogs scamper excitedly along the pavement. Yes, you love London at this time of year. Parties, lunches and walks in Hyde Park. And what makes it all the better is that the criminal fraternity of the great metropolis usually throws an intriguing case your way too, just to add to the seasonal festivity.

'Yes, Miss Haverstock,' you say, walking to the neat little room where her filing system is legendary and the ornate Russian tea samovar – a present from an exiled archduke – is always on the boil in the corner.

'Will you be attending the opening of the Golden Star this evening?'

'I will. Johnny McAlister's pumped all his savings into the club so the least I can do is show up.'

'I've heard there will be some press there from the *Daily Mail* and the *Evening Standard*.'

'However do you hear these things?'

She peers at you through her thick spectacles. 'I have my ways, Dr Tenor.'

Yes, she certainly does. Her intuition has matched your powers of scientific deduction on more than one occasion. She's been with you through thick and thin for years as you've been lauded by the press as the brilliant police pathologist who has cracked cases when the official detectives were stumped. 'Well, I shall be accommodating.'

'They will doubtless want to ask you about the case with the Treasury minister.'

'Doubtless. But my lips will be sealed while the trial is ongoing. I shall save my testimony for the judge and jury.'

'Did he do it?' she asks.

You lean in close and lower your voice. 'Between you and me, Miss Haverstock, he's as guilty as sin.'

'I thought so. Eyes are too close together if you ask me.'

You smile. There's no one quite like Miss Haverstock.

'And I always will ask you.'

Just then, the door buzzer sounds and Miss Haverstock goes to answer it. Half a second later, your mother bustles in like a navy destroyer. Her visits are rarely an unmitigated joy.

'It's about time you thought about marriage,' are her very first words upon seeing you. She orders Miss Haverstock to bring her tea with lemon and stands before your fireplace like a demon before the gates of hell.

'I thought about it,' you inform her. 'Then I thought about lunch instead.'

'You're twenty-nine.'

'I'm aware, Mother.'

'And a police doctor, of all things. Associating with the criminal class.'

'The police like to think of the actual criminals as being the criminal class. They tend to put them in prison.'

'You could catch something.'

'I could catch something at Queen Charlotte's Ball.'

'Don't be coarse!'

'I'm not at all. I could easily catch diphtheria, tuberculosis, scarlet fever. The list really does go on, Mother. I shouldn't like to imagine the state of the water supply in Kensington Palace.'

'Oh, you're a lost cause.'

'Probably right. Best to throw in the towel, eh?'

Truth be told, it isn't always easy working for the police. Many of them are a bit suspicious – or outright contemptuous – of you. And they only get worse when you show them up by noticing the details they have missed. Still, you take the rough with the smooth. And a certain degree of amusing fame has come with the territory.

'You . . .'

'Mother.' You hold up your hand. 'I am sorry to cut our interview short, but I have a prior engagement and

I can't possibly be late. Miss Haverstock will bring your tea. Good evening.' And at that, you grab your hat and saunter down the stairs, pursued by the sound of your mother's fury.

'Gosh, you're Kinn Tenor,' exclaims the blonde girl seated to your left half an hour later as you sink into plush seats done up in golden velvet.

'Yes, I am,' you tell her. She's a good-looking thing turned out in the latest flapper fashion, with a white beaded dress and daringly high hemline.

The band on the stage blasts out a hot new number and the air hangs thick with cigar smoke as the brightest young things of the age press up close to each other on the dancefloor. Though you've caught a few inviting glances, for now you're keeping your seat and watching.

'I read about you in the *Express*. There was a case of robbery and murder in a Brighton hotel that the police couldn't solve, and then in you stepped and you cracked it and caught the criminal before lunch.'

It was actually before breakfast – you were booked for a game of tennis against the Comte de Reims at lunchtime and you didn't want to miss it, but you don't feel the need to point that out.

'It was all quite simple once I had established that the thief left no fingerprints because his hands had been covered in paint, and that inevitably led me to the decorator. It seemed obvious then that he had hidden the necklace inside the bedroom wall and plastered over the crack so it couldn't be found on him.'

'How peachy,' she says, with deep admiration in her eyes.

'Dr Tenor!' Johnny calls as he approaches. 'Thank you for coming.' He drops into the seat at your side. 'A bit of criminal intrigue about the place does wonders for custom. Hello, Annabelle,' he says to the girl beside you.

'Hello, Johnny.'

'Have you been pumping Kinn for the latest hot gossip about his cases?'

'I would love to hear more,' she replies.

'We were at Oxford together. Kinn was the most brilliant medic in our year.'

'Oh,' you say, 'hardly.'

'No, no, credit where credit's due. The most brilliant medic in our year. Though you did have something to prove, didn't you?'

'Did you?' Annabelle asks, curious.

'The Duke and Duchess of Aston weren't too over the moon about their only child going into medicine,' explains Johnny. 'Not quite *becoming*, they said.'

'Oh dear. Well, they must be proud now.'

'Not really. If Kinn's mentioned in a newspaper, they ban it from the house for life. I think they're currently left with the *Daily Telegraph* and *Sporting Life*.'

'Actually, only the *Telegraph* now,' you say. 'Ever since that embezzlement case at the English Cricket Board.'

'Did you solve that one before lunch too?'

'The second innings.'

'Why not the first?' Johnny asks devilishly.

'Because I was called upon to act as umpire during the first. And I can't be in two places at once.'

A waiter arrives with a round of dark hooch in highball glasses. Yours catches your reflection: tall, slim, with soft brown hair and dark eyes. You down your drink in one – a habit from medical school – and take a second.

'Do keep up,' you instruct Johnny. He does as he's told and drains the dregs of his glass.

'Crikey,' says Annabelle.

'Bottoms up,' Johnny adds, knocking back a second to keep pace with you. 'Do you have plans for the weekend?' he asks, setting his glass back on the waiter's tray. He looks a little cross-eyed.

'Johnny, are you tight already?'

'Not a but of it,' he says. 'I mean a bit of it.' And he shakes his head as if trying to dislodge something perched on his scalp.

'Well, Algy Hurley has invited me down to Hurley Court for Christmas.'

'Oh, how is Algy these days?'

You consider the question. 'You know Algy. If brains were dynamite, he couldn't blow his hat off.'

'That's true. Are you going?'

'Well, I said I would. Apparently, there's something amiss at Hurley Court.'

'Oh, what?'

'Yes, do tell,' Annabelle adds excitedly. 'Is it a case?'

'It could be.'

Yes, it certainly could. Algy was distraught when

he telephoned you this afternoon. 'We've been getting poison-pen letters. Accusing us of all kinds of stuff. I don't know if it's just someone's idea of a joke, but it's pretty horrid,' he whispered. 'And I don't know where else to turn. Oh, Kinn, can't you come down? We're having a little house party over Christmas anyway. And you see, it's . . .' And then his tone changed – someone else must have come into the room. 'Oh, hello. Erm, yes, fifty more hundredweight of apples. And some hay. Lots of hay. Yes, Thursday, please, Mr . . . Grass. Thank you very much.' And at that, he hung up.

'Well, well, well,' Johnny says, intrigued by the story. And he sits back, lost in thought for a moment. 'The funny thing is, I was rather hoping for a bit of your brain power myself.'

'Oh, yes?' You lift an eyebrow.

'Yes, I'll admit it. I had an ulterior motive inviting you along this evening.'

'Tell me.'

He looks past you to the back of the room. 'I'll do better than that. Come with me.' The two of you leave Annabelle to go back to her friends as you step lithely through the throng, heading for a small table where a handsome woman in a daring dress is sitting with a Scotch in her hand. Another glass on the table and a burning cigarette in an ashtray beside it indicate that she has a companion who is currently absent. A lack of lipstick on the cigarette suggests that her companion is male. The woman is in her mid-thirties, you would guess, and has a discreet wedding ring with a small ruby on her finger, which reveals that any money is from her side of the family, not her husband's. 'Kinn Tenor, my cousin, Melissa Thresh.' You shake hands. She has a firm grip. Yes, she's a girl with an air of confidence – adventure, even. 'Kinn's the one I told you about. Who sets the coppers right.'

'Oh, I was hoping to run into you,' she exclaims. 'I've got an exciting little story to tell.'

'And what is that?' you ask.

'Someone seems to be "tailing" me.' She smiles genially.

Those words will always pique your interest. 'How so?'

'Well, it could be nothing, of course. But let's hope it's something. It was the other day, I was just coming out of Selfridges, when . . . Oh, drat, it's the old man.' She wiggles her ring finger and nods towards a large, bald chap with the appearance of a tank striding towards you all. 'He says I'm going barmy. Tell you what, can we meet, say, tomorrow? I'll give you all the juicy details. How about at the Burlington Arcade at nine?'

You had planned to drive down to Hurley Court in the morning to keep your promise to Algy. But Melissa also needs your help, and it sounds like it could be more urgent. What will you do?

To attend the house party at Hurley Court and look into the case of the poison-pen letters, turn to section 11

To stay in London and talk to Melissa, to find out whether someone really is following her, turn to section 34

2

You trot out and into York itself. What a spectacular city it is. Gothic stone arches soar overhead, cars tootle over cobbles and shoppers hurry in and out of buildings that have served as shops for five hundred years. You cross the bridge from the station into the town centre and see the river, the Ouse, surging underfoot, fat with the winter rains. Luckily, today's weather has turned to a light dusting of snowfall, and kids are stamping about in it and trying to catch individual flakes dropping from the clouds overhead.

You reach The Shambles, a picturesque twist of lanes lined with market stalls and drinking halls, which was once the butchery centre of York – these gutters once ran red with blood, not with the crystal-clear water of melted snow.

Your attention is grabbed by a stall selling orange segments dipped in chocolate – the stallkeeper has offered you one and the combination of tart orange and rich dark chocolate is somehow intoxicating – when you notice, on the other side of the road, the familiar hawk-face of Inspector Reeves. This time he hasn't seen you, it seems. He is nonchalantly looking through a set of glass *objets d'art* and you know that William Reeves has about as much interest in glassware as you have in the Chinese mining industry. No, he's watching someone, that's for damn sure. And you would bet all the money in your pocket book that it's the same member of your party that he was keeping tabs on earlier.

'Tell me,' you say to Melissa as she takes one of the orange segments that you proffer her. 'Have you ever met Inspector Reeves of Scotland Yard?'

'Gosh, these are rather heavenly, aren't they? I'll take two dozen,' she tells the stallholder, who happily hands her a box covered in silver paper. 'These will do for Nanny Tiggy. I told her we would meet her at the Minster. No, never heard of the inspector. Should I have?'

'Probably not. Special Branch. Sensitive or major crimes.'

'Gosh. Do you think he would be interested in my little predicament?'

'I think he might already be connected to it.' And at that moment, Reeves lifts his eyes to meet yours and inclines his head a little to acknowledge you. You do the same, and then you both go back to the items in front of you, allowing another professional in the business of criminal investigations to go about their work unheeded. 'Can you think of anyone in our group in whom he might find an interest?'

'Well, I don't know what Nanny Tiggy has been up to on her Thursday afternoons off, but I can't imagine running a major criminal empire has been part of it.'

'Tim has a secret.'

She stares at you. 'Now, whyever do you say that?'

Her words make you pause. They're not a denial, no *I can't believe that!* Does she know something?

'His neck tie.'

She blinks in befuddlement. 'I have no idea what you mean.'

'At this time, neither have I.' No, an hour ago you thought his evasiveness about the subject was curious, but probably of little importance. Now, since one of his magic act props has been used to send a potentially murderous threat to Melissa, you feel it might actually be of some importance after all. 'Who do you know the least?'

'The least? Oh, I suppose it's the Yarrows.'

'Tell me about them.' Out of the corner of your eye you watch Reeves amble past the Georgian window of the Walnut Tree tea room and glance inside. He seems satisfied by whatever he sees, as he strolls on a few paces to a table selling antique books. Whoever he is following is inside and showing no indication of running off, by the look of things. Reeves picks up a thick volume and flicks through it. You have never known him to show any interest in literature, either.

'Pererin has been Tim's secretary for a few years. Very efficient, Tim says, she reads absolutely everything and absorbs it like a sponge. Now, I've only met her hubby a couple of times, but he seems from a different world. You know what these football players are like. Jack the Lads always ready for a bit of cheek. These things just can't be predicted, I suppose. We all have our funny little peccadilloes, don't we?'

'Do we?'

'Kinn, you enjoy haunting the scenes of horrid murders and chatting to the killers.'

'Usually only if they're likely to incriminate themselves.'

She looks at you sternly. 'The word "usually" suggests not always.'

'Oh, no,' you concede, perfectly happily. 'I've met some utterly charming murderers in my time. Some of them I would be delighted to bring home to meet my mother.'

'Do you get on with your mother?'

'Not one bit. That is why I should like them to meet her.'

She lifts an eyebrow. 'That's a wicked thing to say.'

'And yet perfectly honest. Now, would you like to be introduced to one of Scotland Yard's finest officers?'

'I certainly would.'

'Excellent. That's the chap over there, trying extremely hard to look casual. And I wouldn't be surprised if that's the first book that he has opened this year. After you.'

She politely thanks you, and you both walk over to the policeman. He sees your approach and walks quickly away.

If you follow him, turn to 25

If you check inside the tea room, to see who he was following, turn to 17

3

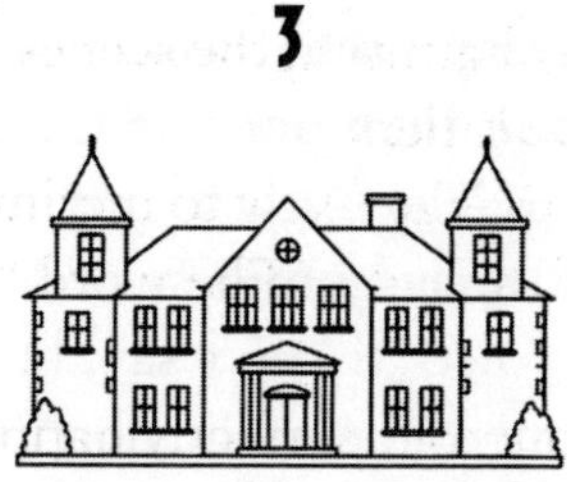

The pub is absolutely heaving. You have to fight your way in, pressed up against hot bodies clinking glasses together and shouting out Christmas songs. You grin and return all their bids of 'Merry Christmas!'

You manage, just about, to get to the bar. The barmaid asks you what you want while pouring a pint of beer from a huge jug. 'Another of those,' you tell her. You have a bit of a talent for accents and you put on the local drawl, so you sound like you're from nearby.

'Right you are,' she says, and pours another.

'I was looking for someone. John Finney. Works as a butler at the big house.'

'John? Hasn't been in today,' she answers. 'Not that I miss him.'

'What do you mean by that?'

'I mean,' she says, leaning in, 'that if I never see John Finney again, it will be too soon. There's something about him that . . . well . . .'

'That what?'

'That gives me the heebie-jeebies. Don't like him. Never have. No matter how much money he's splashing about the place.' Aha!

'Has he been doing that?' you say as you hand over the cost of your drink and a whack more as a tip.

She glances about, then pockets the cash. 'Been doing it a lot of recent, yes.'

'Where's he getting it from?'

She lowers her voice. 'I can't say, but last month he'd had a few too many and says he don't need to be in service anymore. He's got some business on the side and he reckons it'll make him a fortune.'

Well now, that's interesting. You could stay for a while and make some more enquiries among the pub clientele, or you could head to Oxford.

If you stay, turn to 76

If you drive to Oxford, turn to 13

4

'What have you found?' asks Tim.

'Nothing,' you say, pulling back from the cabinet.

'You're hidin' something from us!' snaps Simon. 'Come on, out with it!'

'Not yet,' you tell him. 'Perhaps later.'

'What a little sneak you are,' burbles Freddie, as he collapses heavily into a plump leather seat, sloshing half a tumbler of clear liquid over his knees.

'I am what is necessary. No more than that. And you really should stay off that stuff.'

'Oh, should I?' He bounces an inch or two into the air as the train bumps over some points. 'I should think that's for me to decide.'

'The police will want to speak to you. And it won't do them, or you, any good if you're three sheets to the wind.'

'My wife. My wife is dead, and you want me to stop drinking? Is that what you're telling me?'

'That is precisely what I am telling you.'

He glares at you, puts the drink to his lips and takes it all down in a single draught. 'I feel much better,' he says bitterly.

You watch him for a few more seconds but he seems to have made his point, so you address the carriage.

'I believe it is worth stating the facts as they stand now. Someone has killed Melissa, almost certainly with a fast-acting poison.' Even though they all knew this, your announcement still sends a shiver through the car. 'When we reach Harrogate, they will question each one of you. But before then, I would like to ask a few questions.'

Julia looks around, concerned. 'Isn't it better to do this with us, well, apart from each other?' she asks. 'Only,' she glances at the other faces before her, 'there are some things that we don't want to raise in front of everyone, isn't that right? And besides, who's to say we're telling the truth?' A few searching stares make her change her tune. 'I mean, of course I will, but someone else might not.'

'And who are you talking about?' Pererin pipes up, her tone very prickly. 'Do you have anyone in mind?'

'Well, you wouldn't . . .'

'Oh, wouldn't I? Am I a liar?'

Julia looks startled. 'Oh, now, no, I don't mean that. Only that . . .'

'We know what you mean.' Pererin folds her arms and Julia's cheeks turn plum-red.

'Now, look!' Constantinos says, standing up. 'You're badgering her.'

'You sit down, mate!' Simon orders him, puffing out his chest. 'You just sit down!'

'Don't tell me to sit down. Do you know who you are speaking to?'

'I don't know an' I don't care. What I do know is that I'll knock your block off if you don't sit yourself down right now!'

But Constantinos isn't to be pushed around either and takes a step forward, his chin jutting out as if daring Simon to carry out his threat. Simon matches the pace and they're no more than twelve inches apart, lips turning into snarls. 'Back down, or . . .'

Simon's fist smacks into Constantinos's ribcage, folding him over. Constantinos grunts in pain, but he has more steel than you realized and launches himself forward like a torpedo, his head crashing into Simon's chest, his arms reaching round to bind them together as they bang into the disappearing cabinet, knocking it off its table and tumbling it to the floor. You check it – it's an invaluable piece of evidence – but it's unbroken.

'How about you two stop that,' you say, irritated, as they grapple like teenage boys on one of the seats, neither getting any clear-cut blows in.

'Oh, don't stop them, it's a distraction, isn't it?' sneers Freddie as he reaches over to the drinks bar and lifts a small unlabelled bottle with a little clear liquid at its bottom.

'It's not especially helpful,' you mutter, as Julia and Pererin rise to stand behind their menfolk, shouting encouragement.

'Who's to say?' He unstoppers the bottle and sniffs the contents. 'Ah, amaretto. I didn't know we had any.' He lifts it towards his lips.

He thinks it's amaretto, the almond liqueur. Will you let him drink it or will you stop him?

If you let him drink it, turn to 48

If you stop him, turn to 69

5

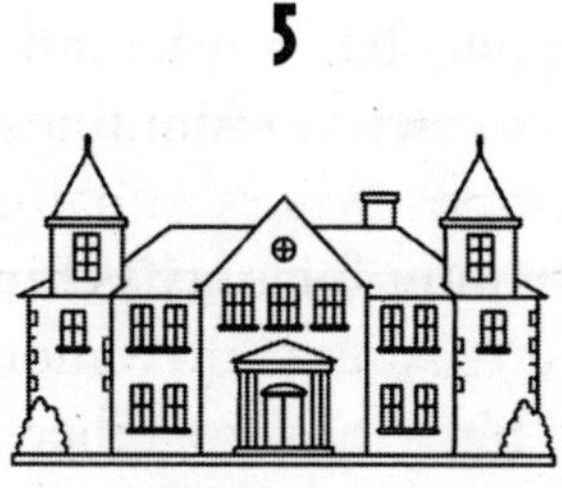

In the drawing room, the household is assembled under the beady eye of one Inspector Rollinson.

'We're all very lucky that the inspector happened to be at the station when I arrived,' says Gervaise. 'He was there to follow up on some fraud case – is that right, Inspector?'

'It is, sir,' says the skinny officer in a local accent. 'Now, I would like to see the body.'

You inform him who you are and, like clockwork, he views you with suspicion. No matter where you are, it seems, the police just don't like you poking your nose in.

Oh, well. With the officer projecting more suspicion onto you than onto every other person there, you take him outside to the body, which lies just as you all left it. 'Thank you, Dr Tenor. We shall handle it from here,' Rollinson says. 'The crew to take the deceased away will be here in a few hours, I expect.'

'And in the meantime?'

'In the meantime, I shall conduct my investigation. And I should advise you not to impede it.'

'It wouldn't even cross my mind, Inspector.'

Well, no, it wouldn't. Because you have your own enquiries to make.

So far, you have only had a brief talk with Gervaise.
If you want to question him more, turn to 19

If you want to hunt for Algy's diary, turn to 78

6

'The best thing now is to wait until we arrive at Harrogate,' you inform everyone. 'There I shall speak to the police and between us we will unmask the culprit. I give you my word.'

Suddenly everyone is talking at once. The Yarrows agree with you, the Georgious disagree vehemently. Tim is asking everyone to calm down, Freddie is glaring at everyone. Nanny Tiggy looks distraught. You gaze out of the window at the dark. You can't see a thing out there. And suddenly, something throws you forward. No, it's that the train has abruptly halted with a screech. Someone has pulled the emergency chain, you guess, and the lights have gone out, causing utter chaos. But you don't get a chance to discover what's the matter, because you feel a sharp prick in the back of your neck, and then there is nothing but blackness for evermore.

Now, go back to the beginning and start again

7

'Would you mind if I stay for a few minutes while the scene of death is examined? I have some expertise that might prove useful,' you say. The policeman looks doubtful, but your position as a medical examiner for Scotland Yard sways him and he agrees. 'Thank you.'

You climb back inside just as the photographer's flash bulb pops, briefly turning the whole car white. When your vision returns, Melissa looks more tragic than ever, now that her friends have departed and the only people present are the police and you. And you barely knew her. You drop heavily into one of the seats. As you settle against the plump leather you feel a scratch on your thigh. A sharp little pain. You glance down to your legs, but before you can even see what has happened, the whole world is turning black. Somehow the taste of almonds is in your mouth.

Now, go back to the beginning and start again

8

You wait in your room until the allotted appointment – some time alone is welcome for you to have a chance to think, anyway. A maid brings you some tea and you gaze out at the Christmas landscape, mulling what has happened and what might happen now.

Eventually it is nearly noon and time for your rendezvous. You steal down the stairs, not wanting anyone to see you leave, and jog to the church, your breath turning to fog on the way.

The church is open when you arrive. It's gloomy inside, the weak winter light struggling to penetrate the stained-glass windows. You see a figure in the front pew, wrapped up in thick coat and scarf, with their back to you. This must be whoever has invited you.

You approach carefully, hearing your feet tap on the flagstones like a dancer. 'I'm here,' you say, though they don't turn around. The closer you get, the more you begin to wonder if you have made the right decision. But it's too late now. And then, as you reach them, you realize what has happened, how you have been set up.

You shake the body. It falls to the floor, a puddle of red liquid seeping across the flagstones. The knife – that silver-bladed knife that has done such harm to this family – is plunged into the gut of Gervaise Hurley, the new lord of Hurley Court. You grab the hilt to keep it stable. But it takes you less than a second to see that the man is dead.

'Gervaise,' you say. 'Good God, man.'

And then you feel a rough hand grip you hard on the shoulder. 'That's it. You're under arrest.' You spin around and see Inspector Rollinson. But before you can say anything, he sees the bloody knife in your hand and wrestles you to the floor.

'Don't you—' you yell, but the handcuffs are already snapping on your wrists. 'I'm here to investigate this case.'

'I'm sure you are. Want to explain that?' he says, pointing to the knife.

'It wasn't me!' you cry, now terrified as to where this is leading.

'Save that for your trial,' sneers the policeman. 'You'll need a defence.'

You're held there for an hour, while a police van is called. You're pushed in, no matter how many times you tell them to call your contacts at Scotland Yard, and locked in a police cell, where you remain until the magistrate says you're to be held until trial.

Three months later, you're in the dock at the Old Bailey. It's a popular spectacle: the police pathologist on trial for an especially brutal murder. Some of your old colleagues give evidence in your favour, one or two give evidence against you. The prosecution suggests that all those cases where you attended have turned your brain and you became obsessed with seeing death up close. 'Is it so hard to understand that? No? Then it cannot be hard to condemn it,' the prosecuting barrister tells the jury.

Over and over, from every angle, you tell your side of the story, but it's to no avail. And when the foreman of the jury stands up, it's to announce a verdict of 'guilty'. The judge shakes his head and tells you that it's a capital crime, but on this occasion, he will be lenient, given your years of service to the Crown. Life in prison, with possibility of parole after thirty years. You will have a long time to contemplate where you went wrong.

As you are led back down to the cells, you see someone who was at Hurley Court with you. They are laughing at you. Again and again and again.

Now, go back to the beginning and start again

9

'Freddie!' you call.

'Oh, it's you,' he mutters as you catch up with him.

'Yes, me. And I want to know what just happened.'

'Do you now? Why?' He doesn't care about being rude.

'Call it intellectual curiosity.'

'I'll call it many things, but not that,' he sneers. You wait for him to continue. 'All right. It's her. Pererin Yarrow.'

'What about her?'

'Yes,' he muses, kicking his feet irritably. 'What is it about her? I don't even know myself. But she knows what she's doing.'

'Care to enlighten me?'

'She's a little minx. Looks like butter wouldn't melt in her mouth. But it would. And that great heap of mud of her husband knows it too. I don't think he even minds. Some men get a kick out of it, I suppose, seeing their wives drive other men crazy.' You look at him with a mix of disapproval and pity. 'Oh, don't bother with that. I know what I'm doing.' He laughs at you. 'Whatever I get into, I'll get myself out of it again. I've had enough practice.' And he chuckles to himself and walks away.

You let him. You've had enough of his presence for a while, and treat yourself to a sticky bun at the tea room. After ten minutes' thought, you follow in Freddie's footsteps, back to the train.

Turn to 70

10

'Come, come, the truth!' you say. 'I know that is a lie.' But the effect is only to make Nanny Tiggy burst into tears. Julia goes to comfort her, looking daggers at you. You feel a little guilty.

Yes, it probably is time to let everyone have a moment to mentally deal with what they have just witnessed. You gaze from one to another, then at the terrible sight stretched out before you on the table: a beautiful, vivacious young woman whose future has been cruelly and violently stolen from her.

For twenty minutes that feel like hours, you are all quiet, alone with your thoughts. Six of the seven people before you are remembering, regretting, celebrating and saying goodbyes. And one of them is plotting, scheming, mocking and quietly rejoicing at the scene that they have engineered.

When you finally roll into Harrogate station it feels like a blessing. The wheels squeal to a stop and you shout to the platform guard to fetch the police. He looks befuddled, but you repeat the instruction and he scurries off. Until the officers arrive, you let everyone mill about on the platform, but you will allow no one to leave the station. Simon grumbles but no one tries to defy your order.

A bobby, as surprised as the station guard, nearly falls over when you tell him what has happened, and even before you have finished explaining, he is sprinting away to bring a senior officer. While you all continue to wait, Tim sidles up to you. 'Look,' he whispers, 'between you and me, I think there's something up with Miss Tiggworth.'

'Oh?' you reply.

'You know how she didn't want to tell you where she really was when Melissa was nearly run over?'

'Yes.'

'It's – I don't know if it has any bearing, but it's just so odd.'

'Out with it, man.'

'Well, she's been asking me recently about adoption agencies. She thought I might have some influence because of my position at the company. I think she wants to adopt a child.'

'At her age?' you ask sceptically.

'I know. I said that myself. Couldn't put her off it, though. Very odd.'

'Very.'

A Detective Inspector Wilkes arrives and takes charge efficiently, bringing with him a photographer and an ambulance. He takes everyone's details and addresses, making no comment about your costumes and how absurd you must all look, given the circumstances. But he is most interested in Freddie – for a police detective, a drunken husband might as well have a hand-painted sign saying 'murderer' hung around his neck.

Wilkes orders everyone to the police station to give statements.

If you agree to go, turn to 68

If you ask to stay behind and observe while the scene of the crime is examined, turn to 7

11

'Sorry, I made a promise to another chum,' you tell Melissa. 'And I'll never break a promise if I can help it.'

'Oh, well, I don't expect it's much anyway.'

'Probably not. It will all come out in the wash. Now, Johnny, how about a Buck's Fizz?'

Turn to 55

12

You accept Pererin and Simon's offer. Freddie's seems less than wholly sincere and you could do without Nanny Tiggy fussing over you.

You walk to their home, a neat little terraced house on a gentle hill. It's the sort of street where everyone knows everyone.

You're tired and hungry. Pererin fetches you all some soup and bread, and you listen to the wireless for a while. You've had enough of asking questions and following lines of enquiry. You just want to rest, and so you all head to bed.

You have a little box room at the back, with a bed that only just fits in it. But it's warm and comfortable enough and you're dead tired, so you drift off to sleep almost immediately.

That's why when you're woken maybe an hour later, in the pitch black, you're so groggy that you look the figure standing over you up and down, wondering where you are, instead of grabbing for the small revolver pointing straight at your heart. And when it fires, it's like you're falling asleep again.

Now, go back to the beginning and start again

The drive up to Oxford is a three-hour journey if you're going fast. You drive like an absolute demon and make it in two, nipping past carloads of families off to visit grandparents for Christmas. As you pull into the old university town, you feel a bit nostalgic for your student days. Such high times! Well, you're past that now and so park your little Roadster in front of a fine-looking pub tucked away behind Hertford College, which a painted sign announces as the Turf Tavern. Raucous music is playing, and laughter and singing is spilling from every window. A chaotic mass of students trips out from the front door, pouring drinks down their throats. One of them spies your car.

'Crikey, chaps, have you seen this little jalopy?' he yells to the others. 'MG Roadster. Latest little model.' He turns to you. 'I say, any chance of a quick spin?'

This is just what you need. 'Certainly,' you say. 'Hop in.' You hit the accelerator hard and burst out onto the road as if the devil himself is after you. 'Hold on.' You roar a high-speed circuit of the city, past the snow-covered colleges and full-to-bursting churches, so quick your companion can barely keep his breath, and then skid to a stop back outside Hertford College.

'Come on in!' cries your delighted new pal, who mentions in passing that his name is Canute, like the doomed king. 'Let's get to the bar before it runs dry.'

'Don't mind if I do. Actually, I'm trying to track down an old chum. Was here somewhere between 1923 and 1928.' Judging by Leaner's appearance, that would have been his time here.

'Old Boy, eh? Well, let's call in at the Porters' Lodge and they can tell you.'

You stop off at the lodge just inside the imposing entrance arch, where the bowler-hatted porters politely do as Canute asks and allow you a peek at the college records. You hunt through a huge leather-bound book with lists of names going back a hundred years in increasingly faded ink. But it's pretty clear that no W. Leaner was a student here during the years you check, and you look at a few years either side to make sure. But then, in the list of students matriculating in 1925, you do spot a name that rings a distant bell: D. Vickers.

'Good Lord,' you whisper to yourself.

'Hmmm?' asks Canute.

'Oh, something I wasn't expecting at all.' Your mind is ablaze with a chain of events, and you laugh and slam the book shut.

'All finished then? Well, let's go up to the party!' Canute says happily.

'Thanks, old chap. But I've got somewhere else I need to be. And it's not going to be a party.'

You speed back to Hurley Court. Along with what you discerned at the pharmacy, you have learned some interesting things today.

A few hours later, you are driving through the village, which is quite dark by now, with light leaking from the houses. Passing along the High Street you notice a familiar face coming out of a little tumbledown cottage: Rebecca the maid. And you know that she has seen you because she suddenly jumps back inside and shuts the door. You drive on, making no sign that you saw her, but then pull into a side street with a hardware shop and kill the engine. You creep back to the corner and watch Rebecca emerge furtively from her house and tramp quickly in the direction of Hurley Court. You think for a minute. It comes with your job that people are often less than happy to see you, but this was quite a strong reaction.

If you stop and investigate, turn to 88

If you go straight to Hurley Court, turn to 38

'All right,' you say. 'Go ahead.'

Tim steps forward and yanks on the red chain. For a few seconds, nothing happens. And then there's a screaming of metal as the brakes engage hard on the wheels. You're all thrown forward as the train judders to a halt. The lights go off and you're left in perfect darkness, only the twinkling stars through the windows showing any light.

'You idiot!' yells a man's voice – Simon, you can tell. 'Now what're we going t'do?'

There is the sound of shuffling and complaining as people try to get to their feet.

'Does anyone have a light?' you say. No one speaks up, which tells you all you need to know.

'You got us into this, you get us out of it,' Simon grumbles.

The driver is in the locomotive. You should tell him what's happening.

If you try to get out of the carriage and round to the driver, turn to 102

If you sit tight until he comes to you, turn to 42

You don't move, you can't risk anything somehow contaminating the body. Pererin, who looks very pale but is keeping herself together, tends to Nanny Tiggy. 'It's all right,' she says. 'She's breathing fine. Just fainted.'

'Give her some brandy,' you say, and return to Melissa's body. She's still as warm as life. You check her over and find nothing to note, until you come to a strange abrasion on her back. A little spot leaking ruby-red blood into her fine dress. You have seen countless little marks like it. Doctors and nurses make them all the time.

'What's done that?' Simon asks.

'It looks like a hypodermic needle.' And it fits with the way she has died. Had she suffered a heart seizure, she would have made more noise, thrashed about, even. But a lethal injection could have killed painlessly in seconds. The question is: how could anyone have done it in plain sight?

You check inside the box. You are as thorough as can be, making sure there are no more hidden compartments, holes or flaps. You're convinced: there's no needle here. And even if there were, how could anyone have administered the injection? It's conceivable that it was done before she entered the cabinet, but barely credible that she wouldn't have felt it and started in pain – the prick of a needle in your flesh is hard to ignore. It's also a bit far-fetched to think that no one would have noticed one of you walking around with a full syringe. No, how Melissa was killed is, at this time, inexplicable.

'A needle?' Julia asks faintly, desperately. 'But she was always afraid of them. Said she hated the idea. She couldn't possibly have.'

'I don't think this was her doing.'

Julia puts her hand to her mouth. 'You mean she was . . .'

'Murdered. I believe she was murdered.'

'Oh!' cries Tiggy, who has regained consciousness. 'My girl. My little girl.'

'But she can't have been,' gasps Tim. 'How?'

'That is what I intend to find out,' you tell him earnestly.

The train shudders and it feels like it is being shaken by an angry god.

'It was . . . it was one of us?' Tim blinks in amazement.

'I can't jump to that conclusion. But it seems so.'

'No, but no,' Julia insists. 'Someone else. It must have been someone who . . . who got the train or . . . or . . .' She is beginning to panic now.

'Look around you, do you see anyone else?'

'Bet you it was 'im,' mutters Simon, narrowing his eyes at Freddie. In answer, Freddie stands and silently squares up to his employee's husband.

'I . . .' Julia stumbles to the rear of the carriage and checks through the luggage compartment, wildly throwing bags aside as if she will discover someone lurking beneath them. You all watch her in silence. She soon gives up and simply stares at her friend, tears making her mascara run. Constantinos goes to her and pulls her into his chest.

'She is at peace now,' he says.

'We have to stop the train!' Tim says, lunging for the emergency chain.

If you let him halt the train, turn to 14

Or do you want to continue on? Turn to 98

16

York Minster looms above you, its square towers stretching almost to heaven itself. A guide book that you pick up from a hawker outside tells you that it was built in stages, beginning in the thirteenth century. And today it is mobbed by a mix of religious worshippers and tipsy tourists.

You have to fight your way in, there are so many either desperate to say silent prayers or to coo at the arched roof. Every pew is full and the service is ending, with a terribly handsome priest in his mid-twenties conducting the affair. He smiles broadly, enjoying himself by the looks of things. Perhaps at this time of year he lets his hair down a bit – it's blond and curly, so letting it down suits him – and has a jolly time along with the congregation.

You find Nanny Tiggy at the end of a pew, staring transfixed at the divine as it all wraps up and the worshippers begin to drift away chatting, replaced in their spots by the out-of-town gawpers. 'Isn't he marvellous,' she whispers.

'Who? The vicar?' Melissa asks, sounding surprised. 'Never had you pegged as a religious sort, Tiggy. I don't recall you so much as setting foot inside a church.'

'Oh, well, times change,' the old servant replies, flustered, tearing herself away from the vision before her.

'Shall we head out for afternoon tea? Where do you fancy?'

'Oh, I'm not so hungry, Mrs Thresh. Why don't you young people go out and have a nice time without me. I'll be happy here by myself.'

You glance at the good-looking priest, who is chatting to a couple of the congregants and shaking hands. There's a bit of a fan club around him, made up of ladies young and old. He does his best to give them all a little of his golden time but eventually he has to remove himself.

'Is there another service soon?' you casually enquire.

'Oh, well now, I think there is,' Nanny Tiggy replies lightly, avoiding your gaze.

'And would that priest be the one conducting it?'

She clears her throat and hesitates before answering. 'I really couldn't say.'

'I'm sure you could if you wanted to,' you tell her, doing your best not to smile. She simpers self-consciously. 'Melissa, we know when we are not wanted. Let's be off. Your husband must be more in want of our company than your old nanny.'

'Now I see why you wanted to come to York, Tiggy, old thing,' Melissa says, screwing up her face as she tries not to giggle fondly at her love-sick old servant. 'All right, we'll be off to track down Freddie, in the vain hope that he hasn't already got himself into trouble.'

She threads her arm through yours and you leave the grand old church.

'Was it her idea to come here, then?' you enquire as you stride through the cathedral precincts.

'Yes. She said she's wanted to visit the Minster for yonks, but now I see there's another attraction to be found.' And this time she lets out a full-throated whoop of laughter. 'Now, it's about time we headed back.'

You agree and saunter through the pretty highways and byways of the old town. The light is beginning to fail and the shop windows glow with electric lights. The shoppers and joy-seekers draw their coats tighter – and glance harder at Melissa's thin covering – as the chill finds its way down collars and between layers of fabric. The cocoa sellers and roast chestnut-mongers do a roaring trade as people filter away back to their homes and their hotels, keen for one last sweet mouthful before an evening of carols and children who won't go to bed.

The white blanket crunches thicker as you wend your way back to the station.

'. . . and it's going to be such fun. Do you know, we've been practising for a month. Now, it won't be Theatre Royal standard . . .' Melissa is saying as you emerge onto the concourse. But you aren't listening to her, you're focusing on another sound nearby. Voices are yelling, two of them. One sounds threatening, the other demanding calm. You peer over to the corner where the station pub – The Huntsman, according to its cheaply painted sign – is situated. And you recognize the three people working out their differences.

Simon Yarrow has thrown aside his jacket and has the dishevelled figure of Freddie Thresh pinned against the brick wall of the saloon bar. 'Come close to 'er again and I'll break yer neck, you little . . .' Simon is yelling.

'For God's sake, Simon,' Pererin says as she tries to pull him away. 'You're as drunk as he is.'

For his part, Freddie seems half-cut even while he sneers, 'You don't know what she . . .' He breaks off when he sees you and Melissa, and his head hangs down.

'My God, look at him,' Melissa says contemptuously. 'What a buffoon.' She stares at him for a moment, then turns and strides towards the train, her heels clicking on the damp floor.

Simon lets go and Freddie slumps down, coming to rest on his haunches. Simon takes Pererin by the arm and steers her back into the pub, leaving Freddie to sort himself out.

You walk over and he slowly lifts his face until he is looking up at you. You see he has a split lip that is leaking a little blood. 'Spare a hanky?'

'I don't have one. You might not need one if you leave other men's wives alone.'

'You don't understand.'

'Don't I? Would you care to enlighten me?'

'She led me on.'

'I'm sure she did.'

'Very flirtatious.'

'Of course.' You glance through the window of the pub. It takes a while for your eyes to penetrate the thick mist of smoke, but then you make out, in a corner, the Yarrows talking, their heads close together. Pererin's anger at her husband seems to have gone. She takes a drink from a glass – there's a large collection of empties in front of them – and goes back to speaking with an earnest look on her face. 'She's a pretty thing.'

'And she knows it,' he mumbles, but the words trail away into a deep sigh. He looks as if he's about to fall asleep but shakes himself back awake. He rolls onto all fours then pushes himself to his feet, swaying a little like a branch in the wind. 'All is well.' He snorts in derision at his own predicament and walks unevenly towards the train. Something tells you it's worth talking to the Yarrows. But that would mean letting Freddie stagger on to the carriage, where Melissa is probably on her own. God knows what that would mean.

If you pursue Freddie, turn to 9

If you go into the pub, turn to 89

17

It's packed inside with jolly tourists and a few locals grumbling about the tourists. You look around but can't see a familiar face. 'Over there,' says Melissa, digging you in the ribs. Yes, in a corner, half-hidden by a large wooden seat that looks like it has been ripped from a castle, is Constantinos Georgiou. He's deep in a conspiratorial-looking conversation with a fat man sporting a huge, bushy white beard and whiskers. They seem to be arguing over something and at one point Constantinos slams his palm onto the table, only for the other man to grab his wrist and pin it down, remonstrating with him. You can't hear what they're saying above the general din in the tea room, but you can tell by their facial expressions that it's not entirely friendly.

Constantinos tears his hand away and jumps up angrily from the table. You and Melissa quickly turn your backs and huddle behind a table so that he doesn't see you as he storms out of the shop.

You glance at each other in surprise. Then, without consulting her, you immediately follow.

Turn to 22

18

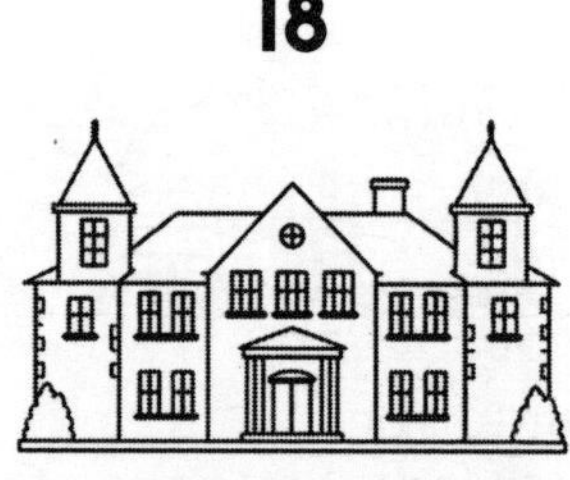

You watch as the two men leave. Algy finishes talking to his friends and returns a minute later. 'What's the matter with you?' he asks, having seen your face.

For some reason, you think it's best to keep to yourself the fact that there are two men looking for his brother. And you have something else to deal with right now.

Turn to 114

19

'May I have a few words?' you say to Gervaise, finding him smoking in the dining room.

'Oh, if you must.'

'How about outside, for a little privacy?'

'Sounds delightful.'

You both go out of the back of the house, into the kitchen garden. Gervaise lights another cigarette and tosses the spent match aside. 'This is the bit where you grill me. Am I correct?'

'As it happens, you are not,' you say. 'But I do have a few questions to put to you.'

'Put away, dear Doctor, put away.'

'Your newspaper. Doing well, is it?'

'Wonderfully well. We have upset all the best people, and made all the worst chuckle.'

'And into which camp do you fall?'

He grins. 'Do you know, I like the cut of your jib. You should write a column for me. *Murderers I have known and liked*. Shall we say a guinea for five hundred words each week?'

'From what I understand of your finances, a shilling would be a stretch for you right now.'

'Touché. Your spies tell you right. Yes, dear Doctor, the cupboard is largely bare.' He taps ash from his cigarette. 'But we really have put the wind up some insufferable bores, so it was all worth it, in the end.'

'To whom do you owe the money?'

He takes a thoughtful drag on his cigarette. 'I suppose there's no harm in telling you. I had a deal going with a turf accountant.'

'You mean a bookie.'

'I do mean a bookie. We were going halves on a racehorse. Only I had a bit of a cashflow problem and I had to temporarily divert the funds that he was putting into it.'

'And now he wants his money back.'

'With knobs on. But poor old Mickey Plank, he won't be seeing it for a long while. He's vowed revenge upon me, of course, but I'm not too worried. He's all mouth and no trousers.'

You change tack. 'How did you get on with your father?'

'Couldn't stand him. Next question.'

'I intend to keep on this one. What couldn't you stand about him?'

'Oh, the archaic thoughts, the priggish attitude to my

business venture, the way he treated my mother. All of the above and more, now I come to consider it.'

'And what action did you take?'

'Well, obviously I attempted to stab him to death in the church, and when that didn't work, I bopped him over the head with a hammer. Is that right? Is that what I'm supposed to say?'

'No,' you sigh, 'but it's what I expected you to say. Lord above, Gervaise, you're predictable. And so utterly dull for it.'

He smiles ruefully. 'You know, sometimes I forget that you're not one of the coterie around here. You actually have something going on upstairs. All right, if you want to know something, I've suspected for a while that Finney's up to no good.'

'What do you mean by that?'

'I mean by that that he seems to be passing little packages to old Major Tun-Hurley. I've seen it twice. Little parcels wrapped in brown paper. All done in the shadows. Now, the old major's as straight as an arrow in his dealings, from what I can tell, so God only knows what that's all about.' He blows little rings of smoke that drift in the air. 'Now, may I depart? I have a glass of brandy warming by the fire.'

'Yes, go.'

He saunters off, and you mull what Gervaise has said. You suspect there's more to it than he is letting on. Yes, it's time to look into Gervaise's affairs. And that means a trip to London, you think.

You head up to your room to change into your travelling clothes. But before you so much as discard your jacket you spy something on your bed. It's a note folded in half. You open it. The writing is in a barely legible scrawl – a first impression would make most people think it was written by a young child, but you know the truth: someone has written it using their weak hand in order to disguise their handwriting.

Come to the church at noon. Not before.

You glance out into the corridor. No one about. Hmmm, what to do? If you drive up to London, you will miss this appointment. But you do suspect there's much to be discovered in Gervaise's murky business dealings, and if you wait until after meeting this shadowy note-writer (who may or may not turn up, anyway), it will probably be too late to get up to London, poke about and come back down before the roads are too dark and snowy to make the trip.

If you go to the church, turn to 61

If you drive to London to investigate Gervaise, turn to 82

20

You and Algy head for the billiards room. It's a gloomy chamber, with the lights on the walls heavily shaded.

Also on the walls are at least two dozen oil paintings. One of them draws your eye. It's of a fine-looking hunting hound; only there's something not there: the dog's body is missing from the neck down and there's just a large brown splodge on the canvas where it should be. 'Algy,' you say, 'have you been trying out this Cleano stuff on your family pictures?'

'Where better to prove its worth?' he replies eagerly.

You point to the painting. 'You cleaned away Fido.'

He looks a little sheepish. 'Ah, yes, I didn't know just how powerful Cleano is. It really is the business, isn't it?'

'It's massacred a loyal hound, Algy. That dog has stood up there for two hundred years waiting for a word from its master, ready to hunt a fox or bite an intruder. And now you've left it bereft of its main form. It won't be guarding anything now except its own head from your dratted Cleano.'

'A little calibration of the amount you put on the sponge, that's all it will take, and then it's the most wonderful tool for the housekeeper or bachelor with limited time for cleaning,' he replies confidently.

'A little calibration of your head is all it will take and then it will be the most wonderful tool for not destroying your family heirlooms on a whim.'

'I'm a little hurt by that comment, Kinn.'

'Not as hurt as Fido is by the damnable Cleano.' You rack up the billiard balls. 'Now, what about these poison-pen letters, eh?'

He looks pained. 'Yes, the horrid things started turning up a few weeks ago. A few times each week.'

'But not all of you each time.'

'No, whoever it is seems to pick his victims at random. Sometimes it's only one or two of us, sometimes it's been all of us at once. As I said, usually we all get the same message, but sometimes one of us will get something special. Always a bit vague, though.'

'Do you still have the ones you received?'

'Yes, hold on, I'll go and fetch them.'

He scampers away and returns a minute later with a bundle of five typewritten letters. You carefully examine them one by one. There are no distinguishing marks on the yellow envelopes, and the postmarks vary – two of them were posted in the village, one was sent from Whitechapel and one from Rochester, which you estimate to be an hour's drive from Hurley Court. There is, however, a watermark on the letter paper, reading: 'Foeman's'.

The messages are short: 'You will get your comeuppance.' 'Cheats never prosper. You should have learned that in school.' 'Death awaits.' 'Do you think you are safe? Think again.' 'You can't hide your deeds for ever.'

Now, Algy's an affable sort, but even affable sorts have their secrets. 'Algy, old man. You know you can tell me anything, right?'

'I wouldn't keep anything from you, Kinn.'

'Good show. And anything you say will be in the strictest confidence.' He looks at you expectantly. 'Your pal here seems to think you've got something on your conscience.'

'Scout's honour, I have no idea what he's talking about.

Unless it's that time I stole a handful of sweets from the village shop.'

You consider this briefly. 'I doubt it, Algy. Nicking a shilling's worth of sweets when you're a nipper doesn't sound like the sort of thing our friend has in mind.'

'It was last month.'

'Algy?'

'Sorry, Kinn. I really wanted them and I had no money with me.' You raise an eyebrow. 'I'll give Mrs Blenkins the money next week.' You wait, with your eyebrow raised. 'And say sorry.'

'That's better. But I still don't think that is what these letters are about. Have you spoken to the police?'

'No, of course not. My father wouldn't allow that sort of thing.'

You ponder for a while. 'Algy, I'm just off to make a telephone call.'

'Oh, right you are, Kinn.'

You call an old friend of yours who works in the paper-making industry. He's proved invaluable on a few occasions. 'Hello, Derek. A quick query for you,' you say, describing the letter paper and asking him to identify it. He agrees and says he will call you back as soon as he can find out. It won't take long.

Turn to 113

21

Hurley Court is a magnificent old pile, but it's not built for the modern age. It's like an ice box at night. The walls seem to be more holes than bricks, and there are one or two furry creatures who fancy bedding down in your chamber rather than taking their chances outside.

It's not long before a blizzard whips up across the open fields, and when you draw back the curtain, you see that the whole of the sky is a cauldron of white, spinning and blasting about. Something scampers through the drifts on the ground – a fox trying to get back to its den before it loses its way. It's at times like this, when you can't feel your feet, that you wonder why humans ever migrated to the rainy north of Europe. What was wrong with putting down roots in, say, Monte Carlo, or Florence? Delightful weather, agreeable locals (mostly), excellent culinary ambitions. But no, your ancient ancestors decided to up sticks and swim across the English Channel. Well, might as well make the best of it. You return to bed, draw the topmost blanket up to your chin and close your eyes to sleep.

Before long you're in the middle of the strange Oath of Fealty again, only now you're one of those taking part – you're Gervaise, then you're Mina, but also Colonel Hurley too. And then the lights are out but the snowstorm is inside and you're being whirled about the room, avoiding giant daggers and old religious oppression. You begin to inform whoever's in charge that this isn't for you when a creaking sound makes you shake your head. It comes again, more loudly this time, and you wake up, blinking in the darkness of your room.

It's still there.

The sound is coming from your ceiling. There's something – or someone – moving about in the attic of the house. It could be the ghost of the wicked Bloody Thomas pacing up and down in search of his silver dagger, but it sounds a damn sight more mortal than that.

You jump out of bed, throw on your clothes and light a candle. You don't have the knife for protection, so you'll have to rely on your fists if it comes to it. You slip out of the room and find your way to the back stairs, which must lead up to the attic.

If it's cold in the main house, it's downright arctic on the bare stone back stairs, which connect the servants' quarters with the main house. You stand with the candle flickering in a thousand draughts and strain your hearing, but the only sound is the wind howling around the house. Then suddenly, there's something else: a door banging closed. It's below you, you're certain, at the bottom of the stairs. But the creaking was overhead. What should you do?

If you go downstairs to find which door has slammed closed, turn to 92

If you continue up to the attic, turn to 77

22

Once outside the tea room, you have to hurry, because Constantinos is setting quite a pace. You wind back through The Shambles, keeping your distance so he doesn't spot you.

You walk right through the city and approach a bridge over the river, towards the train station. You speculate that he might be headed back there.

He strides over the mediaeval stone bridge and you follow in his wake, hoping that he doesn't have cause to stop and look behind him – though you could always tell him that you're heading back to the train too, which is quite plausible.

You're halfway across and glancing down into the black, fast-flowing water below your feet when you feel a sudden thudding pain on the back of your head, knocking you against the low parapet wall. You've been battered by something hard and blunt, leaving you stunned. The next thing you know, someone with great strength is lifting you up. Up and over. Over the parapet and down, down into the cold water below.

Now, go back to the beginning and start again

23

'You disappoint me, Algy,' you say.

'What?' he gasps.

'All those years I thought you wouldn't hurt a fly, and then you turn around and do this. Your own father.'

'I . . . I never touched him,' he gabbles.

'I know he was an overbearing, dictatorial sort. A bad father, perhaps, but patricide?'

'You're . . . utterly wrong,' he stammers. 'It wasn't me.'

'Come, come.'

'It wasn't!' he cries. And he breaks down in tears. 'I had nothing to do with it!'

You have seen many killers confronted with the truth, and some have admitted their guilt, some denied it. But you have always seen the truth in their eyes. And this time, you can see it in his. You've made a mistake!

'I think, sir, you should keep your accusations to yourself. And let the professionals do their job.' Inspector Rollinson is striding into the room, looking irritable. 'And you, Dr Tenor, are getting under my feet. Please depart or I'll have to arrest you for perverting the course of justice.'

You have little choice but to comply. You have failed miserably and even lost a dear friend.

Now, go back to the beginning and start again

24

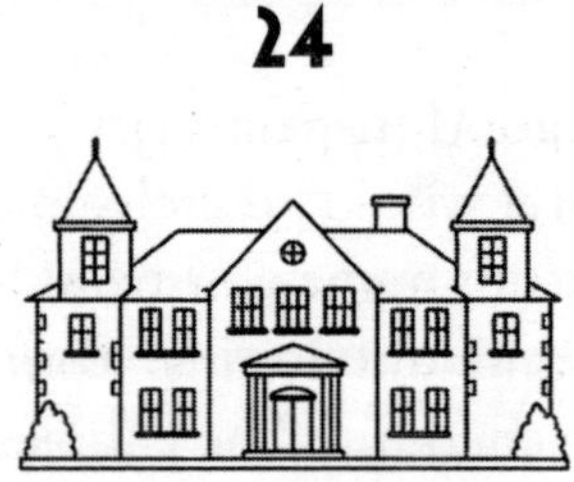

As soon as you enter the hall, Finney hands you a note, saying that Derek Mills has called. 'The letter paper company is Foeman's Stationery. It is common enough. Manufactured in Birmingham. It sells all over the country and is cheap,' the note reads. 'Call back if you need to talk.'

Not the most helpful information, but all information has its use. Right, time to get ready.

Turn to 115

25

'It looks like the good inspector isn't in the mood for a chat,' you say. 'But it would be such a pity to bump into an old friend so far from home and pass up the opportunity for a chin-wag. Let's put our shoe leather to the test.'

'I'm with you.'

You pick up the pace and pursue the errant copper along the road and into a side lane. You find him waiting for you with what passes for a look of irritation on his inexpressive face – the subtlest pursing of his lips.

'Dr Tenor,' he says in an Ulster accent. 'And Mrs Thresh. May I help you with something?'

'Such a nice coincidence running into you here, Inspector,' you reply. 'Are you up for the shopping?'

'No.'

'Sightseeing, perhaps?'

'I am not.'

'Following someone with whom I have recently shared a train carriage?' He makes no reply. 'Yes, I thought so. Whom, may I ask?'

'You may ask, Dr Tenor, but since it is an active police matter, I will not answer.'

'How about a hint?' you suggest. 'Twenty questions?

Are they animal, mineral or vegetable?' His face does not change.

'Perhaps I should speak to Sir Philip Game,' pipes up Melissa. 'Your commissioner is an old friend of mine.'

'Go ahead, Mrs Thresh,' he says without concern. 'I will wait.' He has heard many such threats in his time, and they bounce off him like rubber.

'What a pity,' you say. 'Well, I think we will just have to return to the scene and see for ourselves.'

'Quite right,' Melissa confirms as she follows in your wake.

You pace back to the Walnut Tree and enter. 'No word about the good inspector. If they ask, it's just luck that we came into the same tea room as them,' you instruct her.

'Understood.'

You quickly scan the cafe. But there's no one you recognize. You order coffee and wait ten minutes in case they appear from some cubby hole, but no luck. 'Drat,' you say. 'They must have left.'

'You think they saw us outside?'

'Or they saw someone watching them. Or it was just time to move on. Either way, we're no closer.'

At that, Reeves himself enters. He too checks the room minutely and comes to the conclusion that his birds have flown. He comes over to you. 'You have just interfered in an important police investigation and you're lucky that I'm not taking you in as accomplices. You may tell that to the commissioner.' And at that, he leaves.

'Hmmm, that puts the tin hat on that,' hrumphs Melissa. 'Now what?'

'The way I see it, we have two options. We can either go and meet Nanny Tiggy as planned, or we can turn the tables on Reeves and call your friend the commissioner.'

'Cop the copper?' she shrieks in joy. 'That does sound a hoot. But I'll leave it to you as to which course to pursue.'

If you want to meet Tiggy, turn to 73

If you want to call the commissioner, turn to 79

26

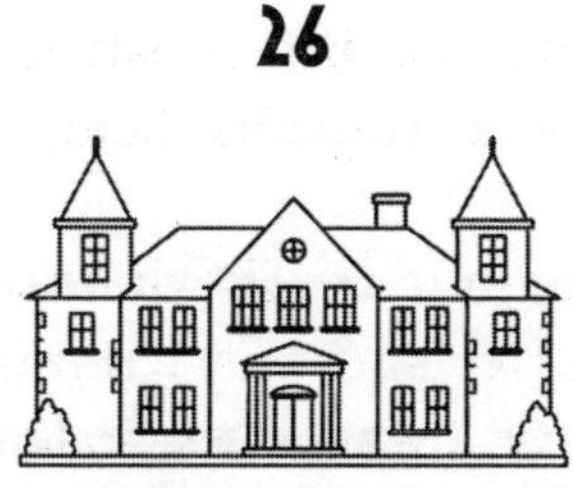

The light through your window is eye-achingly bright when you wake up. It's eight o'clock on Christmas morning and it's so bright because it's reflecting off a sparkling sheet of snow that covers the land as far as you can see. It's all very pretty – there's the church with a thick white blanket on it, skeletal brown trees with a powdery dusting on them. Hills in the distance. The sun is low but shining, and the sky is blue and empty. You toy with the idea of going for a stroll in the grounds – a chance to clear your head of the fog from last night.

Somewhere in the house, you can hear Christmas carols

being sung – a gramophone, you are sure, unless a band of rogue carol-singers has broken in to serenade the household.

You jump out of bed, take a shower-bath and head downstairs, to find Algy giddy with excitement.

'Christmas Day, Kinn, old fruit. Christmas Day!' he exclaims. His excitement is infectious and you can't help but feel a bit of a thrill too. 'Now, the plan for the day is to nip up to the church, say a few quick prayers, sing "Good King Wenceslas" around the drawing-room piano and then lunch and presents!'

'It all sounds marvellous.'

'Yes, it does. Righto, are you coming in to breakfast?'

You're quite peckish, but the weather is so inviting that you're keen on a bit of fresh air.

If you go in to breakfast, turn to 56

If you go for a walk outside, turn to 109

27

'First off, Simon. You seem to think Freddie's behind this. Why would you say that?'

'Stands to reason, don't it? He's the one who's gonna inherit all her money.'

'Money? You cretin,' Freddie spits. 'There's no money. When will you people get that into your skulls? *No money.* We're broke. You might as well head off to the coal mine. Leave me alone. Leave her alone.' He reaches for a bottle on the bar. He unstoppers it and sniffs the contents. 'Ah, amaretto. I didn't know we had any.' He lifts it towards his lips.

If you let him drink it, turn to 48

If you stop him, turn to 69

28

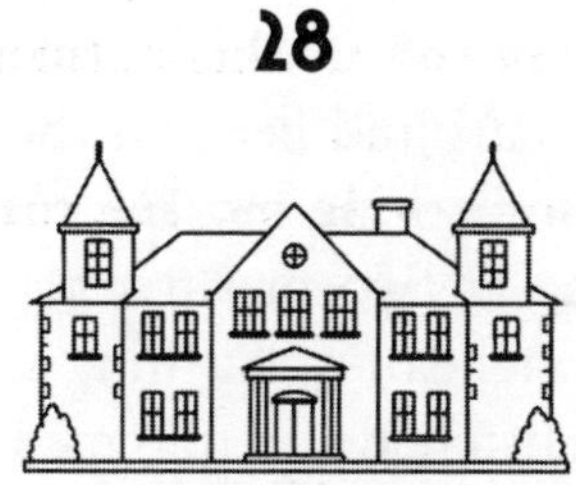

'I think most of you should go back to the house and call for the police,' you say. 'But a few of us should have a quick look around here. Just in case there's anything that turns up. Algy, Gervaise, can you stay?'

'Of course,' Algy says. Gervaise just nods.

You manage to relight one of the torches. While everyone else leaves, the three of you tramp through the snow around the church.

'Any idea what is going on?' you ask Algy.

'I wish I knew.' And you stop as you round a corner. Someone is standing there, shivering. Mina.

'I didn't want to do this,' she says.

'Do what?' You're ready for a confession, but of what sort?

'The ceremony.' She wraps her arms tighter around her chest. 'And something has been wrong here for a while.'

'What do you mean?'

'Yes, what do you mean, Mother?' Gervaise asks.

'I mean there have been . . . movements. At night.'

'Please explain,' you say.

She hesitates. 'I sound mad, I know I do.'

'I'm sure you aren't.'

'Are you sure? I'm not,' she bursts out. 'I don't want to be mad. I don't want to be.' She is becoming worked up. Algy puts his arms around her and she calms down. 'At night. I've heard something moving about in Harrison's study. It wakes me at two or three in the morning. It's pitch black, but I can hear it. Shuffling around. I've woken Harrison, but he's listened and told me I'm hearing things and gone back to sleep. Four or five times it's happened. I'm so tired, I'm not sleeping. Can you help us?'

'I'll try.' And at that, she nods, comforted.

You all finish looking around the church but find nothing, and if there were any footprints, they have all been obliterated by the falling snow. You follow the others back to the house.

Turn to 37

29

'You, Pererin, and you, Simon. In cahoots.'

'You what!' demands Simon, leaping up. But Pererin catches hold of him and prevents him from confronting you physically.

'It was you. You murdered Melissa Thresh for money.'

'What money? There isn't any money.'

'Ah, but there will be, won't there? When Hilkodine hits the market.'

'Hilkodine?' blurts out Tim. 'But it failed.'

'It failed as a treatment for angina. It works very well as an arthritis remedy. It will be a very lucrative asset!'

'How on earth would we know that?' Pererin asks coldly.

'Because it was down to you to filter all the reports that came across Tim's desk. He said himself that he relied on you to do it because otherwise he would be swamped by the paperwork. You simply failed to pass on the documents that told of the great, unexpected potential of this medication.'

She stares at you without a flicker of emotion. 'All those reports are sent to Mr Thresh too.'

You were ready for this. 'Yes, they are. But he doesn't read them, do you, Freddie?'

For once, he looks sheepish. 'No. I can't make head nor

tail of the scientific stuff. I just run the business. Money in, money out.'

'So what?' she snaps. 'We don't own the bloody company, do we?'

'Ah, but there was another weakness of Freddie's that you were planning to exploit.'

'Oh, God,' he says, understanding.

'Yes,' you tell him. 'Your weakness for her.' You turn to Pererin. 'Murder Melissa and then take her place, that was your plan.'

'Whatever do you mean?' she sneers.

'Presumably, divorce and then marriage to Freddie. You've convinced everyone that you and Simon loathe each other. And then after marrying Freddie, maybe he also meets with an accident, leaving you to rekindle your relationship with Simon. But much, much richer, thanks to Hilkodine.'

She snorts in derision. 'How clever you are. And what brought you to this insane idea of yours?'

'It was that you were wearing your winter clothes, even over your costumes.'

At that, Simon laughs out loud. 'So what? It's cold. We weren't the only ones with warm clothes on.'

'You were the only ones making sure to wear gloves.' You gaze around the carriage. 'Gloves. Just what you would need if you were handling a tack poisoned with cyanide, ready to use it to kill Melissa.'

'Rubbish!' he spits.

'Is it? Do you have your gloves with you?'

'I do. So what?'

'May I borrow them?'

'No.'

'Hand them over,' Constantinos growls. Tim and Inspector Wilkes move to stand behind him, backing him up.

Simon pulls the gloves from his jacket pocket and flings them to the floor. You lift them and draw them onto your own hands. 'Thick leather. Very sturdy,' you say. 'Would you be so kind as to stand up?' He is about to protest but Constantinos and Tim look ready to throw him out of the seat if necessary and he stands up, scowling. 'Thank you so much.' Very, very carefully, you ease your fingers down the side of the seat cushion, exploring your way down, feeling for anything hard and metallic. Nothing, nothing. And then something. Yes, hard to the tips of your fingers, right at the back of the seat. As carefully as you can – this could well be the instrument of death, ready to take another life – you place your fingers on either side of the round base and pluck it out into the light. A simple brass drawing pin. Nothing much to look at, but there's a spot of red on the tip that could be blood, and you have a strong suspicion that a toxicology test will prove positive for hydrogen cyanide. Simon glued it to the inside of the disappearing cabinet, knowing that Melissa would have to press herself tightly inside and prick herself on the poisoned tip. When you turned your attention to Nanny Tiggy when she fainted – as Pererin ensured you would – he removed it, leaving the greasy mark on the wood.

Simon snatches for it, but you draw it out of his reach at the same second that Constantinos and Tim throw their arms around him. 'I would be careful if I were you,' you say.

'There's probably still enough poison to kill you if you cut yourself on it.' You're a little tempted to prove your words.

But you might not get the chance! Someone has grabbed hold of your arm and is trying to bend the lethal pin towards your neck. Pererin is using all her strength to end your life out of nothing but spite. For a second, the poisoned weapon is dangerously close to your flesh until you chuck her off.

She throws back her head and laughs. 'Well, doesn't it look like I'm for the gallows?' she cries.

'I would say so,' you reply frostily. 'You really shouldn't have made up that story about seeing Tim at his desk in the hotel yesterday morning. It wasn't a bad plan – give him an alibi and, crucially, give yourself one while you're at it – but it was just a bit too convenient for my liking.'

She gets to her feet and smooths back her hair. 'Well, I'll go game. It was a good plan.'

'It was that,' Simon says, settling against the wall, no longer struggling against the two men holding him.

'Just bad luck we got caught.'

'That's all it was. Bad luck.'

She blows him a kiss and he smiles. There's something deeply unsettling about this pair. You've brought many killers to justice, but few seem to have seen their deeds as nothing more than a business venture – an enterprise that had a certain amount of risk, a certain amount of reward. No, when you see the prison van doors close on Pererin and Simon Yarrow, you'll feel the world is a safer place to be.

THE END

30

You squirm about on the floor, trying to find the lighter with your hands.

'My stomach!' yells the man who had cried out in pain. 'Mother, where are you?'

A melee of footsteps in all directions. Luckily, you find the lighter right beside you. You flick the wheel once, twice; a spark, a flame, and then you hold it up to see a strange scene.

You and Gervaise are the only ones still close to where you were before; all the others have stumbled about or retreated to the walls. Leaner is on his hands and knees behind a pew in the nave like a fox hunted down. Mina is cowering against a wall.

And at your feet is Colonel Hurley, with the dagger in his gut. He's holding the hilt.

Finney goes to grab the weapon. 'No!' you shout, stopping him.

'Don't touch it!' Tun-Hurley, the old soldier, says. 'You could kill him.'

'Give me more light!' you demand. Finney runs to the vestry and turns on the electric lights. Instantly the room is flooded and your eyes smart. You stoop to examine the wound. 'Don't move,' you instruct Hurley. He whines in pain. 'Give me a handkerchief, something clean.' Finney hands you one. You open the colonel's shirt and dab away a little of the blood. You quickly realize that he's been lucky – the wound isn't deep and he has a bit of a spare tyre around his waist, so the weapon can't have caused too much damage. You gently wrap your fingers over the hilt, above his. 'You can let go,' you say. 'I don't think it's very serious.'

He glares at you as if you are trying to kill him yourself, then relents and lifts away his fingers. Slowly you draw out the knife. The wound is shallow.

Once the knife is clear, he collapses back, pressing the handkerchief to the wound, which is leaking but not gushing blood. 'You'll be fine. I've seen worse in kitchen accidents.'

'It's not your damn gut, is it?'

'You must have had worse in France,' you say. There's a time and a place for sympathy, but this isn't it. Especially since you know that now your medical skills have had their moment, it's your deductive skills that are required. Someone just attempted to murder Colonel Hurley. Six of you were within arm's reach, and no one saw a thing.

'Who did this?' demands Tun-Hurley. He attempts to grab the silver-and-gold dagger from your hand, but you twist it away from his grip.

'Not so fast, Major,' you say. 'I don't know that it wasn't you.'

'Preposterous!' he splutters. 'Hurley and I were in France together.'

'Maybe that's where this all started.'

'How dare you!'

'I dare because someone just attempted to kill Algy's

father, and until I know who it was, you're getting nowhere near this knife.'

'You'd best stay back,' Algy confirms.

Tun-Hurley looks around, but you can tell everyone is on your side. He throws up his hands. 'And how do we know it wasn't you?' he growls.

'I suppose you don't, though my connection to the family is slight and I have no reason to kill Colonel Hurley. And I didn't even know this ritual was to take place until tonight, so I couldn't have planned this assault. But either way, this is a job for the police.'

'That's right,' says Hurley, pulling himself to his feet with the aid of his elder son.

You notice something out of the corner of your eye. 'Look,' you say, pointing. 'The door.'

The outside door is wide open. 'Someone could have come in and left that way.'

'Seems far-fetched,' Gervaise mutters.

'But possible. Algy, go look for footprints,' you instruct him, while you keep everyone else under close observation.

He hurries to the door and peers at the ground. 'Lots of them, but I can't say which are ours or someone else's. And the snow's still coming down, so it's all a bit of a mush. What shall we do?'

If you say you should all go straight back to the house and call the police, turn to 37

If you think you should check around the church, in case there's something to find, turn to 28

31

In the morning you wake, wash and dress. Freddie is severely hung over and points to a loaf of bread and a butter dish. You eat your scant breakfast and follow it with water that you trust has no trace of all the chemicals washing about the building.

'I must go out,' you tell him.

'Enquiries?'

'Quite.'

'Well, I hope they bear fruit.' He rests his jaw on his hand. 'I feel seedy.'

'You look it.'

'That will be why.'

'May I have Nanny Tiggy's address?'

'In my address book.' He points to his study. You go, copy down the address and return to the dining room.

'Is there a good hotel in town?'

'The Old Swan is a decent place. Don't tell them I sent you. They won't let you in.'

'Quite the recommendation. Cheerio, Freddie. And pull yourself together, old man.'

You pack your bag and go out onto the street, where you hail a cab to the hotel.

Once settled into the thankfully empty drawing room, you request a telephone, which is brought to your table.

A quick word with the operator, a transfer to a London exchange and then you're through to the General Medical Council in London. Luckily, there is a skeleton crew keeping the doctors' body running on Christmas Day for urgent enquiries. You've been suspicious of Tim since you saw him wearing a St Thomas's medical school tie but he denied being a doctor and insisted that he'd just bought it in a shop. Pull the other one, Tim. It's got bells on.

'Registry, please,' you say. You're connected to a confused, ancient and apparently profoundly deaf old man. 'I'm calling about a student at the school. Timothy Fortiswood,' you say, for the third time.

'What's that? Your name is Timothy Portishood?'

'Fortiswood! F-O-R-T-I-S-W-O-O-D.'

'Ah. Well, Dr Fortiswood. How may I help?'

You're about to correct him, when it occurs to you that the confusion is without doubt in your favour.

'I would like to amend my address. I shall be moving to Manchester.'

'Let me find your records.' There is the sound of the receiver being plonked onto a desk, then ten minutes of silence. This is abruptly ended by, 'How dare you!'

'Oh, yes?' you reply, intrigued.

'You try to pull the wool over my eyes? Do you take us for fools?'

'Heaven forfend. Am I out of luck, then?'

'Of course you are. Once you are struck off, you are

struck off. That poor woman in Dover. Your error cost her her sight. Your *drunken* error!' he snaps.

That's interesting. 'It's a fair cop, guv, but society is to blame. All the best, toodle-pip,' you say, and hang up.

Yes, very interesting. A drinking problem and a shameful history. But Tim isn't the only one on the train with something to hide.

Nanny Tiggy's neat little house – two up, two down – is close by. It has window boxes full of winter pansies hung on the sills. You rap on the door and the old nanny answers promptly.

'Dr Tenor, good morning.' She sounds a little taken aback by your unexpected presence.

'Good morning, Miss Tiggworth. May I come in?'

'Of course.' She stands back, and you enter the front parlour. There is a little wooden tray on a settle, with the remains of toast and marmalade upon it.

'I am sorry for interrupting your breakfast.'

'That's quite all right.' You can see she's nervous.

'May I sit down?' She indicates that you may, and you take a seat on an upright wooden chair. 'There's something that's been troubling me.' Her hands move nervously. 'It's that you're not a religious person.' She blinks. But the fact that she doesn't look utterly bemused by your comment tells you that you're on the right track.

'Why do you say that?'

'Come, come, Miss Tiggworth. I think we both know.' She gazes at her feet. 'I took little notice of it when we met you at York Minster and Melissa said that she "never had you pegged as a religious sort". Now, isn't that a strange thing, when you come to consider it?'

'Is it? I don't know.'

'I think it is. You raised her from when she was a little girl, and she never saw any sign that you were religious? No prayers, no reading of scripture. And yet you are so devout that you attend church on Christmas Eve. That seems unlikely, doesn't it? Unless, of course, you aren't religious at all and have another reason for attending the service.'

She smiles – well, she attempts to smile, but you can see through it. There's no crinkling around the eyes, that's the giveaway sign. 'Oh, well, you have found out my secret. It's that handsome young priest. Even at my age it's . . .'

You hold up your hand. 'Nanny Tiggy, save your effort. I can predict where this is heading. You wish me to believe that you are taken by the curls of that young man and that is why you were besottedly staring at him while he led communion. But that's not it, is it?'

Her eyes narrow now. Does she realize that she has been found out? Perhaps. But she won't go down without a fight.

'I don't know what you are suggesting, Dr Tenor, but I would like you now to leave my house.'

You wait for a moment, deciding what to do.

If you go as she asks, turn to 66

If you refuse, turn to 107

32

You walk quickly and quietly through the silent house, picking up a heavy electric torch in the hallway. All the way you know that he or she might be watching your progress. This time you turn on the lights as you go but still keep a sharp eye on the dark corners, ready for anything, thankfully regaining the feeling in your frozen feet. You walk cautiously through the kitchen, wary of the many weapons on racks and hooks, but no cleavers swipe at you, and you make it to the back stairs. Up to the attic. Just in case they have returned to the scene of the crime, you very cautiously enter with the heavy torch ready to be used as a club. But you breathe a sigh of, well, relief mixed with disappointment that whoever the thief – or would-be murderer – was, they have gotten away with it. For now.

Your torch beam sweeps over familiar sights: grimy boxes, the tailor's dummy draped in green and a mass of forgotten toys. You see the wooden shield that might just have saved your life. You rummage through the clutter, but find little to tell you what your assailant sought – presuming they were seeking something specific and not just out for a strange stroll among the rafters of the house; or something even creepier, such as boring holes in the ceiling to look down on everyone as they sleep.

You're freezing and decide it's time to rouse the household to make them aware of what has happened. You're just leaving when you shine the torch on the spot where your assailant was hiding when you came in. The beam falls on something yellow and crumpled. You stoop and pick it up.

It's a page from a newspaper, *The Times*. The story at the top is about the government's plans for taxation; the one below it covers a production of *Macbeth* in Birmingham that has gone horribly wrong. At the bottom of the page is something much more significant, however. A report of heroism on the Western Front in 1916.

> Three British soldiers have been hailed as heroes for fighting off a gang of Germans attempting to rob a church near the strategic city of Ypres in Belgium. One, Pte Bob Vickers, was injured in the fight and was taken directly to the nearest hospital.
>
> The other men were Majors Harrison Hurley and Wilfred Tun-Hurley. The officers are cousins, serving with the Coldstream Guards. Vickers was their driver.
>
> On the night of 5 September, the two officers were returning from a conference outside the town of Brandhoek. They saw lights on in a church that had been abandoned. They went to investigate, leaving Vickers to guard the car.
>
> They stealthily approached the church and witnessed a gang of four or five German soldiers, including one captain, emerging from the church crypt. They were carrying objects and were obviously robbing the church

of its treasures, which had been hidden in the hope of preserving them during the War.

Majors Hurley and Tun-Hurley relied on their service revolvers and the element of surprise to bravely challenge the Germans. A fight ensued.

The Germans managed to get away with a few items, but dropped most of what they had taken.

While they were fighting, another German struck Vickers from behind, knocking him unconscious.

Vickers was taken to hospital with concussion and remembers nothing of the event. Sadly, the injury has left him unable to walk and the doctors are uncertain that he will ever regain the ability.

The local Roman Catholic diocese later thanked our soldiers for their bravery. They were also commended by Brigadier Pulley, their brigade commander.

Major Hurley said: 'We saw the Hun at work through the window. We soon put a stop to their game. They are all yellow at heart. Robbing a church – how low can they sink? Utter swine.'

Major Tun-Hurley said: 'They only put up a short fight. They didn't want to stick it out, they just wanted their booty. So off they ran as soon as we started firing.'

Pte Vickers said: 'I'm grateful to the officers for finding me and taking me to get patched up.' He is now looking forward to some home leave with his mother, Lilian, 46, and his brother, Dennis, 9.

The local bishop, Hendrik Meijer, said: 'We thank the British soldiers for defending our country and our church.'

You carefully fold up the newspaper and place it inside your pocket. You are sure it was what the intruder came for, and that it therefore holds some significance.

It's time to wake up the household. Turn to 57

33

'You, Freddie. You wanted Melissa dead so that you could run off with Pererin Yarrow.'

'Oh, don't be ridiculous,' he says. 'Run off with her? Melissa was kicking me out as it was. She would have loved it if I was gone.'

'I wouldn't touch him with a bargepole,' Pererin splutters.

'Looking a bit stupid now, aren't you, Dr Tenor?' Freddie sneers.

'Wait, let me think it through,' you say. 'Well, then you did it for money.'

'What money?'

'Hilkodine. Everyone thought it was a failure. And it was as an angina medication, but it's very effective for arthritis. It was going to be a very lucrative asset.'

'That's news to me. But then I wasn't involved in the research. I just ran the company.'

'That's true,' says Tim. 'He never read any reports, he relied on me to fill him in. And what do you mean it was a success?'

You're losing this. You're beginning to doubt yourself. And before you can form any kind of reply to Freddie's denial, someone else forces their way into the conversation. 'He's not the killer, but I know who is.' You look around to see Inspector Reeves standing in the carriage doorway.

'Inspector?'

'I've had just about enough of you. You've been getting in my way. Boys!' Two constables enter the carriage. 'Escort Dr Tenor off the train. I've got police work to do.' The two coppers push you out of the carriage and you can only stand on the platform feeling foolish while the true culprit is revealed.

Now, go back to the beginning and start again

34

'Well, it has been a while since I had a case of a mysterious follower,' you say. 'I shall be there at nine.'

Melissa's husband reaches you and gives you a curious look. He looks like he was a handsome fellow a while back, but he's a bit fleshy around the jowls now. 'This is Johnny's friend, Kinn,' Melissa says. 'My husband, Freddie.' You shake hands, and Johnny makes some excuse about showing you around the club to take you away.

It's likely that there's nothing much in Melissa's belief that she's being tailed, but you'll find out tomorrow.

Turn to 58

35

'I would like to speak to a few of you before the police arrive,' you announce.

'Is that legal?' Tun-Hurley asks.

'Perfectly legal, Major. And I should be most indebted to you if you would be the first. In the billiards room.'

'I have nothing to hide,' he says as he comes forward. 'Lead on.'

You head for the billiards room, where the walls are lined with oil portraits of Hurleys long expired. And in the centre of them all is Bloody Thomas, who might have come back from the dead, judging by the terrible work of the morning. He holds in his hand the knife that now lies outside in the snow. For a second, you are lost in thought. What is Bloody Thomas in all this? You wonder if whoever killed Colonel Hurley – on the second attempt – has been using the story of that wicked dead squire as a bit of a blind, a way to distract you all from the simple facts of the case.

'Ask away. Nothing to hide,' Tun-Hurley repeats, snapping you out of your deliberations.

'It's a strange crime, isn't it?' you say.

'Nasty one on a good soldier. Something festering, if you ask me. I don't like the kind of man who lets things fester. Act. Someone's done you wrong? Challenge them, face to face. You think they took something from you? Take it back. Don't let it twist your guts until you bash a man from behind like a coward.'

He comes across as brash, but you can't help feeling that, underneath, Major Tun-Hurley is mostly just plain-speaking and plain-thinking.

'Were you always friends with Colonel Hurley?'

'Known each other since we were nippers, of course. Had the odd falling-out, like any boys. But never lasted long. Then we served together. We risked our necks for each other more than once. Nothing ever breaks that bond.'

You want to believe him. But there's nothing to stop a good soldier also being a good liar; you only have his word for it – and that newspaper cutting – to say they were friends in the trenches.

'I read the story of how you stopped the Germans looting a church in Belgium. It was quite a heroic act.'

'Did you?' He looks a little embarrassed by the memory.

'No need for modesty, Major. The local priests said they were in your debt.'

'A soldier sees an enemy and attacks. Simple as that.' His voice drops a little. 'Truth is, no one wants war less than a soldier. We know what it's all about. We've seen it up close. Boys read about it in their books and think that there's glory in it. There's anything but.'

'Did you suffer, sir?'

For a moment, his lips seem to quiver. Then he regains control of himself. 'I lost my son.'

It's a tragic thing to hear, no matter how often you hear it. 'I'm very, very sorry.' Algy had mentioned that his cousin had died in the War sometime after holding that silver-bladed knife when he went through the Oath of Fealty.

He sighs. 'He was a good lad, Terence. Joined the Artists' Rifles. It wasn't long before the Armistice. Just bad luck, really.'

Just bad luck. Well, the whole thing had been just bad luck, hadn't it? 'I'm sure he would have been a fine man.'

'Thank you.'

'Can you think of anyone who would have a grudge against Colonel Hurley?'

He considers this for a moment. 'A man goes through life, he picks up a few enemies here and there. Can't say Harrison was always the easiest man. No one would say that. But someone who would kill him for it? No. Can't think of any.'

'Are you aware of any trouble that the colonel had? Money?'

'Money? No. Not like his son.'

'Algy?'

'No, no. The wastrel. Gervaise. That boy goes through it like water, throws it away on that dreadful newspaper of his. Utter trash. Do you know what it printed about the King last year?'

'I don't.'

'Doesn't stand repeating. Utter drivel.'

'Well, I will ask him about it.'

'Don't trust a word he says, that's my advice to you.'

You thank the major for his time, and ask him to be so kind as to send the two maids in to see you.

You have a few moments to collect your thoughts after he strides out, a little stiffly on his leg with the old shrapnel wound. Major Tun-Hurley comes across as solid and dependable, but with a pall of sadness regarding his son. Poor man.

A minute later, the two maids enter. You haven't paid too much attention to them as yet, but you can't rule anything out, and so set to learning who they are. They are both from the village. Rebecca is nineteen and has been in service since she was fourteen, first for the local vicar, and then, for the past year, for the Hurleys. She has an unusually round face and rosy cheeks like a doll. Sally is a year younger, with greasy skin, and has been at Hurley Court for three years, since her mother had a sixth child and Sally had to go out to earn her keep.

'Have you seen anything unusual or suspicious around here recently?' you ask.

'Always something unusual here, Dr Tenor,' Rebecca replies. 'Some of 'em quite batty, if you ask me.'

'Batty, yes,' adds Sally.

'Any in particular?'

Rebecca answers again. 'Well, Mr Gervaise sometimes looks like he would swallow you whole. Then there's Mr Algernon.'

'What about him?'

'Well, th'other day I saw him watching a squirrel runnin' up'n down a tree for an hour. A blessed hour. Some folks don't have much to do, I s'pose.'

'No. They don't,' confirms Sally.

'Have you noticed anyone acting differently recently?' The two girls lock eyes, then look at the floor. They don't want to say. 'It will remain completely between us,' you assure them.

'Well,' says Rebecca.

'Say it,' says Sally.

'It's Mr Finney. He's got . . .'

'He's got what?'

She goes to the door, checks outside to see that no one is listening and comes back. She whispers in your ear. 'He's got a tart.'

'How do you know?'

'Seen him gettin' ready. He wears aftershave water and spends an hour looking at himself in the mirror in his room.'

'How do you know that?'

They glance at each other again. 'Looking through his keyhole.'

You tut, but the information is useful. 'Do you know who it is?'

They shake their heads. 'He walks out and comes back a couple of hours later. Always looks pleased with himself, don't he?'

'Yes,' Sally confirms.

'Also,' begins Rebecca – you get the feeling that she's the repository of any illicit information in the household – 'he's got ever so much money these days.'

'He has,' adds Sally.

'Always jangling in his pockets when he goes out to The Plough.'

'Anything else odd?'

Rebecca thinks. 'Yes. Someone's torn up the colonel's copy of *A Christmas Carol.* Ripped two or three pages right out,' she says.

'Probably nothing,' you tell her. 'All right, that will be all. Please ask Mr Leaner to join me.'

They bob curtseys and leave. You have a minute to yourself. So Finney is conducting a secretive affair – and has come into some wealth. The two might be related, they might not. But it's worth looking into.

Leaner raps on the door as he enters, pulling you out of your deliberations. 'You wanted to see me?'

'Do sit down,' you say. He takes a chair. 'You haven't been here long, have you?'

'No, matter of weeks,' he says. 'Mind if I smoke?'

'Go ahead.'

He thoughtfully pulls out a pipe, knocks it on the grate and stuffs it with tobacco. You can smell cherries even before it's alight.

'Yes, matter of a few weeks. Gervaise Hurley invited me down to profile his father.'

'And what is your conclusion?'

'Of him, or of the family?'

'Both.'

'Well, he's an absolute tartar and they're not happy together.'

'I'm sure that's an accurate assertion. Have you seen anything suspicious?'

He's silent for a moment, with an expression on his face as if he is struggling with the answer. 'It seems so petty,' he says.

'What does?'

'To accuse a maid.'

One of the maids? 'I think you should tell me what's on your mind.'

He sighs. 'You're right, of course. It's that one, Rebecca, who seems to have a chip on her shoulder – last week I happened to go into Colonel Hurley's study, to pick up some notes I had left there, and I found her about . . . well . . .'

'Well what?'

'Well, she had a signet ring of the colonel's and she looked just like she was about to put it in her pocket. I can't think why she would do that, other than to steal it.'

You sit back. 'How certain are you?'

'Fairly certain, I should say.'

'Could she have been cleaning it?'

'No cloth in her hand, nothing like that from what I could see.'

That's interesting. But you're not sure if you should entirely trust Leaner. Maybe you should look into his background. You could start in Oxford with his university time. Yes, that would be a good place to begin.

There is a knock on the door. Finney enters. 'Mr Gervaise has returned with Sergeant Pimm and an Inspector Rollinson. They are waiting for you in the drawing room.'

Turn to 94

36

'You, Tim.' His knees weaken and he grabs on to the disappearing cabinet to steady himself.

'I don't understand,' he gasps.

'But I do. That tie you wear. It's from St Thomas's Medical School in London. You tried to fob me off with some absurd story about having bought it and not knowing what it signified. Hardly. You were a doctor – but no more, isn't that right?'

He hangs his head in shame. 'Yes,' he whispers.

'Why?' you demand.

'I was struck off.'

'For drinking on the job. Admit what happened.'

'I cost a woman her sight. It was terrible.'

'And then, I presume, Melissa found out and threatened to expose you?'

He looks up. 'Melissa?'

'Yes. Melissa.'

'But Melissa always knew. When she gave me the job she knew.'

'She did,' confirms Freddie. 'We all did.'

You are taken aback. 'You did?'

'Of course. Tim wasn't allowed to practise medicine again, but his knowledge was invaluable to the firm.' His voice hardens. 'You fool, Tenor. Tim made a mistake but he paid the price and didn't hide it. No one was threatening to reveal what was common knowledge. It couldn't possibly be any reason to murder Melissa.'

You search for something to say, a justification or an apology. But you never get the chance, because at that moment, a movement makes you turn. Something is moving through the air – an iron bar, and it's swooping down towards your head. You won't survive this.

Now, go back to the beginning and start again

37

You enter the drawing room. Everyone else is standing around, with grim expressions on their faces. The fire in the grate is burning low and Finney throws some more coal upon it. At least you can warm yourself. Once you have done so, you turn around. As the closest thing to a professional, everyone is waiting for you to speak. 'Someone has attempted to murder Colonel Hurley,' you say. 'They may be in this room . . .'

'Nonsense!' Hurley snarls. 'I know my household. My servants, my own family.'

'. . . they may not. But I intend to find out.'

'Have you any idea who it is?' asks Mina desperately.

'Of course not,' scoffs Gervaise. 'Could be any one of us. Could be me.' He grins widely.

'Careful, lad. Not something to joke about,' cautions Tun-Hurley.

'Why not?' says Gervaise, settling into a leather settee. 'Might as well have a laugh while we're stuck in this god-forsaken place with a knifeman on the loose.' He mimes a stabbing motion.

Is this a clever bluff by Gervaise, you wonder? Making

himself such an obvious suspect that you will discount him? You've seen that strategy before.

'I've seen men killed with knives,' Tun-Hurley adds. 'Good men. If you had too, trust me, lad, you wouldn't find it so funny.'

'You're hell-bent on sucking all the joy out of this occasion, aren't you?'

'Nothing to be joyful about. Coward in the dark nearly killed your father. If that doesn't bother you, think about who's next. Could be you! So look sharp.'

'Yes, yes, Uncle. "When we were in the trenches . . ."'

At that, Tun-Hurley, usually so calm, begins to look furious. 'Hold your tongue!' he snaps. Gervaise has clearly found his sensitive spot. Well, no man came through the War without scars. No wonder, given what they saw and what they endured.

'Gervaise, please,' his mother whispers.

For the first time, Gervaise looks sheepish. He seems to realize he's gone too far. 'All right. I'll put a sock in it.'

'That would be for the best,' you say. 'Now, Colonel, I want to treat that wound.' You send for a first-aid kit and take the colonel to his bedroom, where you clean and dress the abrasion. It's quite superficial, and you're not worried so long as it's kept clean. 'Who would do this?' you ask, although you can guess his answer. He doesn't like the idea of a spy in his camp.

'No idea. Madman. Someone watching the house.' He glances at the window. The wind is howling now and the snow is far heavier than it was.

'I believe you remain in danger.'

'I've been in danger before, Doctor, and I haven't turned tail and run away.'

'I insist the police are called.'

'Very well.'

Satisfied, you finish up and tidy away what you have used.

Returning downstairs and leaving the colonel to change his clothes, you pass Mina's room. The door is open and you see her in a wicker chair, gazing out of the window at the night. She notices you and smiles.

'May I come in?' you ask.

'Of course.' You enter and shut the door behind you and take a chair, a twin to the one she sits on. 'The ceremony means so much to my husband's family,' she sighs. 'Even though it's all quite meaningless. That's why I go along with it. They love having a tradition. I suppose it's nice to be part of a tradition, isn't it?'

'Yes, it is.' You guess that she hasn't understood the hidden religiosity of the ritual. It really has been lost in the mists of time. You don't know whether to explain it to them all, or just let it exist as a strange ceremony that will go on and on.

'Funny, but I suppose I'm now more a part of the family than before. Like I have been let into it. You can marry into a family but it's not like being born into one, is it?' she asks.

'Not a bit.'

'No,' she adds pensively. You wonder how much she feels like an outsider, rather than a true part of the Hurley clan. You have often found that people's family backgrounds offer strong clues to understanding them.

'Do you come from a close family?'

'Oh, yes.' She brightens. 'I have three sisters. Four of us in five years. Our mother was quite exhausted, but happy with it. We're all still the best of friends.'

'That's nice. I'm an only child,' you explain. 'All my parents' expectations fall on me. I don't think I fulfil half of them.'

'I'm sure they're still proud.'

'You would be surprised.'

'Oh, living around here, Dr Tenor, nothing surprises me anymore.'

No, you suppose not.

And at that, you suggest that you both return to the others in the dining room.

On your way down, you see Finney pressing and releasing the hook on the telephone in the hallway. The colonel is beside him. 'Hello? Hello?' Finney is saying into the receiver. 'I'm sorry, Colonel, it's dead,' he explains.

'Damn lines must have come down,' Hurley replies, checking for himself.

'Where's the nearest telephone?' you ask.

'Outside The Plough. But the weather has got much worse.' He opens the door a crack and a blast of snow explodes in. It looks like an absolute blizzard out there. Finney forces the door closed against the wind. It's too thick to take a car out, that's for sure.

'Looks like we're staying to take our luck, then,' the colonel says. And you detect a note of satisfaction in his voice.

Turn to 50

38

Hurley Court looks much more foreboding than when you arrived for your stay. The Christmas tinsel inside the hall looks like barbed wire and the taxidermy animals look ready to bite and scratch. Oh yes, it's a different house altogether.

Finney arrives and takes your hat and coat.

'Kinn, where on earth have you been all day?' Algy shouts as he runs to meet you.

'Finding things out, Algy, old chap.'

'What sort of things?'

'The last pieces of this Christmas jigsaw.'

'The last . . .'

'Finney, will you have everyone assemble in the billiards room? I have something to announce.'

'Very good, Dr Tenor.'

Yes, this has been a nasty little crime. But now you're convinced you know who did it and why. You take yourself to the billiards room and fix a whisky and soda while you wait. One by one, they all drift in. Mina looking worried, the maids Rebecca and Sally looking curious, Gervaise contemptuous, Leaner politely affable, Finney suave as ever and finally Major Tun-Hurley, the rigid soldier. They take seats or stand around the room.

'Colonel Hurley lied to me,' you announce.

'How dare you, sir!' his cousin bursts out. 'I won't have his name besmirched in his own house!'

Mina looks quite distressed by your assertion too, and glances at her sons. Gervaise appears coldly irritated, and Algy confused.

'Please keep your seat, Major,' you reply coolly. 'I shall explain how and why he lied.'

'You had better do so quickly, or I shall eject you from this house myself.'

'Hear me out first and then you can send me packing if you wish. All through this affair we have been haunted. Haunted by the ghost of your unpleasant ancestor, Bloody Thomas.' You stare up at the portrait of that most wicked scion of the Hurley dynasty.

'What are you going on about?' Gervaise asks.

'Yes, spit it out,' Tun-Hurley adds.

'Bloody Thomas was known for hunting men down. Blameless men, whom he would chase into a man-trap, so that they would be at his mercy. But he would show them no mercy at all. Colonel Hurley was chased down and caught in just such a fashion.'

'We know that,' the major huffs.

'At first, I thought that the echo of the crimes of Bloody Thomas was a blind, just there to confuse, or perhaps to add some strange layer of mockery over the murder. But I realized that I was wrong. That there was more to it. That the story of Bloody Thomas and what he left behind is absolutely essential to what has occurred here.'

'Kinn, do tell us,' Algy says, in a state of agitation. 'He

was my father and I want to know why someone did that to him.'

'I'm sure you do.'

You look at all the faces laid out before you: Mina, whose life with the overbearing and perhaps even brutish colonel must have been hard. She could have left him, you suppose, but where would she have gone, and what if the colonel refused a separation? Algy. An old chum, and never a great thinker of the age; but then murder never did take brains – all it has ever taken has been jealousy, ambition or revenge. Then there is Leaner, the journalist, a gutter-raker on a most disreputable rag, despite his high estimation of it; he barely knew the victim, though, so could something really have brought him to the point of murder in the few weeks that he had been at the house? Or was it Leaner's master, Gervaise, whose relationship with his father was strained to say the least; and the dead man's disappointment with his heir was plain to see. Tun-Hurley himself claimed to have been friends with the colonel since they were children, but a lot of resentment can build up during a lifetime, and who knows what happened during their war service together? And lastly, Finney. Oh-so-smooth Finney, whose mind clicks away behind that unruffled exterior; there's really no way of knowing what he's thinking.

And you know secrets about all of them.

'Oh, a devilish crime, to go with a devilish forebear,' you say. 'Yes, for a long while I dismissed the key aspect of this case: the history. I concentrated too much on the present, and not enough on the past.' And you turn to look someone in the eye. 'Just as you wanted me to!'

So, the time has come. Who will you accuse of the murder of Colonel Harrison Hurley of Hurley Court?

If you accuse Mina, turn to 100

If you accuse Leaner, turn to 110

If you accuse Tun-Hurley, turn to 93

If you accuse Finney, turn to 49

If you accuse Algy, turn to 23

39

'Going somewhere, gentlemen?' you say, stepping into their path. They look at each other. 'Gervaise Hurley happens to be an acquaintance of mine. State your business with him.'

The one in the yellow suit guffaws. 'Our business? Well, you tell Mr Gervaise that Mickey Plank was lookin' for 'im. 'E owes me fifty nicker and 'e'd better deliver soon if he knows what's good for 'im.'

'That's tough talk,' you say contemptuously. 'But that's all it is.'

'Oh yeah?' He pulls his hand out of his trouser pocket and he's got a set of brass knuckles on it. 'This's just talk, is it?'

'Oi!' It's shouted across the bar. You both look over, and the landlord is pointing a double-barrelled shotgun at the chubby man. 'Want to try your luck, son?' he growls. You always thought the London thugs were hard, but they don't do things by half in the countryside by the looks of it. 'Well, do you?'

The chubby man looks from the barman to you and sneers, but he knows he's defeated. 'You just tell Mr Gervaise I'm lookin' for 'im. And I'll find 'im.' He puts his weapon back in his pocket and he and his mate stride out of the door. You watch the two toughs jump in a battered little van that reads 'M. Plank. Racing bookmaker' and drive off.

You ponder this as Algy ambles back to you. But you have something else to deal with right now.

Turn to 114

'You, Freddie. What did I find hidden in your flat but this bottle.' You lift from within your jacket the bottle marked 'Poison' that you took from the flat earlier that day. 'And what's the betting that if I have the contents analysed, they will show the poison to be cyanide?'

'About zero,' he snorts.

There's something in his confidence that you don't like. 'What do you mean?'

Instead of answering, he looks to Tim. And it's Tim who answers you. 'I'm sorry, it's my fault. That was a joke. It was my Christmas present to him last year – it was gin. Just a bad joke, really. Only, of course, I didn't know any of this was going to happen.'

'Looking a bit stupid now, aren't you, Dr Tenor?' Freddie sneers.

'Wait, let me think it through,' you say, staring at the bottle.

But you never get the chance. Because at that moment, a movement makes you turn. Someone is charging towards you and a glint of metal in their hand tells you exactly what they are thrusting towards your chest. Something that makes the whole world swim until it turns black as night.

Now, go back to the beginning and start again

41

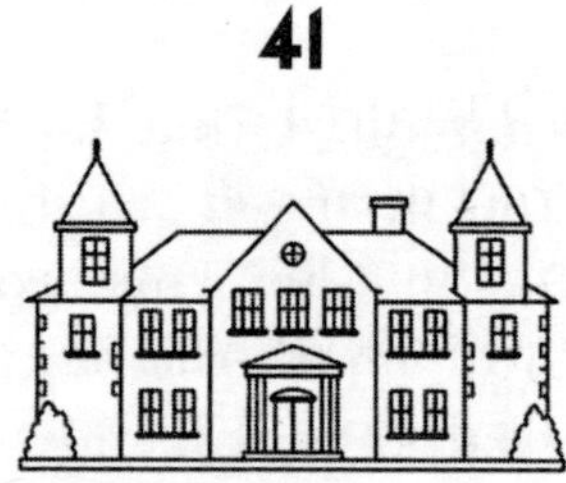

'As I said, Dr Tenor, a mere oversight,' he says. Finney's a smooth operator, but there's a hint of warning underneath his words, as if he's telling you to back off.

Well, it's clear there won't be any more information on the subject, so you tidy yourself up and follow him down to tea.

Turn to 44

'Just remain calm. The driver will come and see what's going on,' you instruct everyone.

But it's the wrong thing to say, because pandemonium breaks out – these people are in no state to sit quietly in the pitch black while Melissa lies dead among them. The yelling gets higher and louder, and you're about to intervene again when you feel something snake around your neck. An arm. It tightens quickly across your throat, and you can't breathe. As the voices snap and shout at each other about what to do, you are feeling your life slip away from you. You won't see daylight again.

Now, go back to the beginning and start again

The streets are empty, but the windows of people's houses are cheerily glowing and the distant sound of Christmas carols drifts in the air with the snowflakes. Christmas Day. A day for peace and joy. But you are on your way instead to Harrogate station. It is empty but for you and your former travelling companions. You all converge at the entrance to the platform and grimly walk the final few paces to the train itself, where Detective Inspector Wilkes is waiting, tapping his foot.

'Thank you for coming,' he says in a gruff, no-nonsense sort of way.

'Didn't have any bloody choice, did we?' replies Freddie.

Wilkes has no time for sarcasm. 'No, you didn't, Mr Thresh. That's the nature of the law. Now, our initial enquiries have told us that we need to know exactly where everyone was when death occurred and the precise order of events. To that end, would you all please enter the car.' You all climb in without speaking a word to one another. Suspicion has taken you over and you regard each other with doubt. 'And now, please take up the places you were in when Mrs Thresh was first discovered deceased.' You are all steely-eyed now – except for Julia, who looks ready to burst into tears – and shuffle into place. You, Simon and Tim are ranged around the disappearing cabinet, Freddie is by the drinks bar, Tiggy and Pererin on the rear seats, Julia and Constantinos on the seats at the side of the carriage.

'Thank you. What I would like to know—'

'Inspector,' you say, interjecting. He doesn't look like he is used to being interrupted, but you put a hand up to quiet him. 'Inspector, I understand your intention, but I am in a position to forestall it.'

'What do you mean?' His gruff manner is even gruffer now, and he looks quite annoyed by the halt to his flow.

'I mean that I can inform you of the who, how and why of the terrible murder of Melissa Thresh.'

He looks gobsmacked. And the gasps from around the room add to the effect.

It's not an unpleasing one.

'You what?' demands Simon.

'You heard me.' You gaze around. 'This was an evil crime. Melissa Thresh was a good woman who didn't deserve what one of you did to her. She had a long and exciting life ahead of her but you cut it short to protect your nasty little secret.'

'Who?' says Freddie.

You pay no attention. 'When Melissa first engaged my services, she thought it was all an adventure, having someone stalking her movements. It never really occurred to her that there would be a serious and ultimately successful plan to end her life.'

'Who is it? Who killed my wife?' demands Freddie.

'Yes. Who? Who would do such a thing? Well, I know.' You look, one by one, at their faces. 'And it was you.'

Who are you pointing at?

If it's Nanny Tiggy, turn to 86

If it's Pererin and Simon Yarrow, turn to 29

If it's Tim, turn to 36

If it's Freddie, turn to 85

If it's Inspector Reeves, turn to 60

44

The tea gathering is in full swing when you arrive. At the head of the table, Colonel Hurley, Algy's father, devours a plate piled high with cucumber sandwiches. He's been through a war or two and has the scars to prove it. Like most retired military men you've met, he doesn't suffer fools gladly. Algy's mother, Mina, is looking a little flustered at the moment. She spills coffee onto the table cloth and looks bewildered as to what to do, until Finney gently places a napkin on the stain.

'Just leave it to the servant, Mother,' instructs Gervaise, her elder son, as she attempts to help the butler clean up the mess. 'It really is what he's here for.'

You have never taken to that boy. While Algy inherited his mother's fine looks and pleasant nature, all his father's brains seem to have distilled into Gervaise, but without any moral direction to them. He owns a small newspaper now, the *Daily Messenger*, whose bland title hides an often-nasty line in scurrilous rumours and sensational reporting of crime and unfortunate accidents.

Finney stiffens a little at what you suspect is more a dig at him than a throwaway comment.

'If you would like me to clear up any other messes, sir, do please ask,' the butler replies.

Gervaise grins at the reply. You guess Algy's brother has left a few untidy situations here and there, and Finney knows all about them. 'Ah, Finney,' he says. 'Sometimes I think we should all just hand over the reins to you. Leave you in charge. You'd make a good job of running us, wouldn't you?'

'I would do my best, sir.'

'Hear that, Father?' Gervaise says. 'Finney's in charge from now on. And I for one am looking forward to a new era of cool-headed efficiency.'

'Stop your nonsense,' his father snaps, sandwich in hand. 'Though God knows you could do with a firm hand.' He takes a bite and glares at his son. 'Wish I'd taken you up more when you were a boy. Someone should have knocked more sense into you. That school of yours didn't.'

'Not for want of trying,' Gervaise says acidly. 'Oh, I don't deny that I put them to it whenever I could, but if you ask me, half of those masters should have been locked up for sadism. And so, here I am, Dad. I am what you and they made me.' He opens his arms to let his father appraise him.

Colonel Hurley, his face turning red, is about to remonstrate with his eldest child when Mina, ever the peacemaker, places her hand on his arm. 'Not now, dear. Guests.'

Hurley huffs and starts angrily buttering a scone.

Turn to 120

45

You put your hands out and blindly step towards whoever is in desperate need of help. You trip over something – a foot, perhaps – but it doesn't really matter what it is, because you fall straight onto the blade of the upturned silver dagger, piercing your chest. You stagger as far as you can and fall behind the church pews. In the dark no one knows that you are bleeding to death. When the torches are alight once more you are found . . . but it is too late.

Now, go back to the beginning and start again

46

Yes, turn up and ambush the ambusher. That's the spirit. You wait in your room until nearly eleven, and then quietly steal out to the church.

Winter light is filtering through the stained-glass windows and sliding along the floor as you peek inside. Empty – as far as you can tell, anyway.

You carefully pick your way up the aisle. A noise makes you stop. What was it? A footstep? Or just the sound of the wind forcing its way through the old stones?

You check over your shoulder. Is there anyone there? No, no one behind you. A glance into the vestry, yes, that's all clear too. You settle into one of the pews and watch the doorway. No one will get the drop on you. No, you—

Your throat! Something gripping your . . . Can't breathe . . . You grab at your neck, find hands there . . .

Twist and struggle and catch a glimpse of someone standing over you, someone who has been hiding longer than you . . .

'I told you to come on time,' they growl. '*I told you.*'

Now, go back to the beginning and start again

47

You're sleepy and decide to avail yourself of the bedroom offered. You take your bags and settle in. It's plain, and doesn't seem to be used very often, but it's clean enough. You lay out your pyjamas and take yourself to the bathroom, where you brush your teeth in front of a large mirrored cabinet. After rinsing, curiosity overcomes you and you open the cabinet. There are a few pill bottles, lotions and potions, but nothing that is of professional interest.

You toddle back to your room. For some reason, the chest of drawers in the corner isn't quite flush to the wall. This bothers you, and you try to push it back, but there's something solid lodged behind it. You get down on your hands and knees and peer into the gap. Whatever's back there looks like glassware. Gently, you pull the chest away, and something – a bottle – drops to the floor with a clunk.

It's a small glass bottle, with a white label. And on the label is a single printed word: 'Poison'. The dregs of a clear liquid flow around at the bottom of the bottle.

You decide what to do. You could wake Freddie and confront him. But maybe that's not for the best right now. No, for now, you will keep your discovery to yourself. After all, there are a lot more enquiries that you wish to make tomorrow.

And so, you turn off the light and go to bed. Making sure that your door is locked.

Turn to 31

You watch as Freddie knocks back the drink. *Wait*, you think to yourself. *The smell of almonds*. Yes. Something else smells like almonds.

And it's about then that you see the first effects. They don't take long – five or six seconds, no more. Freddie is struggling to breathe, his lips are quivering. And then

Pererin is screaming, Simon is rushing to try to help and, in the middle of it all, you're kicking yourself, and smelling almonds – or hydrogen cyanide.

It's more than a professional oversight, though; it's the end of your investigation and, indeed, your career, because as soon as you arrive in Harrogate, you're sidelined and ignored and the case is taken over by the local police, who soon apprehend the killer. You have to crawl back to London with your tail between your legs, where you become a laughing stock in the Metropolitan Police and have to find a new job. Your mother might have been right about your choice of profession.

Now, go back to the beginning and start again

49

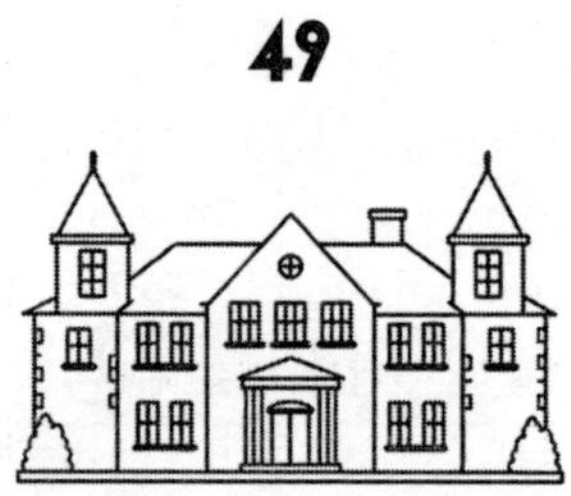

'Finney,' you say. 'From the very beginning I should have suspected you. My first sight when I arrived was of you with your clothes dishevelled. Not what I would expect from such an excellent butler.' And you turn to Mina. 'How long has it been going on?' Mina's eyes open wide and her mouth drops open. 'You might as well tell me.'

'Oh, God!' She looks at Algy, who stares, aghast, at her. 'It was nothing. Your father was . . .'

'Mother!'

Finney smirks and takes a seat on the sofa. He picks a cigarette from a lacquer box on the side table, strikes a match and lights it. 'Is that it?' he asks.

'Hardly. You can also tell me how long you have been selling illegal morphine.' You see Major Tun-Hurley stand, his stiff leg shivering under his weight. 'Yes, Major, I know what you were buying from him. You became addicted due to that wound of yours, I presume?'

Tun-Hurley sits down heavily and slowly nods. 'Ashamed of it. Just ashamed,' he says.

'I presume, Finney, you killed Colonel Hurley because he found out what you had been doing?' The servant is still smirking. He leans back and blows smoke out of the side of his mouth. 'You seem very relaxed,' you say.

'Of course I am,' he replies. 'I'm enjoying seeing you make a fool of yourself. Oh, you're right about my evenings with the widow here.' She covers her face. 'And the dope-head major.' Tun-Hurley opens his mouth to remonstrate. 'Don't bother, old man,' Finney says. 'I'm finished. And so is Dr Tenor. Who is barking up the wrong tree entirely.'

'What are you saying?' you demand.

'I'm saying that it wasn't me. I had nothing to do with the old so-and-so's death.'

'Nonsense!' you insist.

'Oh no, not nonsense. But I have worked out who's really to blame.' He taps his cigarette into a glass ashtray.

'Who?' asks Gervaise.

Finney smirks once more as he lifts his finger and points. You all watch it extend. But not for long, because the accused bursts into laughter, reaches into a pocket and draws out a tiny, two-barrelled Deringer pistol. Two barrels. But one is enough to fire the bullet that means you will never see them face justice.

Now, go back to the beginning and start again

50

Finney wheels a trolley of food into the dining room. It was meant to be for a celebration but now looks cold and unappetizing. People pick at it without much interest before drifting away to bed with little discussion of what has happened.

You are one of the last to leave – you certainly don't feel ready for sleep. Algy bids you goodnight and heads for his room, but something draws you instead to the gloomy billiards room, with its portraits of Hurleys through the ages. You enter and pour yourself a Scotch and soda from the globe drinks cabinet beside the door. Sipping it, you gaze up at the score of family portraits, some dating back centuries.

'Ugly crew, aren't they?'

The words are growled from a dark corner. You see Colonel Hurley with a tumbler in his hand, swirling golden liquid around.

'They won't win any beauty contests.' There are some dressed as Cavalier soldiers, a couple in judge's robes, a priest, but most in civilian garb. The family trait seems to be for prominent ears, which is no great boon to anyone but a spaniel. You fix on one who has the most evil glint in his eye you have ever encountered. He wears fine eighteenth-century garments: a blue silk neckerchief, brocade coat and curling white wig. And you notice something in his hand: a knife with a golden handle and silver blade. He seems to be pointing it straight at the viewer.

'Ah, yes. That one. That's "Bloody Thomas" Hurley.' He knocks back his drink.

'Curious moniker.'

'Curious, you say? Ha! Fitting. A fitting moniker.'

'How so?'

He breaks into a positively Satanic grin. 'Well, I'll tell you how so. It was in the reign of Mad King George. Thomas was the squire here. We've been squires for nigh on five centuries.' He makes a satisfied noise in his throat. 'Bloody Thomas was a hellraiser. Liked drinking, fighting, hunting. Only they say that the hunting got out of hand.'

'And what does that mean?'

'Hares when he was young, then foxes, then stags and finally . . .'

'Yes?'

'People.' You feel a chill draught. 'Local peasants. He would come up with some false offence they were supposed to have committed: poaching, or failure to pay their rents on time. All made up on the spot. He would allow them a ten-minute head start and then give chase with some of his wickedest pals. And he had a special trick.'

'Tell me.'

'I shall. He would deliberately chase his victim along a track where he had placed a man-trap.'

'What sort of man-trap?'

'One of those nasty metal ones with spring-loaded jaws that snap onto your leg and don't let go. Gin-trap, they call them.'

'He sounds quite foul.'

Hurley chuckles. 'You say so? Well, there are many who would agree with you. One of them was the old crone whose son was Thomas's last victim. The lad was twenty, and Thomas was said to be jealous of his fair looks. So one night, in a winter blizzard, he rode through the snow to the lad's cottage. There he claimed the boy had stolen apples from our orchard.'

'Do you even have an orchard?' you ask. You have seen no evidence that there is one here.

'Not now, not ever.'

'I see.'

'So it was the usual business. Ten minutes to make

himself scarce, then Thomas and his gang gave chase. Only this time, they never found him.'

'He survived.'

'Oh, I didn't say that,' Hurley says darkly. 'No, it wasn't the squire that killed him, it was the weather. He was found the next day, frozen in a ditch. Old Thomas was quite disappointed at missing out on his sport.' The colonel's off-hand manner when relating the story is disconcerting, to say the least.

'And what of the dead man's mother?'

'Yes, that's the meat of the tale. It seems she was a local wise woman, suspected of witchcraft. The locals said she had uncanny powers.'

'How nice.'

'Oh, you think so? Well, the squire didn't. Old Mother Glass turned up on Thomas's doorstep, you see, demanding justice. Well, the squire just laughed and threw a basin of water over her so that she would freeze in the cold, just like her boy. Only it didn't happen that way. It's said that she performed a spell, and the moment the water touched her, it boiled and turned to steam.'

'Quite the trick.'

'It was. And then she waved her hands in the air, chanting an ancient curse. There was an almighty cracking sound in the air and the snow clouds turned black. Old Thomas, not a man to scare easily, demanded to know what she had done. She said that from that day on, he would be followed by devils, just waiting for their moment to drag him down to hell.'

'And did he accept his fate?'

'Oh, no. He snarled at her that he was more devil than any she could set on him. After sending her away, he sent for his sword-maker and told him to fashion a weapon so wicked that Lucifer himself would be afraid to come close.' He points to the portrait. 'And there you have it. The Hurley Dagger. A cursed family heirloom if ever there was one.'

It looks it. Your gaze moves along the portraits. Five of them – by the looks of their costume, the five who came after Bloody Thomas – also hold the silver knife in their grasp. Only the three in the most recent clothes, including the picture of your host Colonel Harrison Hurley when he was younger, don't show it.

'We saw its business this evening.'

'That we did.'

'It's been passed down through every generation?'

'Skipped a couple. Disappeared.'

'But you have it now.'

'My cousin Wilfred – Major Tun-Hurley – and I managed to buy it back. After the War. Returned it to its rightful place.'

'What happened to Bloody Thomas?'

'A cheery end to the tale, this. For years he went on as he had before. But always keeping the silver dagger by his side. He would say that at night he could see the devils following him, waiting for the knife to be out of reach so they could pounce. After ten years he became blasé about it. He mocked the black spirits, daring them to come close. But pride comes before a fall. And one Christmas Eve he spent the whole night carousing with his bully friends at a nearby inn. He rode home as the clock tolled midnight. But as he lowered himself to his doorstep he realized to his horror that he had left the dagger at the inn. At that moment, the door blew open and all the black demons poured out, smothering him and wrenching him down to hell.'

'Where is it now?'

He reaches inside his jacket and pulls out the blade, now cleaned of his blood and glinting in the light. 'Always keep it with me. Have to ward off the devils.' He smiles wickedly and you watch each other for a while. Then he pushes himself up from the chair, grunting in pain. 'I shall retire for the night.'

'Very wise, given your injury.'

'Pah. It's nothing. You said so yourself.' He walks slowly to the doorway. 'But know this: Bloody Thomas isn't entirely gone.'

'He's back from hell?' you suggest.

'He never entirely left. His spirit walks the house at night. You can hear his footsteps as he looks for this to protect him in the underworld.' He lifts the blade once more to glint in the light, then slips it back inside his jacket and heads for the staircase. 'Christmas Day tomorrow,' he says as he passes through the doorway. 'Day he's supposed to walk among us.'

Turn to 122

51

When you get outside the snowstorm is still raging, so that your torches seem very weak. Tun-Hurley limps a little on his stiff leg. 'There isn't a chance that anyone is out here, just waiting,' Leaner shouts over the wind. 'He would be dead of cold by now. Let's go back in.'

'Have to check thoroughly. I've seen some tough acts in my time,' Tun-Hurley replies forcefully. He's right, so despite Leaner's objections, you all wade through the knee-high snow. You check the stables, the car garage, an abandoned dairy building and a storage shed. It's all quiet and undisturbed. As you pass on to an ice-bound summer house, you strike up a conversation with Leaner.

'So you work on Gervaise's newspaper.'

'I do,' he says cheerily as you make it into the hexagonal building, half iron and half glass. 'It's a living.'

'How did you join it?'

'Fresh out of Oxford.'

'Oh, yes? Which college? I was at Lincoln.'

'I was at Hertford.' You watch the snowflakes swirling. Tun-Hurley is poking about at the back, checking that no one is hiding behind the stripy deckchairs and wrought-iron tables. 'All my classmates were heading into the Civil

Service or taking over their family estates, some into the Church. It raised a fair few eyebrows when I said I was joining the *Messenger*, I can tell you.'

You're not surprised. Gervaise's paper isn't exactly the respectable end of Fleet Street. In fact, you're surprised it isn't sued every hour on the hour. It really is a poor soup of tittle-tattle, barely credible scandal and outright fabrication. The standard story seems to be that the younger son of an earl has been frequently seen in the company of an actress known to enjoy sniffing laughing gas.

'I read a story last month about the Bishop of Bath and Wells, the niece of Lord Planer and an otter,' you tell him.

'Yes, that was one of mine.'

'Good Lord. Did the otter really do what you said it did?'

He scratches his neck. 'Hard to say. I was a little sceptical myself, but then I saw a photograph and it certainly seemed to do it.'

'Extraordinary. You wouldn't think it would want to.'

'Well, no. Being a primarily aquatic species and all that.'

You both ponder it for a second. 'Do you ever come across information that you can't print?' you ask.

'Oh, all the time. It's all stored up here for later use, though.' He taps his temple. 'One day it'll all come out.'

Turn to 121

52

You're intrigued most of all by Freddie. And the fact that his offer wasn't entirely sincere makes you all the more resolved to take it.

'Thanks, old man,' you say. 'I'm sure yours will be the most convenient for all concerned.'

He snorts a little. 'Come on then. We'll take a cab.' He leads you out to the rank, where a solitary taxi stands idle, the driver looking disconsolately through the windscreen at the falling snow.

He drives you – his downcast countenance not changing one bit – to the Advance Pharmaceuticals factory, which isn't much bigger than a large townhouse. 'We're at the top,' Freddie says, heaving his bag out of the boot and rooting about in it for a bunch of large iron keys.

It's all a little spooky now that it's dark and there's no one around. You follow him through a side door and up three narrow flights of stairs until you land in a comfortable flat, idiosyncratically decorated with curios from across the globe – Melissa's hand, you imagine. A stuffed caiman, tribal masks and wind or string musical instruments that you don't recognize line the walls of the front parlour.

'Drink?' He has a decanter in his hand, unstoppered. It looks like brandy. 'I'm past the point where it's sensible to stop.'

'I imagine you are,' you say, sitting in an unusual seat made of a steel frame with leather stretched across it. 'I'll have one.'

He pours them out, hands one to you and sips his own while staring out at the road.

'What do you think you will get out of me?'

'Some brandy, a pillow for the night. We can take it from there.'

'Ah, yes. Not too optimistic. Probably for the best. Would you like the grand tour?' he asks.

'Why not?'

He shows you around the house. There are servants' quarters, but they are shut up and haven't been used for years by the look of them. The first expense to go when the wolf is at the door.

There is his study, with bundles of scientific papers, clearly unread, stacked on a baize-topped desk. 'I leave all the technical stuff to Tim. I manage the company, rather like I would manage a farm or theatre. Money comes in, money goes out. I can't understand a word of what this says' – he picks up a report and tosses it aside – 'but I don't have to. Money in, money out.' He drains his glass and thumps it down on the desk. 'Problem is, you see, not enough of the former and too much of the latter. *Ergo* bankruptcy.'

'I see.'

'We had a chance to sell out a few years ago. Should

have taken it. Melissa didn't want to – too much family history tied up in the place.' He seems to catch himself and looks at you to gauge your reaction.

'Pererin Yarrow,' you say.

'Ah, yes. I knew we would get there in the end. What about her?'

'Tell me what was between you. And Freddie, one thing.'

'Yes?'

'Don't lie. I'll know if you do.'

He sits behind the desk and places his feet on another pile of scientific papers, rubbing his forehead ruminatively. 'She's enchanting, isn't she? I don't know why. I don't know what it is about her that means I can't just stay away from her. Maybe it's because that lunk of a husband keeps telling me to. Maybe it's because she does the same.'

'You're doing yourself no favours.'

'You can say that again.' He sighs. There's silence for a while. Then he announces wearily that he's going to bed. 'You can have the one at the end of the corridor. There's a sheet and what-have-you in the cupboard.' He drags himself out of the room. You're almost as tired as he is.

If you go to bed too, turn to 47

If you wait around for a while, turn to 54

You drive over to The Plough. It's a pleasant old country inn, with low ceilings, horse brasses on display and pints of warmish beer pulled properly. The atmosphere is all very jolly, packed with locals clinking their glasses together and wishing each other a merry Christmas. You sit yourselves at the bar and chat. The upcoming ritual is uppermost in your mind, though Algy can't tell you much about it. 'I've only seen it done once, when I was a lad and my second cousin Terence – poor chap died at Ypres – underwent it.'

'I see. Now, what about these letters you've all been getting?'

'Ah, yes. I've brought some with me so you can take a peek. These were sent to me.'

He hands over three yellow envelopes, each with an equally yellow page of writing paper inside. 'You think you've got away with it,' reads one. 'Justice will catch up with you,' states another. The third informs the reader: 'Call me your Nemesis'.

'Charming little missives,' you say.

'Put the chills up me, I don't mind telling you.'

'I can see why.' All the writing has been typed. The postmarks say the letters have been posted in the village over the past month, which doesn't tell you too much – it could have been someone local or someone who has taken the precaution of coming to the village to post them in order to cover their tracks. But it's a lead worth looking into.

You take a close look at the notepaper. Holding it up to the light, you find a manufacturer's watermark: 'Foeman's', it states.

'Is there a telephone here?' you ask.

'Out there.' He points to a red phone box on the other side of the road. You head out and he goes over to chat to some friends he has seen on the other side of the bar.

'Metropolitan Police, how may I direct your call?' buzzes out of the receiver when you drop your coins in and tell the operator to whom you wish to speak.

'Derek Mills, please.' A moment's silence before a tired Belfast voice mumbles a hello. 'Derek, it's Kinn.'

'Oh, Lord. What is it now?'

He was always a bit of a wet blanket. 'Notepaper. Sun yellow. Watermark "Foeman's". Find out about it, will you?' You give him the telephone number of Hurley Court and tell him to call when he has some information.

He grunts something like an agreement, and you hang up and return to the pub.

As you enter, a couple of chubby men in loud suits – one is yellow with a red check thread, the other a bright green – and grubby bowler hats approach the landlord. 'Not you two again,' he huffs. 'I told you, I don't know where Mr Gervaise is. Try his house if you like, but leave me alone.'

'We only wants a quiet word with 'im,' insists Yellow Suit.

'That's right,' confirms the other.

'What about?'

One of them chuckles in an especially nasty, gurgling way. 'Mr Gervaise ain't so good at payin' wot 'e owes. An' we don' happreciate people wot don' pay wot they owes. Do we?'

'Nah. We 'ates it,' confirms the other. 'It really gets our goat, it does.'

''E gets the red mist. Don' know wot 'e's doin'. Gets nasty.'

'Nasty. Wiv me fists.'

The landlord is probably used to dealing with aggressive drunks and isn't cowed. 'All right. That's enough. Hop it,' he says, pointing to the exit and glaring back at the two of them.

They gurgle again and make for the exit.

If you let them go, turn to 18

If you jump up and bar their way, turn to 39

54

Your mind is too active to sleep just yet. You take Freddie's place at the baize-topped desk. There's the research report that he tossed aside. It's the final damning report that said the company's new angina medication just didn't work.

'Final analysis: Hilkodine.' You leaf through it. You've seen enough scientific papers to last you a lifetime. But as you glance through this one, something stands out. Hilkodine doesn't work for angina, but it does have an effect. And suddenly something else makes sense, something that you hadn't even remarked on earlier. Tim mentioned that Nanny Tiggy had tried Hilkodine herself and found no side effects. But back on the train she had said she suffered from arthritis. And yet your very first sight of her was her running up the platform to catch the train. And she's been in and out of seats without so much as a murmur.

It seems Hilkodine has no effect on angina, but it works well for arthritic joints.

You are about to replace the report on the desk, but change your mind. Freddie won't miss it. You take it with you when you go to bed.

Turn to 47

55

You wake up with a bit of a thick head – you shouldn't have had that fifth Buck's Fizz – but the fresh air on the drive down to Hurley Court, near Sidcup in Kent, clears it for you. It's a frosty morning and you have to scrape a fair amount of ice off the windscreen before your flame-red MG Roadster can purr into action. It feels good to put your foot down and whip through the narrow country lanes fast enough to scare the locals.

Just after three in the afternoon you skid to a gravel-spraying halt in front of the house. It's Tudor, with an oak skeleton exposed to the elements, and has stood for many centuries. It looks like it will stand for many more.

You've always loved how a house can reflect a nation, as well as the family who live there. Hurley Court is a case in point. Algy told you once that over the ages its owners had fought in the Wars of the Roses, the Civil War, the Napoleonic Wars, the Boer War and the Great War. It has been flooded, set on fire, burgled and bankrupted. And yet here it remains. A bit like England, really: knocked about a bit but still standing at the end of the fight.

'Kinn!' Algy cries, rushing out of the front of the house and tripping over the boot scraper on the doorstep. 'Oh, bother.' He picks himself up and dusts off his knees. You take the opportunity to climb out of the car. 'You came.' Ah, Algy Hurley. No, he won't be winning any prizes for intellect but he's a good-natured thing. Like a puppy that has just about been house-trained.

'You know me, Algy. If there's a bit of a mystery to get my teeth into, wild horses can't keep me away.'

'And there's a jolly odd one here for you. But here's Finney now.'

Finney, the butler, arrives looking as smoothly efficient

as ever. He's a good-looking man, too, with thick, wavy hair that he lacquers back. You notice that although he seems to glide wherever he goes, his shirt studs are currently askew and his shirt slightly lopsided.

'Tsk, tsk, Finney,' you say. 'Did you dress in the dark?'

He follows your index finger and looks down. 'I'm sorry, Dr Tenor, I can't think what happened,' he says, buttoning his frock-coat so that the offending studs are hidden for now.

'Come on, this way, high tea is up,' Algy says. 'We have it in the breakfast room. And on the way, I'm going to tell you how I'm going to be rich.'

'Oh no, Algy. Not another of your schemes. They always end in disaster.'

'Not this time though, this one's a winner.' You sigh and tell him to get on with it. The sooner he explains, the sooner you can tell him the flaw in his scheme. 'Righto. Well, there's a chap I went to school with who's discovered this amazing chemical that he calls "Cleano" and that does wonders for sprucing up the family silver, even your best clobber. Centuries of dirt just wiped away. "One Spray and It's Away!" That's my slogan. I came up with it myself.'

'Very impressive,' you say, suppressing the desire to shake Algy by the shoulders until his brain switches to a higher gear.

There's a compact hallway when you enter through the sun-bleached oak door. An odd Hurley ancestor was obsessed with taxidermy, so the room is lined with bears, stags, foxes, crows and even some poor hamster shot dead during the early reign of Queen Victoria. A hippopotamus's foot serves as a retainer for an assemblage of umbrellas. Algy says he used to give the dead creatures names and pretend to play with them when he was a kid, which is a bit creepy, though when you're in a Tudor manor house two miles from the nearest village, and your only playmate is your nanny (your older brother being away at school), you make do with what you have, you suppose. The hallway is dominated by a staircase of rich elm, which you admire. It leads up to a circular gallery and the bedrooms.

Everything's a bit different today, because the whole house has been given a layer of jolly décor for Christmas, with green and red paper chains everywhere and wooden angels, trumpets and donkeys tied to bannisters and door handles.

Algy heads for the breakfast room, one of the four rooms leading off the hallway – the others being the library, the drawing room and the billiards room – while Finney takes your bags to your bed chamber.

'I'll be with you in a few minutes,' you say. 'I just want to change.'

'Oh, right you are.' And Algy toddles off to tea, while you follow Finney up to your room.

It's a bit heavy on dark wood, but the four-poster looks fitting for a monarch. In fact, two have slept in the house, you know, so maybe old George III laid his mad head on this very bolster. The fire in your grate is pleasingly ablaze.

'Will that be all?' Finney asks.

You're curious about how Finney, who is so particular about his dress, could have missed a shirt stud.

If you ask him about it, turn to 41

If you don't, turn to 112

56

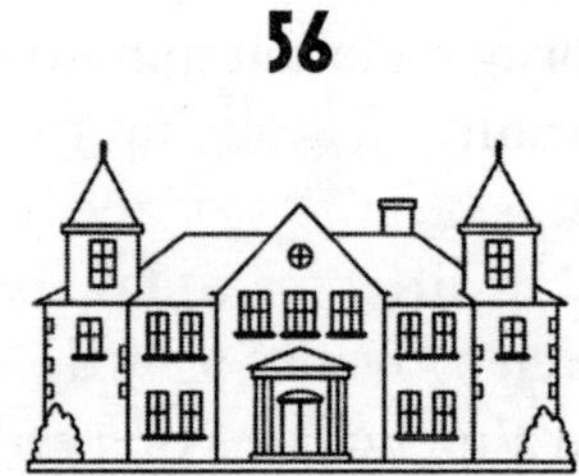

You toddle into the breakfast room. Finney is arranging a dish of kippers. Mina is looking quite beautiful in a velveteen morning dress. Algy throws himself into a chair, beaming at everyone. Gervaise somehow manages to sneer with his eyebrows.

'I say, let's have the first carol of the year!' Algy bursts out. 'Nothing like a good sing-song over brekkie, that's what I say.'

'If that's what you say, then I suggest it is best if you say nothing more,' his brother replies.

'Oh, come on, Gervaise, let's get into the Christmas spirit!'

'Waifs freezing to death with their faces pressed up against sweet-shop windows, mothers of eight cast out of their houses by rapacious landlords, that sort of thing? Well, I can get behind that.'

'Oh, do be quiet, fathead.' And Algy gets up and turns on the wireless, which blasts out 'God Rest Ye Merry, Gentlemen'. 'Oh, now this is wonderful.' He begins to drum on the table with spoons. He drops one on the floor and gets down to pick it up.

'Merry Christmas, everyone,' Tun-Hurley says as he enters the room, his stiff leg, the souvenir of the War, giving him a bit of trouble. Despite that, he is smiling a little more than usual.

'Ow!' Algy says as he tries to stand and bangs his head on the table.

'Harrison not here?' the major asks.

'Out for his morning walk,' Mina replies.

You're just tucking in to some toast when suddenly someone bursts into the room, turning everything upside down. It's Leaner, looking ashen-faced. 'Quick!' he yells. 'This way!'

You don't know what it is, but you can tell it's serious. You jump up and follow him.

The journalist dashes through the house, with you and the others hot on his heels. Even Finney has abandoned his usual suave grace to keep up. You all charge out of the front door and through the stiff snow, around the side of the building. And then you stop short. In front of you, on the narrow gravel path that circles the house, you see a dead man. A man who inherited this pile from his ancestors, some of them good, some of them wicked. A man who survived one attempt to kill him and looks now to have succumbed to a second. Colonel Harrison Hurley, old war horse, master of Hurley Court, lies stiff on the path. A large wound, with blood frozen into black ice, is on his temple. You have seen all of this before in a score of cases, but there's something else, something unique that you have never seen before. For his left leg is clamped in a vicious, evil contraption: a man-trap of two serrated iron jaws that have sprung together to break his limb and hold him down so that a killer can finish the job. It is just how Colonel Hurley's wicked ancestor Bloody Thomas used to capture his victims before killing them.

That's not all, though.

For as you view the body, something beside it glints in the winter sunlight: something silver. Closed in Colonel Hurley's fist is the silver knife with the gold handle that Bloody Thomas had fashioned as protection from the devils sent to drag him down to hell. It did Thomas as much good as it has done his descendant. But you guess from how tightly the colonel's fingers are wrapped around it and the way his arm is outstretched from his body that he was using the blade as a last line of defence against an assailant bent on his death.

You go quickly but calmly to the body, though you know from his open, unresponsive eyes, the grimacing mouth, that there is little point. You are doing it for formality more than anything.

'I'm sorry,' you say, standing, to Mina. 'He's gone.'

'Harrison!' she cries, and rushes towards him. You and Gervaise grab hold of her.

'Please don't touch him,' you say. 'There's evidence there.'

'Evidence?' she says, sobbing, confused.

'He's been murdered, Mother,' Gervaise says as gently as he can, though he glances at the body and winces at the sight. 'Come away.'

He leads her towards the house. 'You found him, I take it?' you ask Leaner.

'I came out for a smoke. Saw him. Realized he was dead and ran straight in. How long has he been like this?'

You take a look. 'It's a bit hard to say. The snow and cold make it more difficult to calculate. Less than an hour though.' You know that that won't help unmask the criminal: even if you could say for certain that it's less than an hour, you doubt anyone in the house will have an alibi for every minute of the last sixty.

'Could it be an intruder?' Algy asks desperately. 'Someone who came across the fields.'

'Not a chance. Look at the snow. The tracks,' you say, pointing to the perfect drifts as far as you can see. The only tracks – Hurley's, yours, everyone's – are between the body and the front door of the house. 'No, Algy, whoever did this is one of us.'

'My God,' he whispers.

'Wait, what's that?' Leaner is pointing to something a few yards away in the snow. You take two paces towards it so you can see it better. A black hammer lies on the ground. And from the blood congealed on it, it's clear that you are looking at the murder weapon. Two gardener's gloves lie beside it, as if to say that there's no point checking the hammer for fingerprints.

Turn to 97

57

You walk back down through the house to the hallway. The dinner gong should be loud enough to wake everyone if you give it a bit of welly.

Bash, bash, bash. A dozen rings and the sleepy inmates begin stumbling down. First to appear is the journalist Leaner, who looks mystified. Then it's his employer, Gervaise, who appears amused by the midnight gathering. 'May we enquire as to the nature of this party?' he asks. 'Is it cocktails or merely warm milk?'

'Do wait your turn, Gervaise,' you reply. 'I'm sure there will be other, less inane questions and I should like to answer them first.'

'As you wish.'

Algy is next to appear, hurrying down dressed in pyjamas and a stripy dressing gown. 'Kinn? Is there a fire?' he asks, staring all around, as if the flames are within reach.

'No, Algy. If there were, then I might think of saying so quite loudly.'

'Ah, yes. Right you are.'

Mina descends, looking quite composed, in advance of her husband, who is glowering like a thunderstorm. 'Who the devil's making that racket?' he yells as he places a slippered foot on the top stair. 'I'll shoot the rascal myself. You!' he snarls, as he sees the drumstick in your hand. 'Out with it. What's the meaning of this?'

'I'm sorry, Colonel, but there seemed no other way.' That's not quite true – you could have been a bit more gentle with the awakening, but there's a little part of you that's enjoying the theatre. 'I'm afraid an intruder is either in the house, or has just left it.'

'Intruder! Where's my pistol? Finney, fetch it now,' he growls. You glance in the direction of the servants' wing. Finney has indeed just arrived, followed by the female servants. He is perfectly dressed, as if he has just finished serving dinner. Perhaps he sleeps in his uniform, in case he is called upon.

'What is it, Harrison?' Tun-Hurley comes into view at the top of the stairs.

'Intruder!' the colonel warns him.

'Where?'

'Don't know yet. Finney, where's that pistol?'

'I shall retrieve it, sir.' He departs for the rear of the house. The two maids are shivering in thin dressing gowns and look confused. Well, they're not the only ones.

'Now speak up!' Hurley demands.

'I was woken about twenty minutes ago by the sound of someone in the attic.'

'Balderdash. Pigeons.'

'I assure you, it was a human being. I went up there . . .'

'Who gave you permission to go creeping about my house at night, eh?'

'I took it upon myself.'

'Yes, that's just—'

'Please let Dr Tenor speak, darling,' Mina says, placing her hand on his arm.

'Well,' he grumbles. 'Go on then.'

'Thank you. I went up to the attic. There, he or she attacked me in the dark.'

'I hope you gave them a good biffing in return.'

'It wasn't so easy, given that we were in perfect darkness.' He mumbles something that you don't catch. 'They then took to their heels, right out of the house and into the snow outside.' You hold up your hand to waylay another word from Hurley. 'Yes, Colonel, I did give chase. But you will note that there is a blizzard out there, and I soon lost them. They may be in this house right now.'

Finney reappears with a revolver and hands it to his master. You see that it's a Webley Mark VI, standard issue for army officers. You recognize a lot of guns due to your work for the police. Hurley opens it, checks that it is loaded and snaps it closed again.

'I hope they did come back,' he says darkly. 'I want to put my hands on the swine.'

'And what if it was someone who is here right now?'

You sweep your gaze slowly over the faces ranged before you. Some are nervous, some are defiant, some are simply tired. Is one of them guilty too? Hurley glares at your companions one by one. And then his voice changes and becomes more quietly threatening. 'If there is a snake, by God I'll . . .' And he cocks the hammer on his revolver.

'Colonel, I must declare that I cannot rule out the

possibility that the person who assaulted me is you.' You await the crash of anger that you expect from your host. You are not waiting long.

'*How ... how dare you!*' he yells, his face turning red enough to light up the room. '*This is my house! My house, damn you! I will not—*'

'Harrison!' Mina insists, raising her voice almost to his level. 'Dr Tenor is quite right to say that.'

'Quite right?!'

Behind her, you see Gervaise desperately trying to stifle laughter at the proceedings.

'It would be irresponsible to ignore anyone. Even you.' She glances all around. 'Although, of course, I know that you are not the criminal.'

That calms him just enough to stop the steam escaping from his ears. 'My house,' he growls, as an aftershock. 'Impertinence beyond anything I've ever heard.'

'Your wife understands my position,' you say. 'Until we discover the truth – and we will discover it, I assure you – we must all consider every possible explanation for what has happened.'

'Well, that sounds very reasonable to me,' Mina adds, smoothing down her husband's dressing gown. 'Doesn't it sound it to you?'

He mutters, irritably, under his breath, before speaking out loud. 'All right. All right. Yes, the camp's been infiltrated. Have to keep a watch all about. So what now?'

You are relieved. That could have gone worse. 'Our target is dangerous,' you say. 'They assaulted me and would have gone further – how much further is impossible to say – had I not fought back. So we must search in groups of at least three with our wits about us.'

You propose that you go with Leaner and Tun-Hurley. You have barely spoken to them yet and it will give you a chance to question them a little. You will search the ground floor. Algy and Gervaise go with the maids to search the servants' wing; Finney and Mina accompany Colonel Hurley to go through the upper storey and the attic. Hurley's finger is on the trigger as he goes. You're sure that if he does come across a fugitive, this time they won't be getting away. Not in one piece, anyway. You tell everyone to reassemble in the billiards room in twenty minutes.

Turn to 74

58

All the clocks in Goldstone's, the finest clockmakers in London, are striking the hour as you saunter through the Burlington Arcade. You do rather like this little enclosed parade of shops – gilded, boutique places to buy brilliantly constructed watches, subtle perfumes, Darjeeling tea. You stroll along, and one of the red-caped beadles who patrol the Arcade tips his hat to you while his eyes search left and right for anyone looking a bit shifty.

You spot Melissa peering into the curved glass window of Dubois of Paris, the leading perfumiers. You happen to know that Pierre Dubois was born Pete Woods in Sheffield and he's seen the inside of Brixton Prison more than once. You've relied on him from time to time for a little information on the activities of his former comrades in the criminal underworld. Every time he begins with, 'I'm goin' straight now, Dr Tenor. No idea what you're talkin' about', but he always comes up with the goods once you mention that your friends in Scotland Yard's fraud department would be interested in how his scents 'direct from France' are actually brewed up in his basement in Pimlico.

'Looking for something sweet?' you ask Melissa.

'None of this suits me,' she replies.

'No?'

'I'm looking for something to ward off the mosquitoes when I paddle up the Amazon.'

'Are you really?'

'I most certainly am. And you have no idea how difficult it is to find good snake anti-venom in London at this time of year.'

'That is true, I haven't.'

She takes your arm and you stroll on. 'Ah, now this I can get on board with.' She pulls you into a store displaying all sorts of ground coffee in tin pots. 'A fine Brazil roast today, I think, Beryl,' she instructs the girl behind the counter.

'Yes, Mrs Thresh. Shall I send it to your house?'

'No, package it up. I shall take it with me.'

'They know you well here,' you say.

'They do.'

You sit on a plush, peach-coloured love seat and wait for the coffee to be prepared. 'Now, tell me the story.'

'Well,' she says, removing her gloves and tossing her hat aside to let auburn curls cascade to her shoulders. 'It's been twice now. We live in Harrogate. I inherited a little pharmaceutical company from my father, and Freddie and I have a flat above the business. I was cycling through the town last week when I saw some strange-looking chap keeping pace with me. I noticed him because he was wrapped up so tightly with a greatcoat, hat and muffler that you couldn't so much as see his eyes. I stopped and looked right at him, and he turned tail and went off. I thought nothing more of it – some oddball watching me hardly worried me too much – until a few days later when we had come down to London to see some chums, and I clocked him behind the wheel of a blue motor car. I was having luncheon in Simpsons-in-the-Strand, you see, and there he was at the side of the road, staring at me through the window and obviously keeping me under watch, decked out in the same gear. I started to march right out to demand what on earth he was playing at, when he stepped on the pedal and chugged off. The very nerve.'

You absorb the information. It strikes you that a man well wrapped up is hardly a rarity in December. 'Can you be absolutely certain it was the same man?' you ask.

She hesitates for a second and ponders, seemingly

beginning to doubt herself. 'Well, I . . . I mean, if you put it like that, then, then I suppose I can't.'

'There was nothing unique about him?'

'Well, no.' She screws up her face a little, as if trying to remember a detail that would prove the two men were one and the same. 'Oh dear, do you think I'm going barmy?'

You lift your gaze to the ceiling. 'I shouldn't like to make such a judgement.'

'No, you're perfectly well mannered, aren't you? Well, perhaps I am. Perhaps it's all getting to me.'

You sense there's something to discover here. 'Exactly *what* is getting to you?'

'Oh, money,' she says, flinging her gloves after her hat. 'Or lack of it, really. Freddie and I have been under the cosh. You see, my family firm, Advance Pharmaceuticals, has stumbled along all right for a long while with Freddie in charge, but times have caught up with us and I'm afraid the whole thing has come apart at the seams.'

'By which you mean?'

'Bankrupt. Liquidation. Every bean spent.'

'Oh dear.'

'Yes. We had one last go at developing a wonder angina medication, but the tests have shown it's useless, and there's nothing left really. We're mortgaged up to the hilt, and all that's left is for the bank to come in and take the premises and stock to pay off some of the debt.'

The ups and downs of enterprise. You're glad you were never attracted to business, though your mother would rather you sold ladies' stockings door to door than work as a police doctor. 'That sounds unpleasant.'

'You could say that. I was dearly hoping to be out of the country paddling up the Amazon when it happens. There's an opera house deep in the jungle, can you believe. Place called Manaus. Rubber barons built it, and it gets some terribly good singers over from Italy for the season. I can't even afford the flights now.' She rallies a little. 'But hey-ho. I've decided to see it out with a bang.'

The girl comes over with a package wrapped in white paper and brown ribbon, handing it to Melissa.

'What do you mean by that?'

'I'm racking up every debt that I can to the firm while I still can. I've chartered a special train to take Freddie and me and some pals up to Harrogate today so we can have a Christmas Eve fancy dress party on the service. A chum's going to do a magic act and I'm going to be his glamorous assistant for the tricks. It will be such a giggle. Why don't you come too? We'll be stopping in York for a trip around the city.' It does indeed sound 'a giggle', but you aren't convinced Melissa is in real danger and you would rather stay in London, so politely decline. 'Your loss.' She shrugs. 'Now I must call into Fortnum & Mason, I want to run up a huge bill on their cheese counter that I'll never be able to pay back.'

'A delightful way to spend a morning,' you reply.

Turn to 126

59

'Let's talk to Julia, see what shakes out,' you say.

'So be it. They were going to visit York Castle, we might catch them there.'

You hurry over to the castle, of which the huge, square mediaeval keep atop a man-made hillock is the most impressive remnant. It was originally built in the eleventh century by William the Conqueror to withstand armies, and for centuries it has done its job admirably. Up until a few years ago, the castle was the town gaol, and it must have been a fearsome sight for any convict brought there in chains.

Climbing a flight of lichen-clad stone steps, you reach the imposing main door and enter. Somehow it seems colder inside the keep than outside – the ghosts of ten thousand lords and ladies, soldiers and peasants are chilling the air, perhaps. Wherever you go, you seem to hear them whispering. You wander through the kitchens, the great hall and what must have been the dungeons, and then rise up the spiralling stairs of the huge eastern tower, which stands over the old city. There are few tourists about and those that are are enclosed in heavy coats and don't tarry, circulating quickly and leaving as soon as they can say that they have seen the main sights. As you come to the top step, an old, thick, oak door that gives access to the battlements is ajar, and from behind it you hear whispering still; but now it sounds more like mortal humans, not spectres from a lawless past. You attune to it, and it becomes more distinct, forming into words and snatches of sentences. And you recognize the speaker: not Julia, but her husband, Constantinos. '. . . that it is time!' he is growling.

What can that mean? You signal to Melissa to stop and be silent while you listen.

'We disagree. If you strike now, you can miss. That would be the death sentence for you.' The voice is husky and sly, and its intonation doesn't seem quite English.

'I am not a coward!' Constantinos snaps.

'You Danes have always been cowards. But someone has to guide your arm. If you try now—' He breaks off suddenly. A second later the door is flung open and you are staring into the dangerous brown eyes of a squat little man with a pencil moustache and an army officer's swagger stick. He glares at you and you ready yourself for violence, but he casts an angry glance behind him, then leaps down the stairs to your side with the agility of a gymnast.

'Let him go,' you tell Melissa, who has started in his wake. You can tell there's a danger to this man.

'Are you sure?'

'Yes. What's going on, Constantinos?' you demand as the squat man disappears wholly and all you can hear are the fading taps of his feet on the stone.

He backs slowly away from you, towards the edge of

the tower, rubbing his jaw as if thinking. 'Tell us what's going on.' You step up onto the platform. A sudden fall of snowflakes is blasted around you by harsh wind.

'No,' he says thoughtfully. 'It is none of your concern.'

'It is our concern,' Melissa interjects, emerging from the stairwell behind you. 'Because someone has been trying to kill me, and here you are meeting a strange man and talking about death sentences. So tell us.'

He draws himself up to his full height. 'You have no idea who you are talking to.'

'I have a damned good idea. And I want my question answered. Now.'

'Peasants,' he snarls. Then he regains his composure. 'I am leaving now. Do not try to stop me or you will regret it.'

At this, Melissa just snorts with laughter. 'What will you do?' He stiffens as if about to attack, but instead makes for the stairwell, pushing past you. You let him go. 'Busted flush, Constantinos!' Melissa yells after him.

He stops and glares back. 'You will see. You will eat those words. You do not know the half of who I am.' And he follows in the footsteps of his companion, out of your sight.

'Golly,' Melissa says, her old demeanour returning. 'That was strange.'

'Strange, yes. And three questions arise.'

'And they are?'

'First, was it just "strange" or is there more than that – after all, Special Branch have been taking an interest in your friend.'

'My friend's husband, really.'

'That is true. And that may be important. But the second question is: who was the other man, and is he a danger to you?'

'Yes, I didn't like the look of him. He had a lethal sort of air about him, didn't he?'

'I would say so. And then the final question, possibly the most important of all: Constantinos is Greek, is he not?'

'Of course he is.'

'Of course he is. So why did the other man say "You Danes have always been cowards"?'

She seems taken aback. 'You think that's the most important question of all?'

'It might be.'

'I can't think why. I suppose the other chap just got it wrong, he thought Constantinos was Danish. So what?'

'How could he be mistaken like that? Even if he didn't know Constantinos at all – and it's clear he knows him well enough – how could anyone mistake his name for a Danish one?'

She shrugs and pulls her cloak tighter around her. 'Honestly, I can't see how it could matter.'

You don't reply. You know it matters. You just don't yet know how.

You look over the parapet around you. At ground level, you see a number of people filtering into a two-storey stone building behind the tower. A flag flutters in the wind. 'Didn't Tim say he was going to the museum?'

'Something like that,' Melissa confirms.

'That's it down there. Let's drop in on him while we're here.'

'If you like.'

Turn to 125

60

'You, Inspector Reeves!' you say, pointing to the doorway. You have seen that man climbing into the car. His inexpressive face barely twitches as he is greeted with the accusation. 'Oh yes, you thought you were oh-so-clever, making up some fake investigation into Julia and Constantinos Georgiou. All a ruse to cover your tracks as you murdered Melissa Thresh.'

He says nothing, but takes a short-stemmed pipe from his pocket, presses some shag tobacco into the drum and lights it with a match. He puffs ruminatively, while everyone else is silent, horrified. 'Now, why might I do a thing like that?' he says calmly. Your mind is a blank. Yes, just why might he do that? You have no idea. 'And, for your information, Special Branch has been keeping a watch on our Greek friend here because he is attempting, from what we can tell, a coup d'etat in his country. Descended from royalty, aren't you, sir?'

Constantinos draws himself up to his full height. 'I am proud to say that I am. And my country needs me now. I place myself at its service. If I am destined to rule, then so be it.'

'Don't think you are, sir. But that's as may be. For now, Dr Tenor, I think the best thing would be if I take you into custody for interfering in a police matter, while I arrest the real culprit, who my boys have identified through good old-fashioned police work.' He beckons to someone outside the carriage, and two uniformed officers enter and place you in handcuffs, roughly leading you away. It's the end of your career, and now you'll have to wait for them to tell you who really killed Melissa.

Now, go back to the beginning and start again

61

Right. You're going to bet on this note being genuine and whoever left it having something important to convey. But the way it tells you to be there at a precise time sounds like it might be a trap. On the other hand, if you don't follow the instruction, whoever left it for you might get spooked and not turn up. What to do?

If you turn up at noon as the note tells you, turn to 8

If you go earlier and wait to see who turns up, turn to 46

62

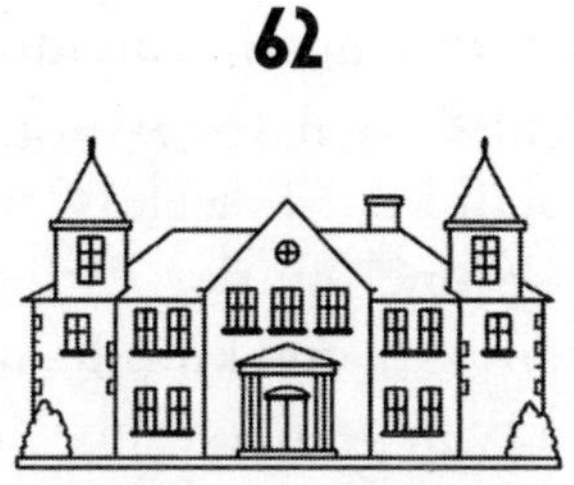

You push back the door. It moves silently and easily – someone has oiled its hinges. Your candle light flickers in the dark and picks out a long, wide room full of ghostly items. At your feet is a pile of children's toys: metal cars, a chess set, a wooden sword and shield. Beyond the pile is a tailor's dummy with a faded green crinoline dress. In the far corner a horse bridle hangs from a rafter. And everywhere there are dusty boxes of all shapes and sizes. Carefully, you step forward, looking for the source of the creaking. You're not the kind of fool who calls out 'Is anybody there?' because if someone *is* there, they're not there with good intentions.

And a second later, you know that for a fact.

Without warning, a hand grabs hold of your candlestick and throws it aside, blowing out the light. They must have been hiding behind the door as you opened it. You whirl around to grab hold of whoever is attacking you, but they have the drop on you and kick your legs away. You fall to the floor, your hands finding something wooden – the toy shield. You grab it and lift it up for protection – just in time, as a fist swipes down towards you. It smacks into the shield – it's thin but does the job it was designed for. Whoever is attacking you gasps out in pain. But it doesn't stop them trying again, thudding into the shield once more. You realize that the wood is splitting – one more strike and you'll be defenceless. And this has to be whoever stabbed Colonel Hurley earlier. You shift your weight, roll onto your side and kick up, cracking into their stomach, and they cry in pain, falling back. You've gained a second's respite and now you can turn the tables. In the dark you spring for where you think they are, but you've miscalculated and instead land on the pile of toys, which scatter under your chest. Hauling yourself to your feet, you ready yourself to give and take more punches. But instead, you hear scrabbling and movement. They're making a run for it. At that, instinct kicks self-preservation out of the way and you launch yourself in their wake, feeling about for the doorway. It takes a few moments, but you locate it and find your way to the top of the stairs. Whoever you are following is scampering down the stone steps quickly – they're more afraid of you than you are of them, it seems.

You give chase through the pitch black. Down a dozen steps, past the landing to the bedrooms – a little grey-blue light is filtering through here, from a distant window, and you catch the silhouette of the person you are following, though it's not enough to make anything out.

You guess that there are only a few more steps, and you increase the pace, charging down. The two of you are racing for the ground floor. They reach the bottom step and burst out, through to the kitchen, where moonlight falls on the big black cooking range and copper pans, neatly arranged by size, hanging from hooks on the wall.

Whoever it is, they seem to know their way around the house, because they jink around the bread oven and head for the corridor into the main house. You pant as you run. Your quarry is fast, and although you get almost within arm's reach once or twice, they make it to the front door, throw it open and sprint out into the blizzard.

If they think you're going to be put off by a bit of harsh weather, they're wrong, however. Into the snow you dash, but immediately it's like you have been plunged into a whirlpool. All you can see is swirling white; it's the air, the sky and the ground. Your target is a dark blur, and then utterly gone, replaced by blank landscape. You stumble on, wiping frost from your eyes, but they're nowhere to be seen. You can only thrash about blindly, cursing them and the weather.

After ten minutes of groping about, you have to accept that it's hopeless. No, your best chance is to return to the building – after all, your quarry might well have doubled back and entered through one of the doors; so you could wake everyone up and make a search of their rooms to see if anyone has snow on their clothes. Or you could go back to the attic and hope to find something incriminating.

If you wake the household, turn to 96

If you return to the attic, turn to 32

63

You tramp around for a while but find nothing. You have lost feeling in your feet, and your hands went some time ago.

'Oh, this is useless,' Leaner shouts over the wind.

'I'm inclined to agree,' you say. 'Major, we're for returning to the house.'

He shields his eyes from the falling snowflakes for a moment. 'Yes, all right,' he relents. 'Let's go back in.'

Turn to 84

It's a little before noon on Christmas Eve and you're in the first-class waiting room at King's Cross station. You have always liked King's Cross, with its soaring steel and glass roof. With a Bath bun at your side, you are engrossed in Alicky's descriptions and photographs of the wonders of Pompeii when Melissa bursts in, dressed as a Renaissance duchess. It's quite the sight among the more sedately dressed ladies and gentlemen on their way home to sober celebrations with their families.

'Why on earth are you dressed like that?' she demands, peering at your normal clothes. 'Don't you have anything suitable?' In reply, you open your bag containing a French mime artist outfit. It was lucky that you had it left over from Finbarr's birthday bash at Monte Carlo in August. 'Ah, good show. Well, let's shake a leg. The train's waiting for us.' Out you both pop, weaving through the crush. 'Ah, there's Tim.' Tim is a rake-thin fellow, aged around thirty, with a long drooping moustache that looks like something from an American film set in the Wild West. He spies you both and his face lights up. He ostentatiously strokes his moustache, proud as punch, inviting you to note it.

'Why is he doing that?' you ask.

'Oh, the weasel? He's glued it on especially for the trip,' Melissa responds.

'And why would he do such a thing?'

'Well, for the act, of course. Oh no, you don't know, do you? Tim is my cousin, and the chief scientific officer of the company. Terribly clever with the drugs, an utter disaster when it comes to anything else in life. Anyhow, he's the one doing a little magic turn at the party tonight and he absolutely insisted on sticking that thing to his face to do it. He thinks it's Oriental.'

'He's not confused with "mental"?'

'No, though I can see why you might think that. He's got card tricks, a disappearing cabinet, silk hankies that appear out of nowhere. Everything.'

'And you're involved in it, you say?'

'I'm to be his glamorous assistant.'

Tim stops waving to you and starts to walk over, opening a deck of cards into a fan, then trips over the trolley carrying his bags and sprawls on the floor, the cards flying everywhere. He tries to stand up and a mass of coins and marbles spill from his pockets.

'Promise me he won't try his hand at sword swallowing,' you say. 'I'm an excellent doctor, but I can't bring a man back from the dead.'

'I'm promising nothing.'

'Then I renounce the Hippocratic Oath,' you inform her.

'You can't renounce it. It's an oath.'

'I see it more as a guideline. It has its limits.'

Tim limps his way to you and holds out a hand. You

check it for any kind of trick – something that buzzes when you shake it or the like – but it seems safe.

'Tim Fortiswood,' he says. 'Pleased to meet you.'

'Kinn Tenor. I understand you are to entertain us this evening.'

'I'll do my best, won't I, Melissa?'

'You'll certainly do that.' You spot Melissa's husband, Freddie, carrying a couple of cases. He looks very moody about the trip. 'Hello, Face-ache,' Melissa says. 'What's the problem?'

Freddie looks you up and down and apparently considers you no threat. 'The problem is that we're on the edge of bankruptcy. Perhaps you've heard.'

'Oh, darling Freddie, we haven't a prayer. So let's run up the old debts since we'll never have a hope of paying them anyway.'

'It's rather lucky you aren't the firm's accountant.'

'Nope. Merely its owner.'

You all head off to platform six, where a shining black locomotive has been coupled to a smart carriage with ivory and plum livery. 'Great Northern Railway' is emblazoned on its side like a theatre playbill.

Turn to 127

65

'Thank you, Miss Tiggworth. A very generous offer, which I shall accept gladly.' She looks pleased with herself, as if she has scored a point in a netball game.

'This way. There are no omnibuses today, I'm afraid, so we shall have to use our feet.'

'Our feet will do very well.'

She leads you to a neat little cottage in a nearby street. It has window boxes full of winter pansies hung on the sills. You settle into the front parlour and she offers you a mug of cocoa, which you accept gratefully.

There are photographs on the mantelpiece of Tiggy with a few bouncing babies. 'Two nieces and a nephew,' she explains. She gazes at them with a smile, but you're a connoisseur of facial expression and you can tell there's something else there. Sadness. A loss, somewhere. She catches your eye and instantly realizes that you have seen something. She bustles away and clears up the cocoa mugs.

'There's a little room at the back. You should just about fit,' she says, directing you up a steep flight of stairs. It's certainly cosy, and after washing, you curl up in the bed and sleep well, dreaming only of trains to foreign holidays.

In the morning, Nanny Tiggy is in the parlour, on her

hands and knees, scrubbing the hearth. She jumps up as soon as you enter. You notice that the photographs of her nieces and nephew have been removed. She has something to hide, that's for certain.

'Good morning,' you say.

'Good morning.'

'You're very sprightly today. Especially for someone with arthritis.'

'Oh, yes, but it hasn't bothered me for a while.'

As a doctor, you're intrigued by this. 'How so, may I ask?' You take a seat at the table, where Nanny Tiggy has set out a plate for you with toast and marmalade.

'Oh, about since I tried that new medicine from the firm, Hilkodine, I've felt a new woman.'

'Very good,' you say. 'Now, I would like to speak to Mr and Mrs Yarrow this morning. Where might I find them?' you ask.

'They live in a house close to the factory.' She writes down their address and that of Advance Pharmaceuticals.

You stroll out. It's a frosty but bright day and the fresh air does you no end of good. Ideas swirl about your head, but one by one you sort them into neat piles. A quarter of an hour later you are outside a row of modern workman's houses, clacking a knocker. Pererin answers the door and shows you in, without a word, almost as if you're expected. When you are inside, Simon appears in a shabby dressing gown – mornings are not his best time of day, you suppose.

'What d'you want?' he says, with no pretence of politeness.

'I want to know what advances Freddie Thresh was making towards your wife.'

Pererin tuts and lights a cigarette, wafting the smoke towards an open window. 'He's tried it on and off for years. Usually when he's sozzled. I don't think he really means anything by it. I used to laugh it off but now it just bores me. I think he's finally got the message, though.'

'Why do you say that?'

'For one thing, he's stopped sending me flowers.'

'So that *was* 'im!' Simon snaps, jumping to his feet.

'Of course it was.'

'You told me it was yer dad.'

'My dad's never sent anyone flowers in his life. Probably couldn't tell a rose from a hole in the ground. I just couldn't be bothered with any of your nonsense, so I fibbed.'

'Well, ain't that the end!' Simon storms out into the back yard. You hear him kick a dustbin.

'Shouldn't you go to him?' you suggest.

She rolls her eyes. 'Oh, for God's sake.' And she strides out in his wake. You hear them have a heated argument about from whom she should be receiving flowers, and you take the opportunity to quickly scout about the house. There's little to be found, though, apart from a box of tacks on the kitchen table, open next to a few notes about the doomed trip – departure time from King's Cross, expected arrival in York and the like.

You slip back into the living room just as Pererin and Simon burst back into the house, arguing as loudly as they had at first. Neither has stopped for breath.

'May I ask where Mr and Mrs Georgiou live?' you interject, forcing them to break off.

'Barney Street. Number five,' Pererin recites off the top of her head. She's certainly an efficient secretary. No doubt she has memorized every word she has read at work.

'Then I shall take my leave of you.'

'Take whatever you want,' she says, staring irritably at her husband.

You find a taxi nearby to take you to the Georgious' house. It's an impressive old place, though it's showing its age here and there in crumbling brickwork.

It's Constantinos who takes you in, leading you through a wide hallway to an old library that's looking a bit threadbare. Many of the volumes have been sold, by the looks of big gaps on the bookshelves, and the windows are grimy.

'To what do we owe the pleasure, Dr Tenor?' he asks, as Julia comes in and stands beside him.

'I had a question for your wife.' She looks nervous. 'Some years ago, Melissa and some friends played a trick on you when you were on a skiing trip in the French Alps. You had gone into a sauna and they pushed you naked out into the snow. She said you disappeared for hours and came back in tears.'

Her jaw drops and she stammers an answer. 'Y-yes. That happened. I don't understand why you're bringing it up now.'

'How deeply did it affect you?'

'I was terribly upset. It was humiliating.'

'Yes, why are you bringing it up?' demands Constantinos.

'I think it affects you still,' you say.

'Affects me? I had completely forgotten it. It's a horrid memory and I don't want to recall it, thank you very much.'

'I think you should leave,' her husband says.

You mull this for a moment, and try asking a few more questions about their friendship with Melissa and Freddie, but they refuse to answer so you agree to abide by their wishes. There seems little more to be gained. As you cross the hallway your ears pick up on a sound: creaking floorboards above you. You say nothing but you can tell that you're not alone in this house.

Outside, the front door closes behind you, but instead of striding away, you surreptitiously skirt the building to the south side. Through a bush you can see into the library. No, Julia and Constantinos are not alone. There's a well-dressed elderly man sitting in an armchair. You can't hear what they are saying, but the strange man reaches inside his jacket and draws out a revolver. You're about to raise the alarm when he places the pistol on a side table and stands back. Constantinos puts his hands on the gun, and his lips move, as if he is swearing an oath. They leave the room and you lose sight of them.

You circle around the house, looking for them. Peering through a small window, you glimpse the kitchen. Julia is taking a jar from what looks like a cold store.

'I'll make stuffed vine leaves,' she calls over her shoulder.

A moment later, Constantinos appears. 'Do not. You do it badly. I will make them myself.'

She looks downcast at the slight. 'I really don't mind trying.'

'If I want you to try, I will tell you to try. This is my heritage, not yours.'

She turns tail and runs out of the room. Constantinos doesn't seem to care and sets about preparing a mix of rice and herbs doused in lemon juice. He looks pleased with himself as he does it.

Well, that's all very odd. But after a while watching Constantinos cook you decide there's nothing more to see, so you wonder if Freddie can throw some light on what you witnessed.

It's about twenty minutes' walk to the factory, which isn't much bigger than a large townhouse. It could do with being repainted – it's clear that the firm is on its uppers.

You ring the bell and Freddie opens the door, looking very much the worse for wear.

'Oh, God,' he mumbles.

'I'll come in,' you say, pushing past him.

'If you must.'

'Ahem!' There's an officious-sounding voice behind you. 'Mr Thresh?' You turn to see a young policeman. 'Detective Inspector Wilkes has asked me to take you to the train station.'

'Whatever for?'

'As I understand it, sir, it's to reconstruct the crime from yesterday.'

'Is it now?'

Good Lord. You don't want to miss this.

You speak up. 'Then you'll be wanting me too, Constable. Dr Kinn Tenor. I was also a witness.'

'I see. Then yes, please come this way.'

Did you see Constantinos meet a mysterious man at York Castle?

If you did, turn to 101

If you didn't, turn to 43

'As you wish,' you say, rising from the chair. You bid her a good day and go out into the street. You decide to walk back to the Old Swan and you are on your way when you pass the town's famous Turkish baths. On a whim, you stop in – a nice steam and sweat will clear your mind, ready for another bout of deliberations on the puzzle before you. It's very quiet today – it's lucky that they're even open – and as you slip into the medium-hot bath you're perfectly alone, which is just what you need when you need to think hard. You close your eyes and let the warm water soak you. It's intensely relaxing. Right up until the time when you feel two hands clamp down on your head and push you under the surface. You struggle desperately, trying to shake them off, trying to call for help, but a hot torrent enters your throat and all you see is a blur of water as you sink down and down and down.

Now, go back to the beginning and start again

67

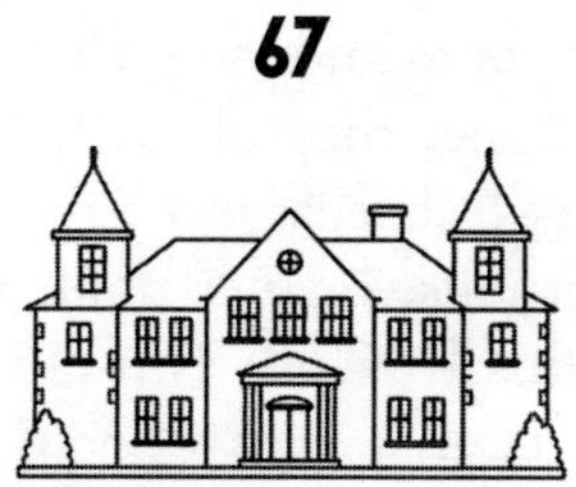

Hurley Court looks much more foreboding than when you arrived for your stay. The Christmas tinsel inside the hall looks like barbed wire and the taxidermy animals look ready to bite and scratch. Oh yes, it's a different house altogether.

'Kinn! Where on earth have you been all day?' Algy calls out, rushing to meet you.

'Finding things out, Algy, old chap.'

'What sort of things?'

'The last pieces of this Christmas jigsaw.'

'The last . . .'

'Finney, will you have everyone assemble in the billiards room? I have something to announce.'

'Very good, Dr Tenor.'

'Kinn, are you going to say who you suspect?'

'I am.'

'Oh, thank the Lord for that.' He stops. 'You don't think it was me, do you?'

'Algy, I would be more likely to accuse the Archbishop of Canterbury than you. You couldn't hurt a fly.'

'Yes, that's true,' he says brightly.

This has been a nasty little crime. But now you're convinced you know who did it and why. You take yourself to the billiards room and fix a whisky and soda while you wait. One by one, they all drift in: Mina looking worried, the maids Rebecca and Sally looking curious, Gervaise contemptuous, Leaner politely affable, Finney suave as ever and finally Major Tun-Hurley, the rigid soldier. They take seats or stand around the room.

'Colonel Hurley lied to me,' you announce.

'How dare you, sir!' his cousin, the major, bursts out. 'I won't have his name besmirched in his own house!'

Mina looks quite distressed by your assertion too, and glances at her sons. Gervaise seems coldly irritated, and Algy confused.

'Please keep your seat, Major,' you reply coolly. 'I shall explain how and why he lied.'

'You had better do so quickly, or I shall eject you from this house myself.'

'As you wish.' You pause. 'All through this affair we have been haunted. Haunted by the ghost of your unpleasant ancestor, Bloody Thomas.' You stare up at the portrait of that most wicked scion of the Hurley dynasty.

'What are you going on about?' Gervaise asks.

'Yes, spit it out,' Tun-Hurley adds.

'Bloody Thomas was known for hunting men down. Blameless men, whom he would chase into a man-trap, so that they would be at his mercy. Colonel Hurley was chased down and caught in just such a fashion.'

'We know that,' the major huffs.

'At first, I thought that the echo of the crimes of Bloody Thomas was a blind, just there to confuse, or perhaps to add some strange layer of mockery over the murder. But I realized that I was wrong. That there was more to it. That Bloody Thomas and what he left behind are absolutely essential to what has occurred here.'

'Kinn, do tell us,' Algy says, in a state of agitation. 'He was my father and I want to know why someone did that to him.'

'I'm sure you do.'

You look at all the faces before you: Mina, whose life with the overbearing and perhaps even brutish colonel must have been hard; she could have left him, you suppose, but where would she have gone, and what if the colonel refused a separation? The maid Rebecca, whom Leaner suspects of being a thief. Then there is Leaner himself, a gutter-raker on a most disreputable rag, despite his high estimation of its worth. He barely knew the victim, so could something really have brought him to the point of murder in the short time that he had been at the house? Or was it his master, Gervaise, whose relationship with his father was strained to say the least; and the dead man's disappointment with his heir was plain to see. Tun-Hurley claimed to have been friends with the colonel since they were children, but a lot of resentment can build up during a lifetime, and who knows what happened during their war service together? And lastly, Finney. Oh-so-smooth Finney, whose mind clicks away behind that unruffled exterior; there's really no way of knowing what he's thinking.

And you know secrets about all of them.

'Oh, a devilish crime, to go with a devilish forebear,' you say. 'Yes, for a long while I dismissed the key aspect of this case: the history. I concentrated too much on the present, and not enough on the past. Just as you wanted me to.' And you turn to look someone in the eye.

So, the time has come. Who will you accuse of the murder of Colonel Harrison Hurley of Hurley Court?

If you accuse Mina, turn to 100

If you accuse Rebecca, turn to 75

If you accuse Leaner, turn to 110

If you accuse Tun-Hurley, turn to 93

If you accuse Finney, turn to 49

68

You and the others tramp to the police station, which is, thankfully, nearby. Harrogate is an attractive and wealthy spa town, built from solid blocks of the local stone, attracting well-to-do northern industrialists who come to take the waters.

'Dr Tenor, I didn't want to say, but there's another reason Mr Fortiswood might have wanted Mrs Thresh dead,' Pererin whispers to you. You can smell her perfume. It's intoxicating. You lift your eyebrows in question. 'I can't say what it is precisely, but a couple of times I've gone into his office when he hasn't been expecting me, and he's had a letter in front of him that he's put away quickly.'

'To hide it?'

'I should say so. Both times, when he was reading it, he's had his head in his hands like he doesn't know what to do.'

You mull this while you're all in the station for hours giving statements. When all's done, you're released together. You're not sure where to go – you were to stay with Melissa and Freddie.

'I expect you're still looking for a bed for the night,' Freddie sneers. 'Well, I'm a hospitable sort. The offer's still open.'

'You can come to ours,' says Pererin. 'It's not so much, but it's private.'

'My little house has a spare bed, if need be,' says Tiggy.

If you go to Freddie's, turn to 52

If you head for the Yarrows' house, turn to 12

If you accept Nanny Tiggy's offer, turn to 65

'*No!*' you cry, leaping over. You have only a second to save a life. 'Stop!' You smack the bottle from his fingers. It smashes against the wall, the drink seeping across the carpet. Freddie looks at you, astonished.

'Amaretto is brown,' you tell Freddie.

'I know, so what?' He's still amazed by what you have done but is regaining his composure. 'This stuff is some clear version of it. It still smells like it, though.'

'Not everything that smells of almonds is amaretto, Freddie,' you warn him.

'I don't understand.'

'No, you don't, do you? You know what else smells of almonds?' He shrugs. 'Hydrogen cyanide.' You both stare down at the wet patch on the floor. 'Drink that, and I guarantee you will never have another worry.'

'That's what killed Melissa?' You look back to the body of his wife, laid out so that she almost looks peaceful. But you know there was nothing peaceful about her death.

'Yes. Whoever killed her somehow injected her with it. And this was the supply. Hiding in plain sight.' Freddie's fingers reach tentatively towards the bottle of Scotch that he has drunk from before, his eyes asking your approval. You nod and he gratefully drinks hard from it, then presses the bottle to his forehead, wincing. He's been through a lot, and the alcohol surging through his veins can only dull so much of it. 'Lay off it now, old man.' He lowers the bottle, having made something of an inroad into it, and puts it back on the counter. But if you think he will be quiet now, you're dead wrong.

'Which of you dogs was it?' he spits. 'Which of you did that?' He points to the dark and lethal patch on the carpet. No one replies. He pushes himself away from the bar.

'Steady,' you say.

'I won't be steady, Kinn, until I've wrung the neck of whoever killed my wife.'

'You wasn' even faithful to 'er,' mutters Simon.

'Who said that?!' Freddie roars, whirling around to face him.

'It's true, isn' it?' Simon glances at Julia. 'Isn' it?' She looks away, out of the window at the blue landscape.

'Freddie,' you say. 'If you keep a hold of yourself, I

guarantee that I will discover who did it. And they will hang.'

'Hang? I'll tear them apart right now!' He furiously sweeps all the bottles off the bar, smashing them to pieces. He's getting out of hand. What do you do?

If you grab him and tie him up for his own good, turn to 83

Try to talk him down? Turn to 91

70

You all climb aboard to find Melissa and Freddie sitting at opposite ends of the carriage. Melissa has fixed herself a huge pink gin, and is looking daggers at her husband, who is slumped in his seat, nearly nodding off. Your arrival perks him up and he grins around. She looks disgusted. The tension is thick as mud and you decide to say nothing.

'Hello, hello!' calls Tim, who enters just as you are all standing, waiting for someone to speak first. 'We're all here, then. Good.' He rubs his hands. 'It's freezing out there, isn't it? Did we all have a nice afternoon?' He looks about, bemused that no one is answering him. 'No? Is there something wrong?'

'Nothing wrong,' Melissa informs him without shifting her gaze from her errant spouse.

'Oh, right then. For a second, I thought I was missing something.'

Somehow his lack of insight puts people more at ease, and you smile to yourself as you fix yourself a Cosmopolitan. You sip it and watch as Simon indicates a seat to his wife. She rolls her eyes but takes off her coat and sits. He sits beside her. 'Who're we still waiting for?' he asks.

'The Georgious. And Nanny Tiggy.'

'Not us!' pipes up Julia as she appears through the doorway with her husband in tow. 'What a nice time we've had here.' She has a pleasant and unconcerned expression on her face, but there is a flicker of suspicion in his looks, watching you for a reaction to what his wife has said about their day.

'Just Tiggy, then. That's odd, though. We saw her a while ago and she knew what time she had to be here.' You peer out of the window. There's no sign of the faithful old servant.

'She must have been delayed,' Tim says. 'It's nearly time for our show. Freddie said he would entertain us with a song, so we can listen to that while we wait for Nanny Tiggy. Freddie? Freddie?' He shakes his friend and employer. There is no reaction. Tim shakes him harder. 'Freddie?' He sounds concerned. You step forward to look closer.

'What is it?' Freddie grumbles, rubbing his face.

'Oh, for a second there . . . well, I was a bit worried.'

'About what?'

'Nothing. Now, it's time for your song.'

'My what? Oh.' He yawns. 'I'm far too drunk for that. Look, I'm off for a snooze. Just entertain yourselves.' He hauls himself up and staggers back to the luggage compartment.

Tim looks a little downcast at the response. 'Right, well. All right.'

'Oh, look,' says Melissa, pointing out of the window. You follow her finger and see Nanny Tiggy trotting down the platform towards you. 'Better late than never.'

A moment later, the old lady is up and in the car, huffing and puffing with the effort.

'So sorry, everybody,' she says. 'I got caught up.'

'In what?' chuckles Melissa privately to you. 'Naughty old Tiggy.'

'Good, then that means we can be off!' Tim says. He jumps out, has a word with the driver and the guard and then bounds back in. It's no more than five seconds before the whistle is blown, the green flag waves and the wheels begin to spin. You're away through the snowy Christmas countryside on your ninety-minute journey to Harrogate.

The landscape is blue now, as the snow reflects a black sky. It's a gorgeous night – between the puffs of snow clouds you can pick out glittering stars. Night birds swoop through the black trees.

'Now,' says Tim, clapping his hands joyfully, then steadying himself as the train jolts, 'we can really get started. Costumes, everyone!' He scurries away to the luggage area and immediately Freddie emerges muttering about how his snooze has been interrupted.

You all pull on your outfits. Your mime get-up is very fine, and you admire the effort that Julia and Constantinos have gone to in their imperial Greek style. Simon looks the part as a football player, which isn't difficult to pull off, and Pererin is a bird with feathery head and cape. Tiggy is a fairy godmother with wand and tiara, which looks charming; Freddie hasn't bothered. No surprise there.

One thing the costumes don't do is protect against the cold – it's not exactly warm in the carriage, and Nanny Tiggy pulls a thick tartan blanket over her lap, while the Yarrows put their coats and gloves back on.

'I imagine Melissa must have been a handful as a child,' you say to Nanny Tiggy to make conversation while everyone settles down.

'That she was. More than once I was this close to giving up and joining my sister in her grocery shop, I can tell you.'

'But you didn't.'

'No, she's a dear at heart. And I was made to be a nanny. I know that. I could tell myself I would be happy doing something else, but I never would. Silly of me, really.'

'Not at all,' you say. 'It's a gift to know where you're meant to be.'

Constantinos kicks the performance off with a medley of Greek folk songs, while Julia accompanies him on the flute and the rest of you down more cocktails. Nanny Tiggy has two port and lemons, heavy on the port, light on the lemon, and you're all having a swinging time when

Tim emerges dressed like the genie in *Aladdin*: a huge glittering turban sits on his head, his long moustache drips unevenly from his upper lip and his upper body is partly clad in a blue sequined bolero jacket, but mostly bare. He isn't a great one for the athletic life, you surmise from his physique. The look is completed by bright yellow silken pantaloons. It is, to say the least, unforgettable.

'Laydees and gentlemens!' he announces in an incongruously French accent. 'I 'ave a spectacle to show you. It weel make you amazed!' He lifts his arms to the roof of the carriage. 'It weel make you astonished!' From his pocket he draws a pack of cards, which he carefully fans out as he walks to the front of the car. 'Peek one.' Pererin takes a card, looks at it and places it back in the deck, as instructed. Tim makes some hand movements and shuffles the deck. 'What was your card?'

'Three of spades,' she replies.

He taps the top card. She turns it over to reveal the three of spades as promised. Everyone is, indeed, quite surprised that it worked. Tim winks at you, getting into his stride. The mood becomes more relaxed and joyous as people laugh and clap when he manages to produce a bouquet of paper roses seemingly out of thin air, then make them disappear again in a bright flash. You have seen flash paper – nitrocellulose – used in crimes. It's quite fun to play with, instantly exploding as soon as it's touched with a flame. Tim uses Constantinos's cigarette and poof! The flowers are nowhere to be seen. The Yarrows stamp their feet and yell for more – Pererin is letting her guard down. It really is so much fun, as you see sprinkles of snow fall past the windows, and the train's chugging and rolling seem to take you to a fairyland. Tim flushes with pride and then he informs you all, 'It ees time for ze big one!'

He pushes a large chest to the front and heaves it onto a sturdy little table. It is polished wood painted in a black-and-white marble pattern, measuring about five feet across, four high and two deep. A door in the front is about four feet long and three high, and hinged at the bottom so that it will fall open.

'For this, I require my be-yootiful assistant. Mademoiselle Melissa!'

Melissa steps gamely forward, curtseying to the audience, who cheer and clap approvingly. Tim waves his hands at the box and unclasps the door, which falls open to reveal an empty black interior. He raps his knuckles on the interior to show that all is solid. 'Mademoiselle Melissa!' She lithely climbs inside the box, blowing kisses to you all. Tim closes and latches the door behind her, and theatrically waves his hands over the box while chanting pseudo-magical mumbo-jumbo. He drums his hands on the top of the box, eliciting an 'Ow!' from inside, so you know Melissa is still in there. 'And now, laydees and gentlemens! The gods of magic have done their work!' he cries, and unlatches the door. It falls open to reveal Melissa has gone! It's the same black interior as before.

It really is an impressive trick. You can see right under the box to Tim's pantalooned legs, so you would have noticed if your hostess had rolled out the back. And the interior is undoubtedly empty – no smoke, no mirrors. For once, Tim has done something quite astonishing. And no one seems more amazed at his success than him. 'Crikey,' he says.

The rest of you clap and cheer with gusto. Tim's face lights up. 'An' now, I bring back the laydee!'

He closes and latches the door, repeats the hocus-pocus and arm-flailing and dramatically drops the door open. You all peer in, expecting a grinning Melissa to throw her legs out and join in the celebration. But all you're looking at is the same empty box. 'Oh dear,' Tim says, a little confused, back in his own voice. 'I . . . I think I've done it wrong. Give me another try.' And he closes up the cabinet and repeats the magical invocations, taking longer over it this time and tapping on the wood. With a furrowed brow, he opens it up.

Nothing. No glamorous assistant. No indication that she has been and gone. A slight pang of concern shoots through your veins.

'Umm, Melissa,' he whispers into the box. 'Are you in there?' The only sound comes from the train wheels rattling over the rails. It was charming and comforting before, but now it is ominous and threatening.

Constantinos and Julia are laughing – they clearly think this is part of the act. But you can tell from Tim's face that it isn't. You stand up and go to the cabinet. 'What's happening?' you ask.

'Ummm. Nothing. No, it's all right.' He raises his voice. 'Melissa? Is everything all right?'

Still silence.

'Open it up,' you say. You don't know how the illusion works, but you know that now is not the time to respect the magician's code of never revealing a trick. And Tim understands that this isn't the time to argue. Now Julia and Constantinos have stopped laughing. They too have realized that the act finished a few minutes ago and something has gone wrong.

Tim reaches into the cabinet and lifts up a thin black horizontal panel in the floor, to reveal Melissa's Renaissance-costume-clad outstretched legs below it, and pulls away a vertical panel along the tall line of the doorway, behind which her body must be concealed. You marvel at the simplicity of it all: around the doorway there is about a foot of space before you get to the actual edge of the box. It is in this space that the assistant hides, hidden under and behind the false panels. It's cramped, but a slim woman can do it without too much bother. Tim pulls out the upright panel.

Julia catches her breath. Nanny Tiggy cries out in alarm. Simon Yarrow pushes forward. And then there is silence. Even the sound of the turning wheels seems to have stopped.

For falling forward, folding at the hip, her face white as the snow outside, is Melissa Thresh. Perfectly dead.

Her fine eyes are open and staring, accusing you all of doing nothing to save her.

Simon rushes forward, reaching for her body as if trying to pull her out of the way of a speeding car, but with quick reflexes you grab him and pull him back.

'What're you . . . ?' he exclaims.

You step forward. You don't have to examine her for long. You look around. 'I'm sorry. She's dead.' For a moment no one stirs. All are struck dumb – you're used to the sight of a dead body, but few civilians are. You glance at Constantinos – he's alert, but not shaking with the shock.

Perhaps he saw bodies during the War. Many men did, and it left them numb to the suffering of others. Julia has buried her head in his shoulder, obviously distressed as can be at the sight of her old schoolfriend without the breath of life in her.

You turn back to the body. Melissa's curling hair has fallen onto her powdered cheeks. She will never again be as lovely as she was in life.

'Dr Tenor! Help!'

The voice is Pererin's, and you spin around to see her standing over Nanny Tiggy, who has slumped against the wall, her hands on her slack jaw, fingers twitching as if trying to grasp her own skin. She raised Melissa from a child and probably saw her as her own daughter. Now her child is dead. She cries out and drops to the floor, looking quite ill, and you are about to go to her, even though the corpse before you demands your attention.

If you stay with Melissa's body, turn to 15

If you go to Nanny Tiggy, turn to 87

‘There’s a mark on the inside of the cabinet,’ you say. ‘A little greasy mark.’ And you are about to tell them all what that suggests – a clever and nasty little method of murder – when you feel a sharp scratch on your hand. You look down to see a pin-prick, and up at the person who made it. ‘Sorry,’ they say casually, pushing past. Will any of the others around you make the connection? It’s doubtful. And even if they do, you won’t be alive to see it.

Now, go back to the beginning and start again

72

‘Something tells me your friends are quite memorable. I bet the waiting staff remember them. Maybe they will have something to tell us,' you tell Melissa.

'Oh, do you think so? You might be right. And so, lead on!'

You enter the tea room and stop the nearest waitress. She looks quite put-upon, balancing a plate of currant buns on one arm and a bowl of soup on the other, with cups of tea in her hands.

'What?' she asks, without politeness.

'A friend of mine was in here a few minutes ago. Greek chap. Did he do anything of interest?'

She stares at you as if you're mad. 'Greeks? What do I know 'bout Greeks? Ernie!' she yells at the portly man at the till. 'They want to know 'bout Greeks.'

''Bout what?'

'*Greeks*,' she yells at him.

'What do I know 'bout Greeks?'

'Tha's what I said.' She turns back to you. 'We don' know 'bout Greeks.'

'So I understand.'

Melissa is trying not to giggle. 'Shall we find Tiggy?' she manages to say as the waitress walks off to do the job that you've interrupted.

'I suppose we must.'

Turn to 16

73

York Minster looms above you, its square towers stretching almost to heaven itself. A guide book that you pick up from a hawker outside tells you that it was built in stages, beginning in the thirteenth century. And today it is mobbed by a mix of religious worshippers and tipsy tourists.

You have to fight your way in, there are so many visitors desperate either to say silent prayers or to coo at the arched roof. Every pew is full and the service is ending, with a surprisingly handsome priest in his mid-twenties conducting the affair. He smiles broadly, enjoying himself by the looks of things. Perhaps at this time of year he lets his hair down a bit – it's blond and curly, so letting it down suits him – and has a jolly time along with the congregation.

You find Tiggy at the end of a pew, staring transfixed at the divine as it all wraps up and the worshippers begin to drift away chatting, replaced in their spots by the out-of-town gawpers. 'Isn't he marvellous,' she whispers.

'Who? The vicar?' Melissa asks, sounding surprised. 'Never had you pegged as a religious sort, Tiggy. I don't recall you so much as setting foot inside a church.'

'Oh, well, times change,' the old servant replies, flustered, tearing herself away from the vision before her.

'Shall we head out for some afternoon tea? Where do you fancy?'

'Oh, I'm not so hungry, Mrs Thresh. Why don't you young people go out and have a nice time without me. I'll be happy here by myself.'

You glance at the good-looking priest, who is chatting to a couple of the congregants and shaking hands. There's a bit of a fan club around him, made up of ladies young and old. He does his best to give them all a little of his golden time but eventually he has to remove himself.

'Is there another service soon?' you casually enquire.

'Oh, well now, I think there is,' Nanny Tiggy replies lightly, avoiding your gaze.

'And would that priest be the one conducting it?'

She clears her throat and hesitates before answering. 'I really couldn't say.'

'I'm sure you could if you wanted to,' you tell her, doing your best not to smile. She simpers self-consciously. 'Melissa, we know when we are not wanted. Let's be off. Your husband must be more in want of our company than your old nanny.'

'Now I see why you wanted to come to York, Tiggy, old thing,' Melissa says, screwing up her face as she tries not to giggle fondly at her love-sick old servant. 'All right, we'll be off to track down Freddie, in the vain hope that he hasn't already got himself into trouble.'

She threads her arm through yours and you leave the grand old church.

'Was it her idea to come here, then?' you enquire as you stride through the cathedral precincts.

'Yes. She said she's wanted to visit the Minster for yonks, but now I see there's another attraction to be found.' And this time she lets out a full-throated whoop of laughter. 'Now, it's about time we headed back.'

You agree and saunter through the pretty highways and byways of the old town. The light is beginning to fail and the shop windows glow with electric lights. The shoppers and joy-seekers draw their coats tighter – and glance harder at Melissa's thin covering – as the chill finds its way down collars and between layers of fabric. The cocoa sellers and roast chestnut-mongers do a roaring trade as people filter away back to their homes and their hotels, keen for one last sweet mouthful before an evening of carols and children who won't go to bed.

'Julia and I were at school together just around the corner,' Melissa says, looking wistful. 'We used to sneak out at lunchtime and go to the pubs.'

'Oh, yes? She doesn't seem the sort.'

'Oh, she's very pliable. And very forgiving.'

Call it a sixth sense, or animal instinct, but you sometimes get a little needling feeling when you hear a comment; it's a little sensation that says there's more below the surface. 'What exactly do you mean by "very forgiving"?'

You catch something shifty in Melissa's eye. 'Hmmm?' she says, as if she hasn't quite heard you.

'I said, what exactly do you mean by "very forgiving"?'

She sighs, considers and draws a gold cigarette-holder from her handbag. She places a long, slim, peach-coloured cigarette between her lips and lights it with a match that she tosses to the ground. 'It's all in the past.'

'Is it?'

'Oh, I thought it was until you dragged it up.' She taps ash onto the ground. 'Six or seven years ago a gang of us went for a winter holiday – skiing in the French Alps. Nice little place that I've forgotten the name of. Log cabins and warm wine, that sort of thing. Well, I'm sorry to say that we all got a little tipsy and some of the others decided to play a prank on Julia. I should have put my foot down and stopped them, but I went along with it.'

'What did they do?'

'There was one of those steam-bath houses where you sit naked and whack yourself with twigs. They tricked her and shoved her out of the door into the snow with nothing on, in full view of all the men. She ran off and we didn't see her for hours. No idea where she even went. She just turned up after midnight, sobbing. By that time I had gone to bed. We apologized in the morning and she seemed to forgive us.'

'Seemed.'

'Well, I don't know!' she says, stamping her foot. 'Yes, it's shameful, but it's all in the past.'

'The past has a habit of coming back to haunt you.'

The white blanket crunches thicker as you wend your way back to the station. Melissa has recovered her good mood and is telling you excitedly about the show she and Tim are going to stage.

'... and it's going to be such fun. Do you know, we've been practising for a month. Now, it won't be Theatre

Royal standard . . .' she's saying as you emerge onto the concourse. But you aren't listening to her, you're focusing on another sound nearby. Voices are yelling, two of them. One sounds threatening, the other demanding calm. You peer over to the corner where the station pub – The Huntsman, according to its cheaply painted sign – is situated. And you recognize the three people working out their differences.

Simon Yarrow has thrown aside his jacket and has the dishevelled figure of Freddie Thresh pinned against the brick wall of the saloon bar. 'Come close to 'er again and I'll break yer neck, you little . . .' Simon is yelling.

'For God's sake, Simon,' Pererin says as she tries to pull him away. 'You're as drunk as he is.'

For his part, Freddie seems half-cut even while he sneers, 'You don't know what she . . .' He breaks off when he sees you and Melissa, and his head hangs down.

'My God, look at him,' Melissa says contemptuously. 'What a buffoon.' She stares at him for a moment, then turns and strides towards the train, her heels clicking on the damp ground.

Simon lets go and Freddie slumps down, coming to rest on his haunches. Simon takes Pererin by the arm and steers her back into the pub, leaving Freddie to sort himself out.

You walk over and he slowly lifts his face until he is looking up at you. You see he has a split lip that is leaking a little blood. 'Spare a hanky?'

'I don't have one. You might not need one if you leave other men's wives alone.'

'You don't understand.'

'Don't I? Would you care to enlighten me?'

'She led me on.'

'I'm sure she did.'

'Very flirtatious.'

'Of course.' You glance through the window of the pub. It takes a while for your eyes to penetrate the thick mist of smoke, but then you make out, in a corner, the Yarrows talking, their heads close together. Pererin's anger at her husband seems to have gone. She takes a drink from a glass – there's a large collection of empties in front of them – and goes back to speaking with an earnest look on her face. 'She's a pretty thing.'

'And she knows it,' he mumbles, but the words trail away into a deep moan. He looks as if he's about to fall asleep but shakes himself back awake. He rolls onto all fours then pushes himself to his feet, swaying a little like a branch in the wind. 'All is well.' He snorts in derision at his own predicament and walks unevenly towards the train. Something tells you it's worth talking to the Yarrows. But that would mean letting Freddie stagger on to the carriage, where Melissa is probably on her own. God knows what that would mean.

If you pursue Freddie, turn to 9

If you go into the pub, turn to 89

74

You, Leaner and Tun-Hurley carefully check the drawing room, the library, the dining room, the billiards room and the breakfast room. You look in every nook and cranny. You can hear the others searching the rest of the house, calling out to each other from time to time. You leave no cupboard unopened, no settee unlifted.

Nothing.

'We should try outside,' Tun-Hurley says. He is less brash than his cousin, but still a firm and reliable military man. He grabs another electric torch from the coat stand.

Checking outside would be a good idea, but you have something else in mind that you are keeping to yourself. It's a trap. You could secretly return to the hallway and leave the newspaper cutting in plain sight and unguarded. Whoever tried to steal it earlier would see it on the way into the billiards room. They might be sorely tempted to steal it again. You would have to make sure you're back before anyone else to keep watch though.

On the other hand, the garden does need to be searched and you're not sure about leaving it to Leaner and Tun-Hurley – you have no idea if you can trust them, and even if you can, they might miss something that your trained eye would spot.

If you set the trap, turn to 99

If you search the garden with the others, turn to 51

75

'No one ever suspects the maid. Do they, Rebecca?' you say. The girl, who is standing at the back of the room, takes a sharp breath in astonishment. 'Not even when they have such a secret to keep.'

'But . . . but . . .' she stutters.

'Rebecca?' says Mina, as amazed as the servant.

'My God!' exclaims Gervaise with a dark expression on his face. 'You little viper!'

'Be gentle,' you warn him. 'You are addressing your half-sister!' At that, he jumps to his feet. But it is the girl's reaction that grabs your attention. She screams in something like agony and half faints against the wall. She is caught by Finney, who looks to you for explanation. 'I met your neighbour today, Rebecca. It was she who told me that no one knows who your father was: a secret that your mother kept from everyone, probably even your father. And who else could that be, but a man so powerful in this part of the country that he could ruin her? A man you took your revenge on after he used your mother with the same disregard with which Bloody Thomas used others from the village. Colonel Hurley!'

She lifts her head and blinks at you. 'No,' she says. 'It's Ron Boroclough from Tunbridge Wells.'

'What?'

'He's me dad. We didn't tell anyone because it's no one else's business. He's a fishmonger.'

Everyone stares at you. You're struck dumb. You can tell by her voice that she's telling the truth. How could you be so stupid?

Then her voice changes. 'But I know who the killer was,' she says.

'Who?' you say.

'It was . . .'

She catches her breath and stares to your side. Out of the corner of your eye you see a poker lifted up high, then come swooping down towards your skull.

Now, go back to the beginning and start again

76

You strike up conversation with a few others in the pub. People are friendly but have nothing to say, until you talk to a squat little man with a bushy beard and a criminal sort of air about him.

'I've been looking for my mate John, John Finney,' you say.

'Oh, aye?' There's a glint in his eye. 'I ken John.'

Something in this man's tone tells you he knows something. You decide to act a little drunk to hide the fact that you're pumping him for information. 'I've got a bit of cash, y'see,' you burble. 'And he said I should come in on his little side business.' And you give a knowing grin.

'Did he now? And what side business is that?'

You tap the side of your nose. 'You know.'

'Maybe I do, and maybe I don't.'

'Ah,' you say, waving him away. 'You don't know.'

'Like I said, maybe I do and maybe I don't.'

You reach into your jacket and pull out a few bank notes, which you deliberately fumble and drop on the floor. You crouch down and pick them up hurriedly. 'Sorry, stupid of me,' you say.

Your new pal carefully checks around and then whispers in your ear. 'Out the back.'

He heads out. You drain your glass, then follow him.

Behind the pub, he's waiting for you. He has a steely look on his face. 'Now, what business are you in?' he says.

'Anything that pays well.' You maintain your tipsy act.

'Let's see your money.'

You hold the cash out, but snatch it back when he reaches for it. 'The goods first.'

'I haven't got it here, have I?'

'I need to see it.'

He stops and stares at you. 'Are you Old Bill?'

'Am I what?'

'A copper. Are you a copper?'

'No.'

'You are! You're a copper!' And he grabs hold of you. You struggle and biff him one on the nose. But he roars and leaps on you. The two of you fall to the ground.

'Oi!' yells someone close by. And then the two of you are dragged apart by the landlord and a policeman in uniform. 'That's it. You're both nicked. Drunk and disorderly.'

Arrested! Well, this is embarrassing. You're dragged off to spend the night in the cells and sleep it off.

You don't get a wink of sleep though, and in the afternoon you're pushed in front of the local magistrate. You're fined five pounds and told to go back to London.

You creep back to Hurley Court, where everyone has heard about what you've been up to.

'Sorry, old fruit, but we've got enough to deal with,'

Algy says when you turn up on the doorstep. 'Finney's packed your bags. Perhaps I'll see you in the new year, eh?'

Well, that's an ignominious end to your investigation.

Now, go back to the beginning and start again

77

You climb the stairs. Luckily your bare feet make no sound on the stone. It's ten steps up to a little wooden door that leads into the attic. What's stored up here, and why someone would want to poke about, you don't know. The candle shows your misty breath in the air as you go, and your mind races through all the possibilities as to what you will find on the other side of that door; when you finally rise up the last step, you're tense as a violin string.

You stand still and put your ear to the door. Another loud creak makes its way through the wood. This is your last chance to go for help.

If you go back down the stairs for help, turn to 92

If you enter the attic, turn to 62

78

What could Algy's diary hold? Well, there's one way to find out. And while you're at it, you might as well poke your nose into everyone's bedroom, just to see what you can find.

You start at the far end, with Mina's room. It's a quiet sort of affair: a little jewellery here and there, a copy of *Wuthering Heights* by the bedside with a leather bookmark halfway through, a few attractive watercolours on the wall that you suspect were painted by Mina herself, but nothing noteworthy. You slip out and into Gervaise's room. It's shockingly austere. You had rather expected something chaotic and monstrous, but it's almost bare, as if he had never even lived here, just passed through for a night. That makes searching it a quick business, however, and you're in and out in a minute flat. Then into Colonel Hurley's room. A regimental colours flag hangs in the corner, and the walls are neatly adorned with photographs of men in uniform and a family tree of the Hurley clan. All is precisely arranged. You set to work, opening a writing bureau to find some correspondence sorted into stacks of 'answered' and 'to be answered'. A letter from his banker intimates that Gervaise had invoked the colonel's name when asking for a loan – you can only imagine the reply that Hurley fired off in return. A display case of his campaign medals sits in pride of place on his bureau. Again, little of interest here.

Next up is Algy's room. Well, if you were disappointed by the lack of chaos in Gervaise's chamber, his brother more than makes up for it. He must have left strict instructions with the staff never to tidy up. It's a havoc of discarded clothes and battered paperback books with bright covers and titles such as *High Noon in Thirsty Gulch* and *The Smoking Gun*. 'Not exactly Shakespeare, Algy, old boy,' you mutter.

In the corner of the room are three small packing cases filled with cans of Cleano, the disastrous cleaning fluid that he thinks is going to make him a mint – although you suspect he's more likely to find himself sued for all he's worth. And you find something else, hidden under his mattress. It's his diary, crammed with doodles and scrawls, including such passages as 'all you *ever* do is humiliate me', 'that's the last time you will mock me in front of Mother' and the like. Well, it's interesting, but after reading it through, there's nothing concrete and you're not sure quite what to do with it, so you place it back where you found it. Doing so, you notice something else hidden under the mattress: a little pewter hip flask. You take the top off. Brandy. Quite good stuff, by the smell of it. Well, it would be a pity to waste it, so you take a good glug. Instantly you feel dizzy. It packs a punch, this stuff. No, there's more to it than that. It feels like your head is on fire. There's something wrong. You can't . . . Poison. It's been poisoned. You drank it. And now you're being torn away from Hurley Court, from life itself. You're done for.

Now, go back to the beginning and start again

79

'Righto, I'll give Philip Game a bell.'

You find a decent hotel nearby and ask to use the telephone. You're shown to a generously proportioned booth that allows you to sit on a little sofa while making the call.

'Hello? I would like to speak to Sir Philip Game,' Melissa informs a distant and bored voice at the other end. 'Melissa Thresh.' You can't imagine how many people and of what sort ask to be put through to the Commissioner of the Metropolitan Police on a daily basis, but Melissa's confidence pours through the telephone and she is connected to his office without delay. One more secretary and she's speaking to the man himself. 'Philip, old fruit, how are you? Hmm, oh yes, that does sound fun. We really must. Now, sorry to cut you off, but we have an odd sort of situation here. Did you know that one of your 'tecs was on my tail? Following me and some chums about in York.' She pauses, listening as the earpiece buzzes with the senior officer's reply. 'Good Lord, really? Who? But why can't you? They've always seemed so staid. Well, no, I shan't. Not unless you tell me why. Well, then there's an end to it. All right, yes, give my love to Gwendolen. Cheerio.' She replaces the receiver thoughtfully. You lift an eyebrow in question. 'Hmmm? Oh, yes. Well, don't ask me why, because Philip was an absolute bear and wouldn't let it slip, but it seems that for some reason, Scotland Yard has a bee in its bonnet about Julia and Constantinos Georgiou.'

'You don't say.'

'But I do say, I very much say. Isn't it so odd? He's a bore, but I wouldn't have thought you could be arrested for being dull. Not that it would be a bad thing if you could – there are oodles of dullards I would happily have chucked in chokey until they became more interesting. But you're not really allowed to do it yet.'

'And what about her? You haven't told me anything about her.'

'Julia, oh, she's quite harmless, of course. Wouldn't say boo to a goose, Julia. You can do anything to her and she'll still be the most loyal friend.'

Call it a sixth sense, or animal instinct, but you sometimes get a little needling feeling when you hear a comment; it's a little sensation that says there's more below the surface. 'What exactly do you mean by "you can do anything to her"?'

You catch something shifty in Melissa's eye. 'Hmmm?' she says, as if she hasn't quite heard you.

'I said, what exactly do you mean by "you can do anything to her"?'

She sighs and draws a gold cigarette-holder from her handbag. She places a long, slim, peach-coloured cigarette between her lips and lights it with a match that she tosses to the ground. 'It's all in the past.'

'Is it?'

'Oh, I thought it was until you dragged it up.' She taps ash onto a brass plate beside the telephone. 'Six or seven years ago a gang of us went for a winter holiday – skiing in the French Alps. Nice little place that I've forgotten the name of. Log cabins and warm wine, that sort of thing. Well, I'm sorry to say that we all got a little tipsy and some of the others decided to play a prank on Julia. I should have put my foot down and stopped them, but I went along with it.'

'What did they do?'

'There was one of those steam-bath houses where you sit naked and whack yourself with twigs. They tricked her and shoved her out of the door into the snow with nothing on, in full view of all the men. She ran off and we didn't see her for hours. No idea where she even went. She just turned up after midnight, sobbing. By that time I had gone to bed. We apologized in the morning and she seemed to forgive us.'

'Seemed.'

'Well, I don't know!' she says, stamping her foot. 'Yes, it's shameful, but it's all in the past.'

'The past has a habit of coming back to haunt you.'

She hangs her head. 'You might be right. Do you think

I should speak to her? Ask if she's behind what's been going on?'

You wonder about bringing it all up. It might be the opposite of what's needed right now – and if Julia is behind the threats and violence directed towards Melissa, is she really likely to admit it?

If you talk to Julia, turn to 59

If you let it go and instead go into the tea room and ask the staff if they remember Julia and Constantinos, turn to 72

You tell the others that you're off to get help. No one offers to come with you; they seem to think it's your fault that they're now stuck in the Yorkshire countryside, even though it was Tim who pulled the emergency communication chain. So off you stride as the snow comes down lightly. Your costume seems a mockery now. There's a path that you follow between two fields, but the snow begins to come down harder and it hides the path and you realize that you're tramping through a field. Now you can't see the railway and you're getting colder and your feet are getting heavier. And you want to sit down to rest but you know that you can't. When you trip over, you find you can't get up again because your limbs are numb and the snow is settling on you.

You wake up a week later in a cold sweat. You're in a hospital with white-uniformed nurses.

'Dr Tenor?' asks one in a Scottish accent.

'Y-yes,' you reply weakly.

'Pneumonia. A bad case. But you'll pull through.

'Oh.' You try to order your thoughts. 'Tell me, I was on a train. A murder.'

'Ah,' says the nurse with a twinkle in her eye. 'Yes, we heard about that. All very exciting. But don't worry. The police caught them. It's all over. They confessed. I'll get you a newspaper, you can read all about it.'

You read all about it. And then, in another week's time, you can catch another train down to London, where your colleagues will have a good laugh at how you got mixed up in another case, only this time you were nearly a second victim.

Now, go back to the beginning and start again

81

'Freddie, would you be so good as to fill me in on your own whereabouts at that time?'

'Drunk, I expect.'

You smile graciously. 'What a morning it must have been. Any more details?'

'I spend most mornings drunk now. I find it's easier to deal with the sense of impending doom.'

'No doubt. Out of interest, does this doom take on any particular aspect?'

'Going to be penniless soon, old chum. Going to be out on the streets.' For a moment, you are reminded of another case, one where a husband disappeared, with the possibility that he threw himself into a lake after his housebuilding business collapsed. It later turned out that his wife had taken out a large life insurance policy on him three months to the day earlier. It's an ugly thought, of course, but then murder is an ugly crime. 'Oh, I've had enough. You want to sit here talking while my wife lies dead two yards away from us?' He winces at his own words. 'I don't. Just let me be.'

Yes, it probably is time to let everyone have a moment to mentally deal with what they have just witnessed.

You gaze from one to another, then at the terrible sight stretched out before you on the table: a beautiful, vivacious young woman whose future has been cruelly and violently stolen from her.

For twenty minutes that feel like hours, you are all quiet, alone with your thoughts. Six of the seven people before you are remembering, regretting, celebrating and saying goodbyes. One is plotting, scheming, mocking and quietly rejoicing at the scene that they have engineered.

When you finally roll into Harrogate station it feels like a blessing. The wheels squeal to a stop and you shout to the platform guard to fetch the police. He looks befuddled, but you repeat the instruction and he scurries off. Until they arrive, you are letting no one leave. Simon grumbles but no one tries to defy your order.

A bobby, as surprised as the station guard, nearly falls over when you tell him what has happened, and even before you have finished explaining, he is sprinting away to bring a senior officer.

When he does, you are rather taken aback to see Inspector Reeves of Scotland Yard's Special Branch arrive.

'Dr Tenor. A word,' he says, taking you aside. Well out of earshot of the others, he tells you something. 'There is an individual in this case who is of particular interest to my colleagues and me.'

'Who?' you demand to know.

'That's none of your concern.'

'It's very much of my concern, Inspector. And I demand to know.'

He is impassive. 'You will be spoken to. But not by me. By Sir Philip Game.' He points to a single black carriage, with all the blinds down, behind a locomotive on a neighbouring platform. 'In you go.'

You clamber into the train and find the Commissioner of the Metropolitan Police drinking tea with a bewhiskered gent who is not introduced to you.

'Thank you for joining us,' Sir Philip says. 'The case that you have become embroiled in is one of national importance, which is why Special Branch will be taking it over. You are relieved of all duties, and your presence in London is required.'

'May I ask what the case is?'

'You may, but I will not answer. You will perhaps be able to read about it in a year or two in the newspapers. Other than that, I have no more to say to you. You are dismissed.'

And that's the end of the matter. You return to the concourse, to find that Reeves has taken away all your former companions. All that's left for you to do is remove your costume, retrieve your luggage and return home, mystified as to what has taken place underneath your nose.

Now, go back to the beginning and start again

82

You quickly throw on your travelling clothes and jump into your flame-red MG Roadster. There's snow on the roads, but they're passable.

You gun the engine and speed off. You're barely out of the gates, however, before you clock someone following you in a yellow van. The name painted on the bonnet says: 'M. Plank. Racing bookmaker'. They're keeping pace with you as you nip along the country roads. You speed up and they speed up; you slow and they slow. Right, that's it. You're going to lose them, you decide. You pump the accelerator and the car leaps forward. You hit fifty, then sixty, as you reach a long, wide stretch of road with no other traffic. Still the van is behind you. And now you're coming up to a bend in the road. You have to slow down. You press the brake pedal but nothing happens. You're rolling at close to sixty. You pump it again. Nothing. You try the handbrake as you're almost at the bend. It pulls up, but there's no resistance. Someone has been tampering with your brakes! And now you're at the bend and you try to steer around it, but it's too sharp and your car hits the corner and turns over in the air, falling and falling and falling, and then everything ends, in the blink of an eye.

Now, go back to the beginning and start again

'Get a hold of him,' you instruct Constantinos and Tim. They grab hold of Freddie. But he thrashes about and is stronger than he looks. He and Constantinos tumble to the floor. For a second you think you have finally gained control of him, but then he starts gasping, trying to speak but unable. 'My . . . chest . . .' he whispers. 'Can't . . .' With a terrible understanding, you look down to the floor. His hand is bloody, the skin ragged. It has been cut on the broken glass from the bottles he smashed, and then soaked in the deadly poison that killed his wife. Freddie has only a few seconds left to live and you know that there is nothing that you, or anyone else, can do about it. He's dying of cyanide poisoning, and you are responsible.

His eyes bulge as his breathing stops. Constantinos, shocked, scrambles away from the man who will soon be a corpse.

Pererin starts to scream. She, and everyone else, can see what is happening, even if it will take them a few seconds to work out why.

And then, with one final gasp, he's dead. The seven of you stare at him and Melissa, two victims.

'You did it,' Tim growls at you. 'Your fault!'

'I . . .' you stammer, unable to form a thought. 'I didn't know that . . .'

'He would have been fine. He just saw his wife die!' he yells. 'You could have let him be!'

There's no point in trying to explain that you were only trying to help – to keep him safe, even.

'Everyone stop!' shouts Constantinos. 'No more. No more. We wait. We will be in Harrogate in twenty minutes. Now we hand over to the police. No more!'

No one argues, no one has any fight left. Tiggy is shaking, Julia is sobbing. Even Simon looks distraught as he places his arm around his wife and they look out of the window, refusing to make eye contact with anyone in the carriage. You and Tim are left staring at each other until the carriage finally rolls into Harrogate station and you can tell the platform guard to bring the police as quickly as he can.

Was Freddie the one who killed Melissa? Maybe you will never know, because when the local coppers arrive you are bundled away by an inspector shaking his head at you like a stupid child.

'You should've left this to the professionals,' he mutters to you as you are led away by an astonished constable. He's right.

Now, go back to the beginning and start again

84

You walk into the billiards room. Everyone has now returned, and the maids are getting the fire going to warm everyone up. All have come back empty-handed, though, having found not a dicky bird on their midnight rambles. There are a few resentful glances in your direction, as if their banishment from their warm beds is all your fault.

'Kinn was quite right to make us check,' Algy announces, reading the room better than he usually does. You appreciate his attempt to speak up for you. 'Just a pity we didn't find the bounder. And I'm sure Kinn's as miffed as the rest of us about that.'

'Maybe even more,' you say.

'I say we all retire,' Tun-Hurley adds.

There is a general murmur of agreement. Everyone is desperate to get back to sleep, and there doesn't seem to be any point staying up.

'All right. Goodnight, everyone,' Algy says. 'Christmas tomorrow. Sleep well.'

Turn to 26

85

Where did you stay last night?

If you stayed at Freddie's, turn to 40

If you stayed at Nanny Tiggy's, turn to 33

86

'You, Miss Tiggworth.' Your eyes meet hers. They open wider than saucers in shock. 'A secret. A terrible secret.'

'What?' cries Julia. 'Nanny Tiggy? I don't believe it!'

'Oh, believe it well,' you tell her. 'You know what first put me on to her?' you ask the gathering. 'It was that Melissa and I had to go and collect her from a service at the York Minster. And it was hard to prise her away. Yet

Melissa said she had never known Miss Tiggworth to be religious; not in all the years she had known her. And then Miss Tiggworth said she had been with Melissa in London when she was nearly run down by a car. But I knew that was a lie because I was there myself!'

'Oh,' pipes up Nanny Tiggy, flustered and red-faced. 'Oh, I'm sorry. I've been a silly old thing, but it's that young priest. So handsome. I quite found in him a new reason to attend church.'

'You found something in him all right,' you say. 'But it isn't a twenty-five-year-old heart-throb.' Now it's time for the big revelation. 'At one point, Melissa mentioned that you had faithfully raised her – except for a year when a much sterner nanny took over. That was when she was ten. How old is she now, Freddie?'

'Thirty-six.'

'Why were you absent for a year twenty-six years ago, Miss Tiggworth?' Nanny Tiggy is speechless, but her face flushes. 'Was it because that priest is your son?'

For a moment, her face turns white with horror. But then her mouth sets with anger. 'So what if he is?' she yells furiously. 'So what if he is?'

'And Melissa had discovered the secret. And you killed her to protect it, to protect him!'

'Absolute nonsense!' she cries. 'Yes, he's my son. But Melissa was as good as my daughter. The archbishop knows he's my son and says it is no sin. That's where I was yesterday, when I said I was in London because I didn't want you prying. So why would I . . . Go on, ask the archbishop. He'll tell you I've spoken the truth!' She breaks down in tears.

You stop. Could you be wrong? It wouldn't be hard to check with the archbishop, so her story sounds plausible . . .

But you never get the chance. Because at that moment, a movement makes you turn. Someone is charging towards you and a glint of metal in their hand tells you exactly what they are thrusting towards your chest. Something that makes the whole world swim until it turns black as night.

Now, go back to the beginning and start again

87

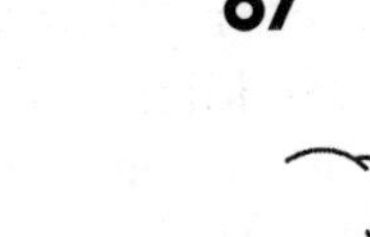

'Miss Tiggworth, are you all right?' you say, rushing over and examining her pupils.

'Oh, oh, yes. I think . . . oh,' she says, as she catches sight of the body again. 'Oh, it's my heart. I have angina. Those pills from Mrs Thresh's company, those pills didn't help one bit. Though my, my arthritis . . .' She's gabbling, in shock at what has just happened.

'Miss Tiggworth, you must try to calm yourself,' you interject. 'This is a terrible situation, but we must try. Can you look after her?' you ask Pererin.

'Yes, of course.' She looks very shaken herself but it's the best you can do.

'Give her some brandy.' Pererin nods and you urgently return to Melissa's body, not wanting to miss anything that might prove vital. She's still as warm as life. You superficially check her over and find nothing to note, until you come to a strange, tiny abrasion on her back that is leaking spots of blood into her fine dress. You have seen countless little marks like it. Doctors and nurses make them all the time.

'What's done that?' Simon asks.

'It looks like a hypodermic needle.' And it fits with the way she has died. Had she suffered a heart seizure, say, she would have made more noise, thrashed about, even. But a lethal injection could have killed painlessly in seconds. The question is: how could anyone have done it in plain sight?

'A needle?' Julia asks hastily. 'But she was always afraid of them. Said she hated the idea. She couldn't possibly have.'

'I don't think this was her doing.'

Julia puts her hand to her mouth, horrified. 'You mean she was . . .'

'Murdered. I believe she was murdered.'

'Oh!' cries Tiggy. 'My girl. My little girl.'

'But she can't have been,' gasps Tim. 'How?'

'That is what I intend to find out,' you tell him earnestly.

You check inside the box, making sure there are no more hidden compartments or flaps, no holes in the wood. Nothing. You're convinced: there's no needle here. And even if there were, how could anyone have administered the injection? It's conceivable that it was done before she entered the cabinet, but barely credible that she wouldn't have felt it and started in pain – the prick of a needle in your flesh is hard to ignore. It's also a bit far-fetched to think that no one would have noticed one of you walking around with a full syringe. No, how Melissa was killed is, at this time, inexplicable.

The train shudders and it feels like it is being shaken by an angry god.

'Was it one of us?' asks Pererin.

'I can't jump to that conclusion. But it seems so.'

'No, but no,' Julia insists, beginning to panic. 'Someone else. It must have been someone who . . . who got the train or . . . or . . .'

'Look around you, do you see anyone else?'

'I . . .' She stumbles, hysterically, to the rear of the carriage and checks through the luggage compartment, wildly throwing bags aside as if she will discover someone lurking beneath them. You all watch her in silence. She soon gives up and simply stares at her friend, tears making her mascara run. Constantinos goes to her and pulls her into his chest.

'She is at peace now,' he says.

'It was 'im!' yells Simon, pointing a finger at Freddie. 'Course it was!' And he leaps violently towards Melissa's husband.

'You think so?' Freddie, who is no small man, snarls in reply.

Tim jumps to keep them apart and just about manages

it. 'We have to stop the train!' he says, grabbing for the emergency chain.

If you let him pull the chain and halt the train, turn to 14

If you want to continue to your destination, turn to 103

88

You watch Rebecca disappear into the gloom. Curiosity takes you and you saunter over to her house. It's a little one-storey place, probably containing just a couple of rooms. Rebecca lives at Hurley Court, so this is presumably where her parents live. It's dark now, though, no sign of life.

'You want her? She's out.'

You look around to see a middle-aged, leather-skinned woman in a housecoat leaning out of next door's window. 'Oh, that's a pity,' you say. 'I had a Christmas card for her.'

'You a friend?' she asks suspiciously.

'Yes.'

'Didn't think Gladys had any friends,' she snorts.

'Gladys? No, Rebecca.'

'Oh!' she says. 'The daughter.' And the way she says it doesn't sound very respectful.

'Yes. Are any of them around?'

'Gladys is probably in The Plough, isn't she? Usually is. Don't ask me about the daughter.'

'What about Rebecca's father?'

She shrieks with laughter. 'You want to know who he is? So do we all. Been wondering that for twenty years, haven't we? Gladys never let on. Probably never even told him.'

'Perhaps,' you reply. They're unpleasant people, gossip-mongers. But it's a sad fact that you need them in your line of work. 'Thank you, goodbye.'

She seems to notice the coldness in your voice and slams her window shut. But the information may be the missing part of the puzzle.

You jump back into your red MG Roadster, gun the engine and head for Hurley Court. You have an accusation to make.

Turn to 67

89

You decide to leave him to it and push your way into the packed pub. A hundred rosy-cheeked men, women and children are putting away the beer. The smoke is so heavy that it makes you light-headed, and the warmth from all those bodies turns the place into some sort of Turkish bath, dripping condensation down the windows.

You don't hide your approach to the Yarrows' table and they watch as you come over. She looks relieved, while he seems to resent your presence. You suppose he wanted to continue his involved conversation with his wife.

'Would you mind if I join you?'

'Glad of it,' Pererin replies, pushing out a chair with her foot.

You sit. 'Think he'll sleep it off?'

'I should've knocked 'im out,' mutters Simon as he downs five inches of yellow ale in one go. He can certainly put the stuff away.

'And what good would that've done us?' Pererin snaps, in what you're sure is a rare burst of anger. 'I need this job.'

'There's limits, girl.'

'Your limits aren't paying our rent, are they?'

'I can earn. I can earn!' he snarls. No, it's not just

Freddie who has had too much. Simon is just better at hiding it, by the looks of things. 'I've just had some bad luck.'

'Bad luck,' she mutters. 'I've never seen anyone with such bad luck.'

They seem to have completely forgotten your presence – or they just don't care. Perhaps they do this so often in private that it's become second nature to them and they don't realize they're now in public.

'Need I ask what Mr Thresh was doing that you took exception to?'

They cast each other cold glances. 'No, you don't,' Simon grumbles. No, it's pretty obvious. 'An' she encourages 'im.'

'I do not!' Pererin snaps back. '*Me* encourage *him*? I do everything I can to keep him at bay. I wear high necks on my blouses and thick coats. He's not even my boss, really.' She throws up her hands. 'Bloody man.'

'Me or 'im?'

'Both of you.' She drains her glass. 'And now I have to spend hours stuck on a train with you both.' He shrugs and she rolls her eyes.

'Have you been married long?' you enquire, searching for a question that might break the tension.

'Long enough,' Pererin grumbles. 'More than long enough.'

Well, the air of married bliss doesn't surround this pair, that's for sure.

'Right, I'm gettin' another round in,' Simon mutters. He doesn't ask what you want, but pushes his way to the bar. You can't guess if he will return with drinks for you and Pererin or if this round is a solo round.

She meets your gaze. 'Yes, I know. But you try being married to Mr "If only I had a bit of luck, if only I'd scored more goals, if only I could find someone who'll lend me a few hundred quid to buy the Fox 'n' Hounds on Wool Street". You try waking up every day and having to slog it out in the office for ten hours, only for him to come home and tell you that he's lost the rent money on a nag.'

'It sounds harsh.'

'It is.' She catches a glimpse of him between the mass of bodies at the bar. 'I sometimes wonder where he went. The bloke I married.'

'Still in there somewhere?'

'If so, he's a bloody champion at hide and seek.' She relents a little. 'Oh, look, I don't mean to be a bear. But it's a hard life when you get hitched on a promise, and that promise falls apart in front of you.'

There's silence until Simon returns. He's brought you both port and lemon, and has a pint of bitter to himself. 'What're you two gossipin' about, then?' He looks suspicious. 'Oh, right. Course. Me. What's she been sayin', then? That I don't pay my way? That I'm not a real man? Well, I'm a real man. And I'll prove it any time she likes.' He shifts about in his seat, trying to get comfortable. 'Never had a cushy life, me. Always had to look out for meself. Right from when me mum chucked me out when I was fourteen.' He seems to have an idea. 'Tell you what, have you got a few quid? Only I've got this opportunity to buy a pub. It's a goldmine. Do you know the Fox 'n' Hounds on—'

'Wool Street?' you suggest.

'That's the one! You do know it!' He looks elated. 'So you know it's a goldmine. A little goldmine. Five hundred nicker's all it takes to get it off Reggie Trait. Come on. What d'you say?'

'I say I'm not in the market to buy a pub.'

'Not now?'

'Not now. Not ever.'

He looks crestfallen. He really did think this was his lucky break. For all his bluster and bullying, he's on his uppers and he knows it. You actually feel a twinge of sympathy for him. His wife doesn't seem to share it.

'Oh, for God's sake,' Pererin mutters, rolling her eyes. 'Come on. It's time.' She gathers up a yellow leather handbag and a soft felt hat that she pulls down tight over her head. Her blouse is, indeed, high-necked, and her coat is thick enough to swallow her figure.

The three of you knock back your drinks and traipse out to your special service.

Turn to 70

You need to return in time to keep watch on your trap. 'I'm sorry,' you say. 'I'm not feeling well. It's because I've been out already, I think. I need to warm up. I'll have to leave you two to it.'

Tun-Hurley raises an eyebrow – he takes a dim view of any soldier not pulling his weight, it seems. But he says nothing.

'All right, we'll go on,' says Leaner.

'I'll see you back inside soon.'

With that, you scamper back into the hallway. You decide the best place to keep watch on the newspaper cutting is from the drawing room. You open the door just a crack and find you have a good sight of the page.

But after a few minutes' wait, you begin to wonder if you have misjudged the situation. Did the intruder really mean to take that page at all? Were they actually looking for something else and this was just a piece of paper that got in the way? Perhaps . . .

Then you stop. Footsteps! You press your eye to the crack in the doorway and stare towards the corridor that leads to the servants' wing. *Tap, tap, tap.* The footsteps come closer. You see Gervaise walking through the hall.

You have no idea how a man can walk insolently, but he manages it. You watch him glance at the cutting on the floor but ignore it and shove into the billiards room. Not him, then. Then it's the two maids who come down the stairs and pad through the hallway, whispering to one another. One of them stops sharply and stares at the page. Her friend continues into the billiards room, but the first maid hangs back, then quickly bends down to the page and picks it off the floor. She scans it, looks all around her, then neatly places it on the little walnut table beside the doorway and enters the room. You feel let down – she was just doing her job. Maybe your plan was a duff one. You might as well give up. You are just about to come out from your observation post when there are more footsteps. You give it one more go, and wait to see who this is.

Ah, the colonel himself. The lord and master of Hurley Court is striding across the tiles. He is about to bash into the room behind the maids when he halts and grabs at the cutting. He must know it well, because he only looks at it for a second to assure himself it's what he thinks it is, then he whirls around, glaring, searching for anyone close. The only sound is Gervaise demanding a drink from the maids.

Quickly, Hurley screws up the paper and rushes towards your hiding place. You have seconds to react, and duck, as quietly as you can, behind a wing-backed chair. The colonel walks swiftly to the fireplace, chucks the screwed-up paper into the grate and hunts around for matches but can't find any.

'Colonel Hurley?'

It's Finney. He is in the doorway, looking quizzical. 'May I help with something?'

'Ah, no, no. Just wanted to light the fire,' Hurley says over his shoulder. He snatches the cutting from the grate and surreptitiously slips it into his pocket.

'I shall have a maid see to it.'

'Good. Right.' You crouch down as low as you can as the two leave the room, and you hear Hurley stride back in his normal manner towards the billiards room. 'Did you find anything on your search?' you hear him ask Finney.

'Nothing, sir.'

You give it a few seconds, then follow on their heels.

Turn to 84

91

'Freddie,' you say, calmly but forcefully. 'You're in no state to go searching for the truth. Leave that to me. Someone on this train is guilty as sin, and I will have them bound and trussed within a week.'

'A week's too long,' he barks.

'And they will be dead for a lot longer when they hang.' He glares at you but says no more, and you take that as some kind of agreement to keep himself under control. You relax a little. 'We will be in Harrogate in twenty minutes, and before then, I want some questions answered.'

'Go on, then,' says Pererin defiantly.

'Thank you. Now, I think we can take it that the bottle that lies in pieces on the floor contained the murder weapon. So, did anyone see who brought it or put it there?' There is a general murmur of 'no' and a shrugging of shoulders. No, it would have been too much to expect that someone had seen the perpetrator plonk it down.

'I don't know anything about that,' says Tim. 'But I do know that someone was messing around with my disappearing cabinet in the luggage compartment. You saw that, Kinn.'

You know what he is referring to – when he showed you the box earlier, he said that the nails on the case it came in had been tampered with. So what does that suggest, you wonder? 'Thank you, that is something to consider. And now, I must ask – and yes, Julia, it is somewhat unusual to do this *en masse*, so to speak – does anyone know of any reason that someone in this train car would have to murder Melissa Thresh?' The wind whistles through the carriage and you could cut the tension with a knife as eyes flick to the person next to them, to the floor, to the body laid out on the table. But no one speaks.

And then a voice, calm and strong, speaks out. 'He did.' It's Pererin Yarrow, and she's pointing a gloved finger at Tim.

'Pererin?'

'I'm sorry, but I have to speak up, don't I?'

'But what can you possibly mean?'

'Sorry, Mr Fortiswood, but it's the truth. Mrs Thresh blamed him for the company going bust.'

'I'm sure she didn't . . .'

'She did, Timmy boy,' says Freddie, regaining some of his composure. 'That drug you developed, Hilkodine, was the last chance for the firm and you blew it. Just doesn't work, does it?'

Tim looks shame-faced. 'We thought it would. No harm in it, though, is there? Even Miss Tiggworth tried it. It hasn't done you any harm, has it?'

'No, no harm,' Nanny Tiggy says, although the strain of the surroundings is obviously taking its toll on her.

'That's hardly enough, is it, old man? "Take our new angina medication. It won't hurt you. It just won't do you any good." For God's sake.'

'We all know what drug you prefer, Freddie,' Tim says angrily. 'The bottle and the bottle and the bottle.'

'It keeps me sane.'

'It keeps you tight. Anyway, what if it were all my fault? That hardly gives me a motive for murder, does it?'

'She was going to tell everyone what a failure you are,' Pererin continues. 'I'm sorry, Mr Fortiswood, but it's the truth.' She addresses you. 'And it was his magic box she died in, wasn't it?'

Tim looks like he could use a whack of the Scotch that he's just derided Freddie for knocking back. 'Maybe it is my fault, I don't know. I couldn't keep up with it all.' He looks at you pleadingly. 'I was working eighteen hours per day. So much paperwork, so many reports on the trials – I had to ask Mrs Yarrow to read half of them for me. I just wasn't sleeping right. And then it all turned out to be worthless. But I didn't hurt Melissa, I swear!'

Your heart squeezes a little at the sight of this seemingly gentle man wrapping his arms around himself for safety. But is it real or is it play-acting? It looks convincing enough to the untrained observer, but you have seen many men shed crocodile tears for their victims about ten minutes before they were unmasked as the killers.

'Buck up, old man,' you say, putting your hand on his shoulder. 'The moment's over.'

If you now sit tight until you arrive at Harrogate, turn to 6

If you ask everyone where they were this morning when a car attempted to knock Melissa down, turn to 108

92

You silently descend the steep stone steps, the candle providing a pool of light so that you don't fall. When a strong gust blows up and extinguishes the flame, you're left groping about in total darkness. All it takes is for you to stumble once, and you fall down in the pitch black, tumbling and crying out.

They will find your body in the morning.

Now, go back to the beginning and start again

93

'It's time to come clean, Major,' you say.

'What do you mean?' demands Tun-Hurley.

'You murdered your cousin, didn't you?'

'How dare you even suggest such a thing!' he protests, squaring up to you.

'Very easily. I know what you've been buying from Finney when you thought no one was watching. A terrible drug, morphine.' His mouth drops open. You see Finney scowl. 'Did you become addicted during your war service? They gave it to you for your leg and you were never able to shake your reliance upon it?'

Tun-Hurley drops heavily into a leather armchair and passes his hand across his forehead. 'Did you guess that?' You nod. 'Well, it's the truth. Foolish thing was, it wasn't even in combat. I broke my leg while hopping into an observation post. Hurt like hell, of course, and they gave me that stuff to dull the pain. From that moment I couldn't do without it. Shame. I feel such shame. Weakness to a bloody drug.'

'Was Colonel Hurley threatening to tell people?'

'What? Of course not. I'll admit to this private weakness of mine, but I never laid a finger on Harrison.'

You have seen many killers confronted with the truth, and some have admitted their guilt, some denied it. But you have always seen the truth in their eyes. And this time, you can see it in his. You've made a mistake!

'But I tell you I know who it was.'

'Who?' Mina demands to know.

He lifts a finger and points. You all stare. But before you know what is happening, there is a glint in the air. It's the silver knife. Why didn't you think to secure it? And it's swiping through the air, towards your uncovered neck.

Now, go back to the beginning and start again

94

In the drawing room, the household is assembled under the beady eye of Inspector Rollinson.

'We're all very lucky that the inspector happened to be at the station when I arrived,' says Gervaise. 'He was there to follow up on some fraud case, is that right, Inspector?'

'It is, sir,' says the beefy officer in a Welsh accent. 'Now, I would like to see the body.'

You inform him who you are and, like clockwork, he views you with suspicion. No matter where you are, it seems, the police just don't like you poking your nose in.

With the officer projecting more suspicion onto you than onto every other person there, you escort him outside to the body, which lies just as you all left it. 'Well, thank you, Dr Tenor. We shall handle it from here,' Rollinson says. 'The crew to take the deceased away will be here in a few hours, I expect.'

'And in the meantime?'

'In the meantime, I shall conduct my investigation. And I should advise you not to impede it.'

'It wouldn't even cross my mind, Inspector.'

Well, no, it wouldn't. Because you have your own enquiries to make.

First off, while everyone is assembled in the drawing room and waiting for the police to talk to them, you take the opportunity to go quietly upstairs to take a look into their bedrooms.

You start at the far end, with Mina's room. It's a quiet sort of affair: a little jewellery here and there, a copy of *Wuthering Heights* by the bedside with a leather bookmark halfway through, a few attractive watercolours on the wall that you suspect were painted by Mina herself, but nothing noteworthy. You slip out and into Gervaise's room. It's shockingly austere. You had rather expected something chaotic and monstrous, but it's almost bare, as if he had never even lived here, just passed through for a night. That makes searching it a quick business, however, and you're in and out in a minute flat. Then into Colonel Hurley's room. A regimental colours flag hangs in the corner, and the walls are neatly adorned with photographs of men in uniform and a family tree of the Hurley clan. All is neatly turned out. You set to work, opening a writing bureau to find some correspondence sorted into stacks of 'answered' and 'to be answered'. A letter from his banker intimates that Gervaise had invoked the colonel's name when asking for a loan – you can only imagine the reply that Hurley fired off in return. A display case of his campaign medals sits in pride of place on his bureau. Again, little of interest here.

Next up is Algy's room. Well, if you were disappointed by the lack of chaos in Gervaise's chamber, his brother more than makes up for it. He must have left strict instructions with the staff never to tidy up. It's a havoc of discarded clothes and battered paperback books with bright covers and titles such as *High Noon in Thirsty Gulch* and *The Smoking Gun*. 'Not exactly Shakespeare, Algy, old boy,' you mutter. In the corner of the room are three small packing cases filled with cans of Cleano, the disastrous cleaning fluid that he thinks is going to make him a mint – although you suspect he's more likely to find himself sued for all he's worth. And you find something else, hidden under his mattress. It's a notebook crammed with doodles and scrawls, including such passages as 'all you *ever* do is humiliate me', 'that's the last time you will mock me in front of Mother' and the like. Well, it's suspicious, but you're not sure quite what to do with it. You place it back where you found it.

The next room is Major Tun-Hurley's. It's a lot like his cousin's: everything in its place, regimented in every way. He apparently sleeps on a folding bed, which must be a habit from his time on the campaign trail, and there's a trunk with most of his possessions – the case seems to have seen as much action as him. Examining it, you find something a bit curious. 'Hello,' you say to yourself as you notice that the curved lid seems very thick. You fiddle with it and manage to twist a metal bolt. The inner side of the lid flips down to reveal a hidden compartment. It's empty but for one thing: a small bottle of brown glass. You peer inside it. There's a little residue at the bottom. You place it in your pocket and put everything else back as you found it. Hopefully, the fact that the bottle is empty means he won't be looking for it.

You descend the stairs and grab your coat and galoshes as Inspector Rollinson slowly informs the family that none of them are under suspicion – but none of them are *not* under suspicion – then slip out the front.

It's a quick drive in your Roadster to the village, where all the houses have little plumes of smoke rising from chimneys. Thick blankets of white snow on thatched roofs, mullioned windows glowing with warm yellow light and a few children fighting with snowballs make for a cheery scene. You park and walk along the little High Street, where The Plough is doing a roaring and noisy trade. A few doors down is the shop you are looking for: the village pharmacy.

It's closed, of course, but you're not to be put off. You knock and knock until a window above the shop opens. 'Don't you know what day it is?' a white-haired, bespectacled man calls down.

'I do, sir. And I'm most terribly sorry. But I'm investigating a murder.'

He looks astonished by your words. 'A what?'

'Murder.'

He stares at you for a few moments more, then his head disappears and the window shuts. After a while the door opens to you. 'Who is dead? And who are you?'

'Dr Kinn Tenor, attached to Scotland Yard. And the dead man is Colonel Hurley.'

He takes off his glasses, squints at you, puts the glasses back, squints at you again and then leads you inside the shop. 'However can I aid you?'

You gaze at the bottle-filled shelves. 'I need forty per cent formaldehyde, ninety-five per cent concentrated sulphuric acid, distilled water and a beaker,' you say.

He looks bemused but fetches the items and leads you to the back room. You are pleased to see a simple but clean little laboratory where you can perform your work at a proper bench. You pour a little distilled water into the bottle that you took from Major Tun-Hurley's case and use it to extract the residue from the bottom, forming a grey-white paste. This you place in a glass dish before mixing the formaldehyde and acid in the beaker.

'Ah, Marquis reagent!' exclaims the chemist.

'Indeed.' And you pour a little of the solution into the dish. The paste turns a deep red.

'The result?' asks the man.

'Morphine. As I expected.'

Yes, morphine. An effective medicine. A dangerous narcotic.

You gaze at the dish, thank the man, pay him for his time and wish him a merry Christmas.

Now you want to head up to Oxford to look into Leaner's background. But you're also a bit curious about Finney. The maids told you some surprising things about him. And you know he's a regular at The Plough. You could stop in there and see what you can find out.

If you call in at The Plough, turn to 3

If you drive to Oxford, turn to 13

95

Ah, England! Such a rich nation. The babbling brooks, the cheery milkmaids, the snow-capped country churches. And the strong booze, which is frequently topped up in your glass by Simon while Constantinos bends your ear about how badly the Greek republic is serving its citizens. Everyone else is chatting away merrily – Melissa has vowed that she will be strolling around York in her Renaissance costume with nothing more than a cloak for warmth, but the rest of you have agreed to don your fancy dress after you return from afternoon tea in York, when you kick off your party with Tim's magic act.

The only person who doesn't seem to be having such a wonderful time is Freddie, who is listening sullenly to whatever Julia is telling him – something about golf, you understand from her mimes of teeing off. Meanwhile, his secret glances are going in quite another direction and landing on the delicately curved back of Pererin Yarrow, who is talking to the old nanny about the weather.

Tim sits beside you. 'Gosh, I'm a little tired already,' he says.

'And you're the one drinking nothing but orange juice.' You point to his glass.

'Ah, yes, best to pace oneself, isn't it?' He lifts his drink in salute, splashing a little onto his tie, which you recognize as that of St Thomas's Medical School. 'Oh, bother.' He dabs at it with a hanky, but the orange is seeping into the white stripes and there seems little hope. 'Bother.'

'You're chief scientific officer for Melissa's company, she tells me.'

'For my sins. Yes. Oh, dear, I don't suppose you have anything to remove orange juice from silk?'

'I'm afraid I don't carry it around with me. I don't have much call for it.'

'No, no. I suppose it's quite specific, isn't it?'

'Is it an interesting job?'

'What, getting orange juice out of a tie?'

'No, being chief scientific officer for the firm.'

'Oh, oh, yes. Advance Pharmaceuticals. Well, I do find it very interesting, yes.' His face falls a little. 'At least, I did until we sort of went bust.'

'What went wrong there?'

'Oh, tried expanding into the wrong areas, got pushed aside by the bigger boys in the market, backed the wrong potential drugs, all went a bit awry.'

'Yes, Melissa mentioned some heart drug you thought would do well.'

'More than that. Hilkodine was our last hope. Five years of research budget down the drain.'

'What will you do now?'

'No idea, to be honest with you. There's not much market for a research scientist whose research tends to end in failure.'

'Could you return to practising medicine?'

His back stiffens at your words and he stares at you. 'I don't know what you mean.'

'You're a physician, aren't you?'

'No, I'm not.'

You look at him curiously. 'Then why are you wearing a St Thomas's Medical School tie?'

His mouth falls open and he stammers. 'I . . . I had no idea that's what it was. I just . . . found it in a shop.'

You pause. It's the least convincing act you have seen in a long time. 'Was it a second-hand shop?'

He hesitates. 'No, I don't think so.'

'Where was it?' you ask casually.

'I . . . don't understand.'

'This shop that sells medical school ties to people who aren't students. Which shop is it? I must stop by and inform them what they are selling without realizing it.'

'Oh, must you? I mean, I don't recall which shop it was. It's probably just coincidence. Those stripes could be anyone's, couldn't they?' He looks at his wristwatch – without actually checking the time – and clears his throat. 'Actually, would you mind? I want to check on all the equipment for our magic act later.'

All right, you think to yourself. *I'll let you off this time.* 'May I come? It sounds very intriguing. I promise not to give away any secrets.'

He brightens and looks relieved. 'Oh, yes, of course. So long as you don't try to unravel any of the mysteries.'

That's what you do for a living. But just this once, you'll leave them ravelled.

'I promise.'

He leads you back to the luggage compartment. There's a jam of suitcases and hat boxes, and to one side a stack of crates with labels announcing 'Shhhh! The Evenlode Magic Company!'

'Evenlode really are the top boys in this game,' Tim informs you happily. He opens up one of the smaller boxes. It contains a mish-mash of conjurors' toys: a bunch of paper flowers, a string of silk hankies and the like. 'Ah, here we go.' He picks out a fairly serious-looking hatchet.

'What on earth is that for?'

'Oh, a trick where I put a glass bowl in a cardboard box, then hack the box to pieces and the bowl's gone. Quite a good trick, actually. All relies on angles, you see.'

'I see.'

'Oh, you'll like this.' He drags out the biggest crate of all, which is the size of a small wardrobe. 'Hello, that's odd.'

'What is?'

He shakes his head. And begins prising up the lid, which is nailed down. 'Oh, nothing. Probably just imagining things. Now, this is my pride and joy. The disappearing cabinet. My assistant gets in, I close the door, tap on it and then poof! She's gone. It really is . . . Oh. Now, look at that.'

'At what?' You stride forward as the train shivers a bit as it rolls on.

'Well, it's just that . . . The lid. I nailed it down myself. I was sure there were six nails to keep it in place. But now there are only four. And inside, it was wrapped in a layer of crepe paper to keep it from scratching. But that's gone.' A grin spreads across his face. 'I know what's happened.'

'What?'

'Someone has been cheating! Peeking at my tricks. One of those rascals out there wants to know the secret of the magic!' He thuds the lid back into place. 'But, oh no! Not while I'm still a member of the Magic Circle. I'll protect the illusions till the day I die. I'm sorry, Kinn, but I can't show you any more, in case you blab.'

'That's disappointing.'

'I know it is, and I'm sorry. But magic is wonder. And you can't destroy wonder.'

'I'm sure you're right.'

'You'll thank me when you're agog.'

'No doubt.'

Turn to 111

96

Right. You're resolved. There's only one thing for it. You enter the hall, take hold of the drumstick for the dinner gong and start bashing away. The copper clangs in the still night like a factory. You keep striking. A minute later Algy rushes down the stairs, dressed in pyjamas and a stripy dressing gown. 'Kinn? What on earth is going on?' he says, startled.

'One minute, Algy. I need everyone here first,' you insist.

Leaner, the journalist, then Gervaise and Mina appear at the top of the stairs and blearily make their way down. Finney glides from the servants' wing, perfectly dressed – you suspect he sleeps in his butler's clothes, ready to serve the house day or night – then the two maids and finally Colonel Hurley, followed by his cousin. Hurley looks ready to tear you limb from limb.

'What the devil's the matter?' he yells as he descends, tying a red woollen dressing gown that he must have bought when he was a thinner man.

'Colonel. I have reason to believe the person who stabbed you is in this house. I have just chased an intruder outside and it is possible he has returned.'

'In this house? The devil he is. I would have broken him in two. I know a criminal when I see one.'

'I understand your gall at the suggestion. Nevertheless, you must check the bedrooms for shoes or clothing which show that the owner was out in the snow.'

'I must, must I? I shall be the one who decides what I *must* do!' he bellows.

Mina goes to him in an attempt to calm his mood. 'Maybe it would be best, just for our peace of mind,' she says gently. A genuine attempt or a ruse to shift suspicion away from herself? You can't tell for certain. He grunts in annoyance but agrees, though he glares at you all the way as you go up the stairs.

As a party you go from room to room, searching for any sign that someone has been outside in the last half-hour. You try every room, including the servants' wing.

But you come away empty-handed. If the intruder is among you, they have either hidden their wet clothes or managed to dry them in time. As you leave the maids' room, the very last to be examined, Colonel Hurley draws himself up to his full height. Mina can't save you this time. 'I have indulged your insulting whim and it has proved you wrong about my household. I expect you to leave this house before breakfast. No matter the weather,' he glowers. You know he means what he says and there's no alternative. You leave Hurley Court under a cloud, watched by the whole household. You can't help but notice Finney stifling a grin.

Well, that's it. You've let Algy down.

Now, go back to the beginning and try again

97

You all reassemble in the drawing room. Somehow the light, which seemed so bright and cheery just a few minutes ago, now feels like a harsh spotlight shining on you all to search out a criminal. Finney calls the maids in too, so that the entire household is there.

Who did it? Well, surely it was whoever attacked the colonel during the Oath of Fealty ceremony. You look from face to face. One of these people, you believe, is a killer. But who? And why?

Mina is sitting, looking utterly distraught. Could it be her? Colonel Hurley couldn't have been an easy man to be married to. Perhaps, even, someone had come into her life, so that she wanted to end things – and Hurley wouldn't have been the sort to just let her walk away.

Gervaise is beside her, holding her hand. It's an unusual act of tenderness and compassion from a man who seems to revel in how obnoxious he can make himself. His newspaper peddles tawdry gossip about the wealthy and powerful, earning him few friends and many enemies. It could be that his mischief-making has rebounded on him and Hurley's death has been a terrible consequence, you reason.

Algy's standing behind them, leaning against the mantelpiece for support. You've known him for years and, for a moment, dismiss out of hand the very idea that he could be guilty of anything more than copying a schoolmate's homework. But then, a good nature has never been a true barrier to an act of violence. Some of the worst killers in history shocked their friends and neighbours with their crimes. No, you can't write him off.

Leaner, the journalist. He's a bit of an enigma, as the one known least to the family. Quite affable, from what you can tell, but it might all be an act. And, despite what he claims about being high-minded and bringing the truth to light, is there any more unscrupulous profession than journalism? And journalism on the *Daily Messenger*, at that?

All through the room, Finney is weaving, serving cups of tea to keep the atmosphere as calm as it can be. He's a smooth one, for sure. Perhaps too smooth, though. Underneath his cool exterior, is his heart cold enough to set a man-trap and beat his victim to death? Maybe. Maybe.

Then there's Major Tun-Hurley. Younger cousin to Colonel Hurley. They came through the War together as brothers in arms. But in that fog of war, anything could have happened to sow a weed of resentment. Especially if the seed already existed due to some old family tension.

And you can't write off the maids. They flit about the house, barely noticed. But therein lies the little niggle of doubt – unnoticed doing what, exactly?

'Finney, is the telephone working yet?' Algy asks.

'I'm afraid not, sir.'

'I see. In that case, would someone volunteer to drive to the village police station and return with Sergeant Pimm?'

'I'll go,' says Gervaise. Everyone stares at him. It is as if a visible cloud of suspicion has suddenly flown in through the window. 'Oh, it's like that, is it?' He stands. 'Yes, it will be a good opportunity for me to flee the scene of my crime, won't it?' he sneers. 'Now, would anyone like to accuse me outright, or do you all want to do it behind my back?' He looks at the faces all around him. 'How about—'

'Oh, please stop, please,' his mother pleads. 'It's all

so . . .' She bursts into tears once more, and Algy puts his arms around her, looking daggers at his brother.

'All right. Well, I'll still go. Give me twenty minutes,' Gervaise mutters.

But you're not going to let him drift away. You follow him out to the hallway. 'Just a minute,' you say as he takes an overcoat from the cupboard.

'Ah, now we get the grilling. All right. Best get on with it. This is what you want to know: up until the time of my father's death I was either asleep in bed or dressing to come down to breakfast. I saw no one and have no idea who it could be. And yes, I will now inherit the estate, and yes, I'm not wholly cut up about his death because he and I didn't get on, but he was still my father and I don't approve of patricide. Does that cover it?'

Almost. 'One more question. You brought Leaner here. Why?'

He responds irritably. 'You know why. We had the idea of a series for my newspaper about old war heroes and their exploits. A few "How I beat the Hun" pieces to keep the readers feeling patriotic.'

'Has he written them yet?'

'He's interviewed my father and the major. Hasn't written them up yet. Now, anything more? I do want to alert the police today.'

You can't think of anything else, so you send him on his way. You step outside to watch him climb into the car. Then you turn to re-enter the house. But there's something odd: glancing at the windows on the first floor above you, you see Finney enter one of the bedrooms. He's carrying something, some sort of package. A moment later it's gone and he's slipping back out of the room.

Whose room is that? You quickly calculate. It's Major Tun-Hurley's. You take a few moments to consider it, but you can't think what it might mean. Probably nothing.

If you have met Mrs Blenkins in the village post office, turn to 116

If not, turn to 119

98

You step in front of him. 'No. There's no point. We should continue to Harrogate. We can alert the police there. What can we do here?' You wave to the window, which shows a dark, blank landscape.

'You're right,' Tim says, dropping his head. 'But it seems so heartless, somehow, to keep on as if nothing has happened.'

'Hardly that.'

'No, I know. It just feels ... we have to sit here for another hour, looking at her.'

'You can all keep looking at her. I intend to drown myself in that bottle.'

It's Freddie. He winds unsteadily towards the bar. He wavers with the movement of the train. But it strikes you that you haven't actually seen him drink anything. He was in the pub with the Yarrows, and there were a number of empty glasses on their table when you went in, but how many were emptied by Melissa's husband, you wonder – especially since the Yarrows themsclves don't seem to be anything more than a little tipsy.

'For God's sake, Freddie,' howls Julia as he unscrews the cap from a bottle of Scotch and puts the neck of the bottle to his lips.

'Leave him,' you say.

'Look, everyone, please! Just . . . please!' Tim calls out. You see tears roll down Nanny Tiggy's cheek. Pererin seems silently shocked and is breathing deeply to control herself. 'Kinn, what should we do?'

Will you ask everyone to stand back so you can take another look at the cabinet – maybe somebody has a torch so you can see it better – or do you want to ask Simon a few questions?

If you ask for a torch, turn to 105

If you interrogate Simon, turn to 27

99

'I'll just be a minute. I'll see you outside,' you tell the others. They grab their overcoats and stomp out into the garden. You check that there's no one around, and you place the cutting on the floor beside the door to the billiards room, as if it has been accidentally dropped. Then you hurry out into the garden.

Turn to 51

100

Your eyes meet Mina's. She looks fragile in her mourning wear. 'Mina. You did it,' you say. 'You were having an affair with Finney and your husband found out.'

'What?' demands Algy, springing to his feet and staring

first at her, then at the butler. For her part, Mina tries to speak but can't, the words choking in her throat. Finney merely cocks a supercilious eyebrow.

'I knew from the first morning when everyone received those poison-pen letters. But you were the only one who wasn't handed one, weren't you? Because you had already intercepted it.' She gasps. 'It was accusing you of a scandalous involvement with Finney, wasn't it?'

And at that, she bursts into tears, which stream down her lovely face.

'Don't be absurd!' Algy says angrily. 'Don't accuse her, she's done nothing . . .'

'I did, I did,' she wails. 'Finney and I were . . . involved.'

Taking that as his cue, Finney smirks and nonchalantly sits on the sofa next to her, placing a hand on her back. He crosses his legs, demonstrating how at home he is, no longer a servant. Mina pulls her hands from her face. 'But I never hurt Harrison. It wasn't me. I tell you it wasn't.' You stop. You have seen many killers confronted with the truth, and some have admitted their guilt, some denied it. But you have always seen the truth in their eyes. And this time, you can see it in hers. You've made a mistake! 'And I know who it was.'

'Who?' Algy demands to know.

She lifts a finger and points. Behind you. You begin to turn your head but feel something snaking around your throat. An arm. One about to break your neck in two.

Now, go back to the beginning and start again

101

The streets are empty, but the windows of people's houses are cheerily glowing and the distant sound of Christmas carols drifts in the air with the snowflakes. Christmas Day. A day for peace and joy. But you are on your way instead to Harrogate station. It is empty but for you and your former travelling companions. You all converge at the entrance to the platform and grimly walk the final few paces to the train itself, where Detective Inspector Wilkes is waiting, tapping his foot.

'Thank you for coming,' he says in a gruff, no-nonsense sort of way.

'Didn't have any bloody choice, did we?' replies Freddie.

Wilkes has no time for sarcasm. 'No, you didn't, Mr Thresh. That's the nature of the law. Now, our initial enquiries have told us that we need to know exactly where everyone was when death occurred and the precise order of events. To that end, would you all please enter the car.' You all climb in without speaking a word to one another. Suspicion has taken you over, and you regard each other with doubt. 'And now, please take up the places you were in when Mrs Thresh was first discovered deceased.' You are all steely-eyed now – except for Julia, who looks ready to burst into tears – and shuffle into place. You, Simon and Tim are ranged around the disappearing cabinet, Freddie is by the drinks bar, Tiggy and Pererin on the rear seats, Julia and Constantinos on the seats at the side of the carriage.

'Thank you. What I would like to know—'

'Inspector,' you say, interjecting. He doesn't look like he is used to being interrupted, but you put a hand up to quiet him. 'Inspector, I understand your intention, but I am in a position to forestall it.'

'What do you mean?' His gruff manner is even gruffer now and he looks quite annoyed by the halt to his flow.

'I mean that I can inform you of the who, how and why of the terrible murder of Melissa Thresh.'

He looks gobsmacked. And the gasps from around the room add to the effect.

It's not an unpleasing one.

'You what?' demands Simon.

'You heard me.' You gaze around. 'This was an evil crime. Melissa Thresh was a good woman who didn't deserve what one of you did to her. She had a long and exciting life ahead of her, but you cut it short to protect your nasty little secret.'

'Who?' says Freddie.

You pay no attention. 'When Melissa first engaged my services, she thought it was all an adventure, having someone stalking her movements. It never really occurred to her that there would be a serious and ultimately successful plan to end her life.'

'Who is it? Who killed my wife?' demands Freddie.

'Yes. Who? Who would do such a thing? Well, I know.' You look, one by one, at their faces. 'And it was you.'

Who are you pointing at?

If it's Nanny Tiggy, turn to 86

If it's Tim, turn to 36

If it's Julia and Constantinos, turn to 104

If it's Pererin and Simon Yarrow, turn to 29

If it's Freddie, turn to 85

102

You scramble through the chaos of tossed-about luggage and magical props until you find the carriage door. You get it open and jump down to the tracks.

'What's goin' on?' yells a voice ahead of you. It's the driver. Your vision adjusts to the dark and you can make him out leaning from his cab.

'Someone has been killed. Mrs Thresh.'

'Jesus,' he mutters. 'What do we do?'

'We should stop here and go for the police.'

'Stop here?'

'Are we close to a village?'

He points to the distance. 'Karleigh's about three miles.'

Three miles, you can do that.

Turn to 80

103

You step in front of him. 'No. There's no point. We should continue to Harrogate. We can alert the police there. What can we do here?' You wave to the window, which shows a dark, blank landscape.

Simon and Freddie retreat, glaring at each other.

'You're right,' Tim says, dropping his head. 'But it seems so heartless, somehow, to keep on as if nothing has happened.'

'Hardly that.'

'No, I know. It just feels . . . we have to sit here for another hour, looking at her.'

'You can all keep looking at her. I intend to drown myself in that bottle.'

It's Freddie. He pushes himself to his feet and winds unsteadily towards the bar. He wavers with the movement of the train. But it strikes you that you haven't actually seen him drink anything. Could it be an act?

'That's not going to help anyone,' Constantinos admonishes him.

'I don't care.'

'For God's sake, Freddie,' howls Julia as he takes the cap from a bottle of Scotch and puts the neck of the bottle to his lips.

'You must pull yourself together,' Constantinos says, starting towards him.

'Leave him,' you say, putting your hand out to stop Constantinos from snatching the whisky away.

'Yes, leave me. My wife. Not yours. Look to yours.'

'And what's that meant to mean?' Julia demands.

'Whatever you want it to mean,' he says angrily. '*My wife!*'

'And my *friend*!'

You've seen it before. The shock hits and those gathered around end up at each other's throats, even as their loved one lies in front of them, almost forgotten in the outpouring of recriminations. It's a mix of adrenaline and pent-up, unsaid emotions.

'Look, everyone, please! Just . . . please!' Tim calls out. You see tears roll down Nanny Tiggy's cheek. Pererin seems silently shocked and is breathing deeply to control herself. 'Kinn, what should we do?'

Will you ask everyone to stand back so you can take another look at the cabinet – maybe somebody has a torch so you can see it better – or do you want to ask Simon a few questions?

If you ask for a torch, turn to 105

If you interrogate Simon, turn to 27

'You, Julia, and you, Constantinos.'

'How dare you!' yells Constantinos.

'I'll tell you how I dare. Your motivation was greed. But it wasn't just greed for money. It was greed for power. You're a greedy man, who thinks he was born to power, isn't that right, *Your Highness*?'

Julia blanches at the final words, but Constantinos stops and looks magisterial. He is enjoying the sound of the title.

'I was born to power,' he says regally. 'Yes, I was. My family had it torn from us but we will take it back.'

'What the 'ell's the bloke talkin' about?' blurts out Simon.

'What I am talking about,' Constantinos informs him, 'is the throne of Greece. The throne that is rightfully mine.'

'Control yourself, Mr Yarrow, you're in the company of royalty,' you say ironically. 'His family were deposed in a revolution in 1924. Since then . . .'

'Since then, there has been anarchy!' yells Constantinos. 'Republicans, fascists, military, fools. A dozen governments, all failures. Failures because they were not born to it!'

'And the men you have been meeting are what?'

'Patriots. Men who believe in their nation. Men who are—'

'Hired guns. Mercenaries,' someone interjects. You look to the doorway. Inspector Reeves of Scotland Yard's Special Branch is stepping in. 'We've been keeping a watch on them and on you, Your Highness. We don't appreciate Britain being used as a staging post for coup d'etats.'

'And who are you?' Wilkes asks Reeves, surprised.

'Reeves. Special Branch at the Yard. I think we'll be taking this over now.' Wilkes isn't happy with that, but he knows his hands are tied. 'Now, Dr Tenor, I should like to know just how you worked it out about our royal friend here.'

'Oh, Denmark.'

'Denmark?'

'Melissa and I happened to observe his discussion with one of those dangerous men that you just mentioned. And that man said, and I quote, "You Danes have always been cowards."' You look around to see if anyone has the first clue of what you're talking about. 'No? Oh, well.

The Greek royal family is a cadet branch of the Danish royal family. They're not even Greek. They were handed Greece in the middle of the last century because no other European royal house wanted it. Oh, control yourself, Constantinos. You know it's true.' He snorts in derision but doesn't dispute what you say.

'But what does all this have to do with Melissa?' Freddie asks, frustration bubbling up in him.

'It was she who informed you about him, wasn't it, Inspector?' you say, turning to Reeves.

'No.'

'What?'

'I'd never heard of her until I came up here and you two started sticking your noses into our surveillance operation. We were actually told about matey here by a bicycle shop owner in Whitechapel. Greek bloke who heard about it from his cousin.'

You're confused. So if it wasn't Melissa, then Constantinos had no motive to kill her. 'Wait, let me see,' you say, stopping and trying to cudgel your brains into picking through this revelation.

But you never get the chance. Inspector Wilkes stops you.

'Dr Tenor, I have been indulgent of your behaviour until now, but I have had enough,' he says. 'You are impeding the investigation. Get out of the carriage. Go back to London, or I'll have you chucked in the cells.'

Faced with a night in chokey, you have little choice but to comply.

Now, go back to the beginning and start again

105

'Would you all kindly give me a little space?' There are many angry glances between them, but they all shuffle away. Simon drops into one of the seats. 'I want to take another look at the disappearing cabinet. Does anybody have a torch?' No one seems to.

'I've got a lighter,' says Tiggy, rooting about in her handbag. She rubs away her tears. 'I shouldn't, really. My doctor says smoking isn't as good for you as people think. I'm afraid it's not the best one.'

'It'll do,' you say as she hands it to you. It's a cheap brass thing. You strike the flint, and on the third go a tiny yellow flame emerges. 'It might do,' you mutter.

You poke your head into the cabinet and look around, feeling the joins in the wood, making sure nothing else comes apart. Yes, all quite solid. You're about to draw yourself back out when something catches your eye. A slight glimmer on the side where Melissa was squeezed in behind the false panel. There it is again. And then gone. You move the lighter. A spot on the wood flashes, but there's nothing there. You reach out and touch the wood. There's a patch no larger than a ha'penny that is greasy and a little bit sticky. It is this that is glinting when you pass the lighter across it. 'Strange,' you say to yourself, wondering if it's anything of importance or no more than something that was on Melissa's dress.

Do you say anything to the others behind you about what you have found, or do you keep it to yourself?

If you tell the others, turn to 71

If you keep it to yourself, turn to 4

106

'I would like to speak to a few of you before the police arrive,' you say.

'I'm not sure that's legal, Kinn,' pipes up Algy.

'There's no law against asking questions.'

'No, I suppose not.'

You might as well start with him. 'Would you be so kind as to step this way?'

He looks surprised. 'Me? Oh, well, yes, all right,' he says.

You take him to the billiards room and try to put him at his ease.

'Don't worry, old chap. Now, you asked me down to investigate poison-pen letters.'

'Yes, that's right,' he says.

'Things are much worse, aren't they?'

'I can't think how they could be any worse than this.'

'No. Listen, Algy, is there anything you aren't telling me?'

'Such as what?' he asks, sounding confused.

'Such as you have a suspicion about who might have sent them. Or who might have attacked your father.'

He groans and drops into a chair. 'It's all such a mess, Kinn. The only thing I have in mind is that Gervaise has some problems with the old moolah.' You raise an eyebrow. 'He even tried to touch me for a few quid. Said some bookies are after him.'

'You don't say.'

'I think he tried to buy a horse with them and the whole deal went queer. I'm glad I don't need to worry about money anymore. Not now that I've got . . .'

'Algy.'

'Yes?'

'Please don't try to sell Cleano to anyone. It really is the most awful stuff.' He thinks about it for a minute, then nods. 'Good chap. Now, how did your father get on with his cousin?'

'The major? Well, pretty well, I should say. They've been chums since they were in short trousers. I've never seen anything amiss between them.'

'And your mother?'

His cheeks turn pink. 'Oh, look, dash it all, Kinn, must I?'

'I'm afraid you must, old man.'

'Oh, all right. Mum and Dad had respect for each other. Not much more than that, if you ask me. But they both seemed content enough.'

'Contentment isn't always enough, Algy.'

'I suppose not. But you'll have to ask her, Kinn.'

'Then I'll do just that. Would you ask her to join us?'

'Righto,' he says, getting up, a little shaken by what you have just discussed.

Turn to 118

107

'I shall remain here until you admit the truth,' you declare.

She puts her hand to her mouth in horror. 'But . . . but . . .' she stammers.

'The truth!'

She looks horrified. 'I . . .' She seems saddened, but stands up straight, drawing herself up to her full height, military-style. 'All right, Dr Tenor. The truth. I . . .' At that moment, there is a knock on the front door. You glance towards it, then back at Tiggy, and you know the moment and the spell have been broken. 'I shall answer that,' she says defiantly.

You look through the net curtain and see a young policeman waiting. 'Miss Eve Tiggworth?'

'Yes.'

'Detective Inspector Wilkes has asked me to take you to the railway station.'

'Whatever for?'

'As I understand it, missus, it's to reconstruct the crime from yesterday.'

'Good Lord!'

Good Lord indeed. You don't want to miss this.

You step out of the parlour. 'Then you'll be wanting me too, Constable. Dr Kinn Tenor. I was also a witness.'

'You don't say.' He rubs his jaw. 'Well, I mean. All right. This way, please.'

You're put in the back of a police car and driven through the quaint roads of Harrogate.

'Is there anything you want to tell me, Nanny Tiggy?' you say under your breath. She stares out of the window and doesn't reply.

Upon reaching the station ten minutes later you cast one final look at your travelling companion. This time she at least acknowledges your unspoken enquiry, before truculently jutting her chin and asking the young constable where you are to go.

'This way.' He shows her towards the same platform where you descended from that accursed train carriage just the previous day.

Did you see Constantinos meet a mysterious man at York Castle?

If you did, turn to 101

If you didn't, turn to 43

108

'There is one more line of questioning I must put to you all,' you announce. 'Does anyone here own a blue car?' This time the only reply is bemusement. 'This morning at half past ten, Melissa was nearly run down by one on Piccadilly in London. I must ask you all to account for your whereabouts then.' It creates something of a stir. Not just because of the surprise that a previous attempt was made on Melissa's life, but because the directness of the question makes the people standing or sitting before you realize that they are all suspects.

'Where was I?' says Tim. 'I was at my desk in my hotel room, staring at my research notebooks.'

'On Christmas Eve?'

'On Christmas Eve. Do you want to know why?' He

doesn't wait for your answer. 'Because I thought maybe if I just sat there long enough and stared hard enough, I would magically come up with some way to save the company. And myself.'

'I take it you didn't.'

'No. I didn't.'

'And can anyone verify that you were there?'

He looks up at you. 'Of course not.' He sighs. 'Not much of an alibi after all, is it?'

'Not much of one, no.'

'I saw him there.' It's Pererin speaking up. 'I passed his door – Mrs Thresh put us all up at the same hotel. We were on our way out and I saw him.'

Tim looks relieved and grateful at the surprise boost to his innocence. 'Oh, thank you so much. So that answers your question, Kinn?'

'Yes, I suppose it does. Was your husband with you?' you ask Pererin.

'Yes. More's the pity. I could have done with a bit of peace and quiet.'

'An' what's that s'posed to mean?'

You've had enough of their bickering. 'May I ask where you were at that time, Constantinos?'

'Bloody rude of you, but I suppose you can.'

'Then where were you?'

'Out seeing a friend.'

'And the name of this friend?'

'. . . is private.' His look challenges you to pursue the line. You do so.

'Nothing much stays private in a murder inquiry. Tell

me or tell the coppers when they have a lamp shining in your face. It's your choice.'

'Then I choose to take my chances with the authorities,' he snarls.

'Constantinos,' Julia says softly, tugging on his sleeve. The look in her eyes suggests that involving the authorities is the last thing that she wants.

'No. Neither you nor the police can make me speak. You will have to wait. It might take ten years or twenty. But you will know in time. Some things are for God, not men.' He points upwards to the Almighty, as if expecting Him to speak up in agreement.

'What about you, Julia?' you ask.

'Oh, me? I was out shopping. Last-minute gifts, knick-knacks, that sort of thing.'

'What shops did you go to?'

'Shops? Umm . . .' She glances at her husband for suggestions. 'I can't . . . Selfridges. Yes, Selfridges.'

'And you bought?'

'Oh, nothing, really. There wasn't anything I liked.'

You pause for a few seconds. 'You understand that that means there's no proof at all that you were there.'

She presses her lips together thoughtfully. 'Well, I suppose not. But I did it.' She looks at you trustingly, as if you will simply take her word for it.

'Dr Tenor, I think you will be asking me next, is that right?' Nanny Tiggy seems eager to get the questioning out of the way.

'I think so. Would you like to tell me where you were?'

'Yes, I would. I was with poor Mrs Thresh just before it happened, you see, before someone tried to run her down.'

You hold yourself quite still, forcing back the impulse to widen your eyes in disbelief at this claim. She clearly has no idea that you were with Melissa then. 'Just before?'

'Oh, just a few seconds before. I said goodbye to her, started to walk away and the next thing I knew, she was flat on her back in the road.'

'I see. And did you help her up at all?'

'Oh, no. There was . . . a young girl in a nurse's cape who helped her to her feet.'

'Extraordinary,' you say.

'Hmmm?'

'Extraordinary luck. To have a nurse passing at just that moment.'

'Oh, yes.'

'And tell me, did you see the driver of the van?'

'The, err . . . van? No, no, I didn't.'

'No, I don't suppose you did.' A look of panic flashes across her face and you wonder if she can tell from your tone that she has been rumbled.

If you press her for the truth, turn to 10

If you turn your attention to Freddie, turn to 81

109

'I fancy a bit of a stroll, I'll be in shortly,' you tell Algy.

'Right you are, Kinn.' And off he goes.

You pull on a pair of galoshes and stride out. It really is a glorious winter day. The sun on your face more than makes up for the chill in your toes. Your feet crunch through virgin snow and, despite the ructions at Hurley Court, you think it's not such a bad old world.

You stroll off around the house, with an idea of walking up to the church, where you will all go later for a service along with the villagers. The local vicar is apparently a bit of a card and tells a couple of jokes to keep the kids entertained – or as much as they can be in a freezing stone building on top of a hill in the middle of winter.

Crunch, crunch, crunch as you round a corner. Then you stop short as something suddenly appears ahead of you. A bloody sight. For ten yards from where you stand, a man lies on the path, a terrible wound on his left temple that looks like his skull has been crushed in. He is on his back, face up as if crying to the sky for help. You have seen corpses before – some of them broken horribly by violence or accident – but never once have you seen something quite like this. Because there is something unique, something wicked about this one. The terrible, bloody corpse is what is left of Colonel Hurley, and clamped to his leg is an evil-looking man-trap of two iron jaws that have snapped his tibia and held him down while someone bashed his head in.

And that's not all that you see. Something glints in the sun. Something held in his left hand, outstretched by the side of the body. Something silver and gold. It is the Hurley Dagger. The knife Bloody Thomas used to defend himself from the devils sent to drag his soul down to hell. And from the look of pure fury on his face, the colonel was trying to ward off whoever – or whatever – was coming after him.

You check around to ensure that you're alone, that whoever did this isn't about to spring out from a hiding place, then dash forward. You can tell he's dead, of course, but it's necessary to make sure. Yes, lack of pulse in wrist and neck confirms it.

The jaws of the man-trap – just the type that Bloody Thomas used to capture his victims – seem to mock their latest victim. A chill runs down your spine – this was a crime hundreds of years in the making.

Turn to 117

110

'Yes, as I said, it all goes back to Bloody Thomas and what he left behind.'

'What do you mean?' Algy asks. 'Tell us, Kinn.'

'I mean the silver knife. The knife that has been passed down through your family, every son using it in the Oath of Fealty ritual.' You pause. 'Except not every son. Because it disappeared for a couple of generations, isn't that right?'

'Yes, that's right,' he says, bemused. 'What of it?'

'Your father told me that he and Major Tun-Hurley managed to buy it back after the War, to return it to the family. Is that correct, Major?'

At that, Tun-Hurley goes to the drinks trolley and pours a large measure of Scotch into a tumbler, knocking it back in one go. He hangs his head. 'That's right,' he replies.

'But is that true? What do you think, Algy?'

Algy blinks; he looks as if he is utterly incapable of forming a thought. 'I, I don't know.'

'But you do know. Because you also told me that you had seen your second cousin, Terence, Major Tun-Hurley's son, take the Oath while holding the dagger.'

'Oh, yes, yes, I did.'

'But Terence died in the War. So he must have taken

that Oath before then. Which means the knife was already back in the family. Colonel Hurley lied.'

'Oh, God,' Tun-Hurley mumbles, rubbing his eyes.

'Why did he lie, Major?'

'It was . . .' He breaks off, unable to find the words.

'Tell us why he lied!' He cannot meet your gaze. 'Then I shall ask Mr Leaner.'

'Yes!' cries Leaner, leaping up and throwing his glass into the fireplace, where the spirit ignites into a billowing flame. 'Yes, feel the shame, *Major*!' And he launches himself on Tun-Hurley, tumbling them both to the floor.

'Stop him!' Mina screams. At that, Gervaise and Finney grab hold of Leaner and drag him away, kicking and spitting. Algy joins the fray and, between them, they hold him down.

'Murderer! My brother was never the same again after what you did to him! Do you know who I am? Do you know who I am!' Leaner screams.

Tun-Hurley pulls himself to his feet and leans heavily against the sideboard. 'Yes,' he mutters.

'Who? Kinn, who is he?' Algy asks you desperately.

'Your father never bought that knife. He stole it back. Major, when I spoke to you the other day you said it was wrong to let things fester. "Someone's done you wrong? Challenge them, face to face. You think they took something from you? Take it back," you said. And you did take it back. You took it back from that church in Belgium, which had gained it God knows how. There never were any German soldiers robbing the church, were there?'

'No,' he says quietly. 'None. We knew it was there and resolved to take it. It was ours by birthright. Our bloody idiot great-grandfather lost it to some crook in a card game, and the crook left it to the church in his will. To clear his conscience, I suppose.'

'You thought it would be a clean crime, didn't you?'

Tun-Hurley turns to face you. 'Yes. Burglary in the night, no violence.'

'But?'

'But we were disturbed.'

'Who by?'

'Vickers. Our driver. We told him to wait in the car. He should have obeyed orders.'

'And you struck him down from behind.'

'Not me,' he says. 'Harrison. But yes, I am just as guilty as he.'

'*Murderer!*' yells Leaner as he struggles.

'I still don't understand,' Algy says.

'I think I do,' Gervaise chucks in. You can see that he does.

'I went to Oxford today,' you say. 'There's no William Leaner who was at Hertford College when he says he was there. But there was a D. Vickers. And the newspaper story, the one that someone managed to find in the attic and Colonel Hurley tried to hide from us, notes how Private Vickers wanted to get back to his mother and little brother, Dennis.' You look at Leaner – or Vickers, as you now know him to be. 'How bad was it?'

'He never walked again,' he tells you, glaring at Tun-Hurley. 'Couldn't work. Took to drink. That ended it for him. All so these two could have their precious heirloom. And we little people had to suffer for it.'

'You thought there would be a sort of justice if you trapped the colonel in a gin-trap, just as Bloody Thomas did, didn't you?'

'Poetic justice, you might say,' he sneers.

'Why didn't you leave it to the police?' Algy asks, clearly distressed by all he has heard.

'Proof, you idiot. No proof, was there? I'm surprised he's owned up to it, after all this time.'

'Gervaise, the series of profiles of old war heroes was Mr Leaner's idea, wasn't it?' you suggest.

'Yes, now you mention it, it was,' he replies thoughtfully.

'All part of his plan to get himself invited down here. And those poison-pen letters were to distract you all while he went about searching for that elusive proof. I think he enjoyed seeing you all squirm.'

'You're the guilty one, not me,' Leaner snarls at Tun-Hurley.

'I'm sorry,' the old soldier says. 'Your brother didn't deserve that.'

'Well, you'll get what you deserve now, won't you?'

The major pauses. 'Yes. Yes, I will,' he says quietly.

So now you see two criminals. Each of whom thought he would commit a crime to right an old wrong. Both of whom are now exposed for what they are. And now justice will have to prevail.

THE END

III

It's a jolly old time puffing along up to York. You've always loved that ancient city – noble England with a Viking heart. As you weave through stone edifices to pull into the station, you see cheery locals, wrapped up like gifts, rushing hither and thither as they scramble for the final decorations and food to complete their Christmases.

Your little special grinds to a halt and the eight of you cry out in joy.

'Right, gang, York!' yelps Melissa. 'We have three hours to sprint around the sights and grab whatever we can to drink or stuff down. Back here at seven, and there's a prize for whoever can find the oddest thing to buy!'

You all spill out, swapping plans. Pererin and Simon Yarrow want to explore the famous local pubs; Nanny Tiggy is all set for the Minster, the cathedral where she hopes to join a Christmas Eve service; Melissa wants to raid the markets and antique shops for curiosities; Julia wants Constantinos to see the sights; Tim says he wants to look at a collection of Roman artefacts in the city museum, which is just behind the castle; and Freddie, last of all, mutters something about just 'mooching about a bit'. Each to their own. You decide to stick with Melissa on her mission to turn the markets upside down.

As everyone talks at once, you watch the hordes of people on the station concourse, many excitedly meeting family members who have been away and are now back in the fold. But then you catch yourself, for among those elated faces, there's one that stands out; one that you know. It's an immensely long and keen face, with a hawk-like nose to go with hawk-like eyes. And those eyes are trained on your little group. *Oh, yes?* you think to yourself. *And what are you doing here?* A moment later, the hawk disappears into the crowd. But you aren't going to forget that you have just seen Inspector Reeves of Scotland Yard's Special Branch. And there's no doubt that he was watching your party.

You decide to let him go. It won't be long before you catch sight of him again, you're sure of that.

Everyone is saying goodbye and confirming that they will be back at seven. 'Oh, bother. I've forgotten my gloves. I just need to nip back on board to fetch them,' Melissa says. She hurries back towards the train while you ponder Reeves's presence. *'Oh!'*

The distressed cry comes from within the carriage. It's Melissa. You leap in, to find her standing with her hands clenched into fists, staring at something stuck to the wall. It's a portrait photograph of her, and it's fixed to the wall by the blade of Tim's hatchet. Someone has swiped that lethal tool right through Melissa's face, splitting it in two. She spins around, and breathes a sigh of relief when she sees that it's you behind her. 'What on earth is this?'

You examine the picture closely. For a brief moment you wonder if it's all some strange theatrical gesture of Tim's, but you dismiss that idea. It's simply too nasty. 'The work of someone with a twisted mind.'

'Twisted? It's a damned corkscrew!' Her shock is turning to anger. 'When I get my hands on them, I'll make them regret this little prank.'

'We'll have to identify them first.'

'Well, come on then, you're the detective. You tell me who it was.'

'In actual fact, I'm a doctor. And I can't tell you who it was because it could have been just about anyone. A stranger, or one of your friends.'

'Impossible!' she cries. 'My friends are very dear to me.'

'Hardly impossible. Or it could have been whoever tried to run you down yesterday.'

'Of course it's that thug!'

You raise your eyebrows. 'But we must also consider that these two parties are not mutually exclusive. The thug, as you describe him, may be one and the same as one of those with whom we have shared a very comfortable carriage from King's Cross.'

She jabs her finger at you. 'I know my chums, Kinn. Not one of them would do such a thing.'

'I have heard similar words from everyone, from a Cornish washerwoman to the Elector of Schleswig-Holstein. And in each case they found they didn't know their friends, or spouses, or servants quite as well as they thought. My advice to you is to have a little think. Have you ever crossed them? Have they crossed you? Has the green-eyed monster of envy entered their bodies?'

'I've hardly got anything to be envious of. We live in a flat above the business, and it's all going to be taken by the bank any day now. Oh, I have fun with my life, for sure, but I doubt anyone's going to knock me off my perch for that.'

You examine the hatchet. You could report it to the coppers, but no crime has been committed unless you count criminal damage, and that would be up to the Great Northern Railway to report. No, it's a case of watch and wait. Whoever is behind it will either slip up or act soon, and you'll be there to catch them at it.

'I think we have to put this aside for now,' you say. 'And just carry on with the day. This won't be the end of things, I can assure you of that. But I'll be close to you at all times.'

'That puts me at ease a little – I won't deny that horrid little messages like this have an effect. But we'll catch the rotter, won't we?'

'We will. You have my word. Now, grab your gloves and let's be off. Mulled wine awaits us.'

Turn to 2

112

'That will be all.'

Finney leaves you, gliding out. You change out of your heavy driving clothes and into lighter, looser garments, then step out of the room. You are about to descend the stairs when something catches your eye below. It's Algy's mother, Mina Hurley – who was considered a rare beauty in her day and is still a handsome woman – hurrying through the hallway, glancing furtively over her shoulder. She pounces on a little low table beside the front door where the maid has left the letters that have arrived with the afternoon post, ready for Finney to take them to their intended and rightful recipients over tea. To your surprise, Mina hunts through them, snatches one out of the pile, dashes into the drawing room and emerges again a few seconds later. She fixes her hair and walks sedately back towards the breakfast room.

Well, that's strange behaviour. And since curiosity has always been your hallmark, you pelt down the stairs.

At the bottom you check around and there's no one watching you. You enter the drawing room to find it full of more festive décor, with a huge fir tree sporting tinsel and brightly wrapped gifts at its foot. You don't have time to get in the holiday mood, though, and you look about for the letter. Given Mina's behaviour around it, you have a feeling in your bones for where it might be, and you're right: it's in the grate. Luckily, although Mina has lit the kindling the coal isn't yet ablaze and the letter is only smouldering at the edges. You snatch it out just as the flames spread to its surface, burning your fingers a little, and hammer out the little waves of fire with your fist. You're left with a letter in a yellow envelope addressed to Mina. Evidently, she has opened it and read its contents. One further glance at the doorway and you draw out the missive inside.

You know what it is even before you read a word. You've seen these half a dozen times in your professional career. A poison-pen letter. This one isn't, as is customary, formed from letters cut out of a newspaper, but neatly typed.

An affair? How shoddy of you. How cheap you are!

You take the letter to the window to examine it under as much sunlight as possible. You carry a jeweller's loupe, a small magnification glass, at all times. The envelope is postmarked 'Sidcup' and the address has been typed on the same typewriter as the note inside. Whoever sent it seems to have gone to some effort because every character has been perfectly formed, suggesting a new machine and ink ribbon, which will make it more difficult to connect the letters to the sender. You fondly remember the Westerham Letters case where the perpetrator – the vicar's wife – had failed to maintain her machine well and the 'k' was always very faint, which led to you unmasking her as the phantom correspondent. That was the end of both her reign of terror and her marriage.

No such luck here, though. All is fresh as a daisy. You slip the note and the envelope into your jacket's inside pocket. You're about to leave the room when you think of something: what if Mina comes back to check the note has burned properly? You quickly search the room for notepaper to throw in the grate. Nothing around. But there's a copy of Dickens's *A Christmas Carol* on a little walnut side table inlaid to serve as a chequer board. You open it, tear out a few pages and chuck them in the fire, which is blazing happily now, and watch as they turn black and curl up. You replace the book and head to high tea, having built up something of an appetite.

Turn to 44

113

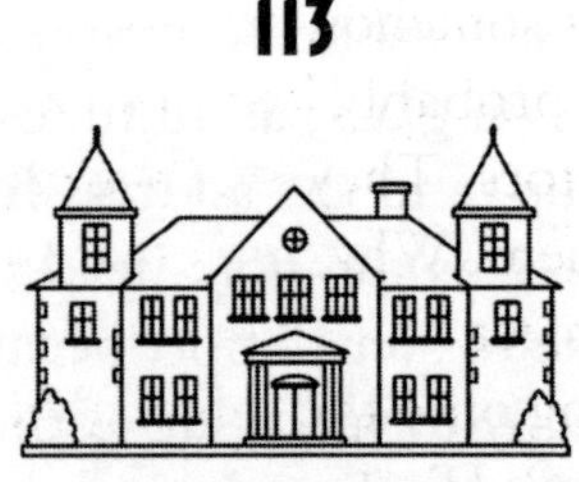

'So tell me,' you say. 'What's this ritual all about?'

'It's actually a little hard to say. I don't really know myself.'

'What do you mean?'

'I mean, no one really knows. At least, I think Father does, but he's keeping it to himself. I've only seen it done once, when I was a lad and my second cousin Terence – poor chap died at Ypres – underwent it; but I couldn't make head nor tail of it then and I still can't. Involves a funny old knife that's been through the family for generations.'

If there's anything that piques your curiosity more than an ancient ceremony imbued with mysterious meaning, you can't think of it.

'What happens during the show?'

'Oh, mostly mumbo-jumbo if you ask me.' Algy breaks and instantly cannons his cue ball into the pocket. 'Oh, bother.'

You chalk your cue and take a more successful shot, potting the red. 'What apart from mumbo-jumbo?'

'Well, there's the knife. At least, there is now.'

'What do you mean, "at least, there is now"?'

'Righto. Well, the knife, you see, was in the family for donkey's years but somehow we lost it, I think. Then we got it back. It was probably lost in a card game, knowing some of my ancestors. They really were a ripe old lot of rogues, some of them. Why, my great-uncle Sylvester . . .'

'Back to the subject.'

'But I was getting onto the subject,' he insists. 'At least, I think I was. Wasn't I?'

'No, you were getting further and further away from it by the second. Tell me about the ritual. Who attends it?'

'By tradition, anyone in the house at the time. If the postman's turned up at that moment, even he's roped in, poor blighter. It's all a sort of "you're either with us or against us" sort of thing. You'll have to be part of it too, Kinn.'

'Will I?'

'Oh, yes, it's that or be tarred and feathered, I'm afraid. Everyone in these four walls – well, however many walls there are, six or seven, I expect – is going to be part of the show.'

You play for a couple of hours, have some excellent brandy after a delightful dinner and then it's time to prepare for the Hurley family's Oath of Fealty ceremony.

Turn to 24

114

'Is the post office nearby?' you ask Algy.

'The post office? A few doors down. But Mrs Blenkins will have closed by now.'

'Let's see if she hasn't.'

You knock on the door of a little village shop, where the windows are stuffed with sweets, cooking pots and wooden toys. The lights are still on and the grey head of a plump woman pops up from behind the counter. She beams when she sees who you are with.

'Hello, Master Algernon,' she says, beckoning you in. 'Is it a quarter of lemon sherbets? I know they're your favourite.'

'Thanks, Mrs B,' he says happily, instinctively reaching out as she opens a big jar of boiled sweets. You clear your throat. 'Oh, umm, actually no, there's something else. This is my friend Kinn.'

'I had an unusual question,' you say as she turns two piggy little eyes on you. 'Letters, Algy.' He pulls them from his pocket and proffers them to her. 'Do you happen to recall whoever posted these?'

'These?' She looks at the letters, a little discombobulated. 'No. I must take in twenty letters each day, and there's the post box at the end of the lane too. I can't say I remember anyone giving them to me.'

'Do you perhaps sell this stationery yourself?'

She opens a drawer behind the counter and takes out a stack of just the same notepaper and envelopes. 'Is this it?'

It is. So whoever sent the letters might well be a local. Something to mull over.

'Can I ask a favour, Mrs Blenkins?'

'Anything for Master Algernon. Such a well-behaved boy.' Algy beams.

'If you receive another of these, could you hold on to it and send word to me at Hurley Court? My name is Dr Tenor.'

She looks shocked. 'Oh, I don't think I could do that.

It would be interfering with the post. Wouldn't it?' she asks Algy.

'Not at all, Mrs Blenkins. I only ask you to hold it for an hour or two. That's all.'

'That's all?' She looks uncertain.

'For me, Mrs B?' says Algy.

She melts. 'Well, since it's you, Master Algernon. All right.'

It's a step forward. Now it's time to return to Hurley Court, for the Oath of Fealty will soon commence.

Turn to 24

115

It's six o'clock and dark as the whole household – family, guests and servants – gathers in the hallway. The Oath of Fealty is a formal occasion, and Mina is wearing a scarlet dress with a white stole, while the gentlemen all wear white tie. The mood is solemn and silent as you all leave the house. On the gravel outside, under a light fall of snow, you form a line, with Colonel Hurley at the front and Gervaise behind him. You each carry an unlit wooden torch, the tip of which has been dipped in kerosene. Finney lights his with a brass lighter and the flames lick upwards. One by one, he lights your torches from his. Instantly you feel the heat in the cold night. Fire and frost vie for dominance but they can only dance around each other.

Colonel Hurley lifts his right hand. In it is a glittering object: a dagger with golden hilt and silver blade that shimmers in the night. The moonlight that reflects off the metal is a perfect white, as cold as the snow that falls upon it. The point is directed at the moon itself, as if to stab it.

You process, slowly, elegantly. The others whisper as you walk. 'Fealty, fealty, fealty,' they say. Then there is a pause and the phrase is repeated again. 'Fealty, fealty, fealty.' It is a ceremony that has lasted generations and so much mystique has crept in that it could have a score of intentions, secrets and hidden depths, but you are unaware of them.

Your feet crunch into an inch of virgin snow, and instantly more flakes flutter down to begin the process of obscuring your steps. The white clouds overhead seem to cloak the ceremony from the world outside.

You haven't been told your destination; you could be heading to the ends of the earth for all you know as the flames flicker. But you fall in, feeling the hands of a dozen generations steering you, pushing you on, demanding silence.

You all circle the house, torches in your hands, passing through a rose garden bereft of flowers, with only twisted stems and thorns that seem to reach for you as you pass. The whispers of 'Fealty, fealty, fealty' grow louder – or perhaps it's just your imagination. Yet every time you try to pick out one of the voices – Algy, Mina, Colonel Hurley, Finney, Gervaise, the colonel's cousin Tun-Hurley, the journalist Leaner – it seems to recede into the mass of the others. You repeat the words and they take on a life of their own. It is self-mesmerism, you tell yourself. And you don't know where it will end.

To the side of the house there is a narrow path that leads up a short, steep hill to a church. The family chapel. Algy's ancestors and their servants must have worshipped here for almost as long as the house has stood. It is silhouetted against the white sky, no more than a mass of jet black; even the moonlight seems to stay far away from it.

The path, a hundred yards long, is made of stones, and the snow upon them turns to slush as your procession snakes up the hill, making you slip so you have to catch yourself. One of the maids falls, her torch dropping into the snow and fizzing out. Finney sends her a dark look and she mouths an apology, before dusting herself down and relighting her torch from his.

On goes your line, whispering the invocation every few paces. As you close in on the old temple, the light from your torches shows a mediaeval square steeple atop a straight nave crossed by transepts. A flash of blue or red picks out stained glass in the windows. Birds – crows – caw overhead, disturbed by the arrival of creatures walking on the ground.

Your light glows brighter on the building, lighting ancient stones. And now you see that the church is surrounded by a graveyard. Headstones with yellow lichen lean at every angle. A few look relatively recent – within the last few years – but most seem as old as the church itself. As you near the crest of the hill you begin to note letters on the grave markers. Here and there they spell a name, a date. A few read 'Hurley', but most have other names, those of the staff or others buried here.

Colonel Hurley reaches the top and lowers the knife to scrape it across the headstones as if trying to wake the dead. He is summoning them, you think, not as spooks, but as silent witnesses from generations past to this latest iteration of a family tradition. It is Gervaise's duty to pledge his fealty – to what, you don't yet know – and theirs to see that it is done.

Your torches light the door, which stands open. With his back to you, the colonel lifts the gold-and-silver knife above his head so it glints again in the flickering torch light. He turns and faces you all, with the dagger aloft.

'This is for the faithful,' he declares to the night. 'Only the faithful may enter.' Gervaise steps forward. His father puts the dagger to his throat. 'Are you faithful?' he demands.

'I am faithful.'

'Then enter.' The colonel allows him to pass. One by one, all have the same demand made of them. When it's your turn, he asks the same question. But this time his eyes are narrower than with the others. It has barely struck you until now how much of an outsider you are. And now you have a man holding a knife to your throat. It's not the first time that has happened, but you're not keen on the situation either way. You discreetly tighten your grip on the flaming torch – it will be a dangerous weapon if you need it. 'Are you faithful?' he repeats, each syllable taking an age. The wind is lifting and the snow is beginning to whirl around you.

'I am faithful,' you say, your hand tight on the torch, ready for anything.

He pauses, looking right into you, this man who has fought in the trenches on the Western Front. You have come face to face with tough men in the past and never quavered, but you wouldn't want to be on the wrong side of Colonel Hurley.

'Then enter.'

Turn to 124

116

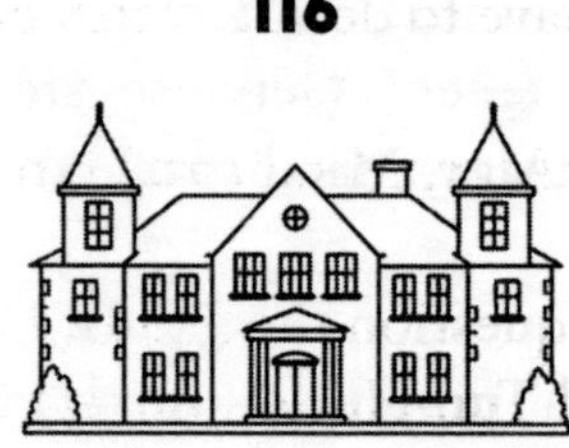

You're about to return to the drawing room when you hear huffing and puffing behind you. Mrs Blenkins, the village postmistress, is striding through the snow, waving something above her head. 'Dr Tenor! Dr Tenor! I have one. It came through my own door this morning. I thought I should bring it right up.'

You see what she's brandishing. It's a yellow envelope, like the others. You take it quickly, thanking her, and look at the address. You're astonished: it's addressed to you at Hurley Court! You tear it open.

You think you're very smart, don't you, Dr Tenor? Well, for your information, there's one much smarter than you around.

Quite incredible. You've never been taunted like this by someone you presume is a killer. Well, given that you've only been at the house a day, it adds to your assumption that the criminal is part of the household.

Now you have to return to the drawing room. If Gervaise will be back in twenty minutes with an officer, you will have to work quickly before the police take over. You probably won't even have time to speak to everyone in the room. Stepping back in, you scan the faces. Yes, you can probably question half of those here in the time you have left. So you have to decide which ones.

If you speak to Algy, Mina and Finney, turn to 106

If you question the maids, Leaner and Tun-Hurley, turn to 35

117

You examine the corpse. No marks on it other than that wound to his temple. Well, it proved enough. And you notice something. In the inside pocket of his jacket you feel a paper. Drawing it out, you recognize it instantly. It's the newspaper report of his exploits in Belgium during the War, when he and Tun-Hurley stopped a platoon of Germans robbing a church. Gruesomely, some of the blood from his head wound has soaked right through his jacket and stained it.

By the state of the body – doing your best to allow for the cold conditions – it's less than an hour since the colonel was killed.

Well, there's little for it now but to inform the next of kin – Mina, Gervaise and Algy. And then call for the police.

You hurry back inside, finding everyone in the breakfast room.

'Kinn!' cries Algy before you can speak. 'Come and have some breakfast!'

'Oh, Algy,' you say. 'I am so very sorry.' The look on your face is enough to make him pause. And the gay conversation over the kippers and toast recedes. Silence falls.

'Whatever do you mean?'

You step properly into the room. 'I have to tell you, Algy, Mina, Gervaise, that Colonel Hurley has passed away.'

'What?!' exclaims Mina. 'What do you mean? No, no, he's out for a walk. His usual walk . . .'

'If this is a joke, I'll throw you out of the house myself!' snaps Gervaise.

'No joke, I'm sorry. I can take you to him. Outside.'

'Outside?' whispers Mina. 'I . . . I don't . . .'

'Kinn?' says Algy in a faltering voice.

It is Tun-Hurley, the old soldier, who takes charge. 'Dr Tenor,' he says. 'I understand what you are saying. Please lead the way.'

At that, you nod and begin to walk out. Behind you, Gervaise helps his mother from her seat. You all – Gervaise, Algy, Mina, Leaner, Tun-Hurley and Finney – quickly leave the house and follow the gravel path to where you left the colonel a few moments earlier. He lies there undisturbed, with the same look of fury on his features and the silver knife in his hand. Yes, it looks like he saw his killer coming and was doing his best to defend himself.

Mina breaks down in tears. 'Oh, Mother,' Gervaise says, comforting her. 'It must have been quick. He wouldn't have suffered.'

You wonder if Gervaise really cares whether his father suffered or not – they were hardly close pals.

'I know, but . . .' And she sobs again, her tears turning to ice on her cheeks.

You explain to them how you found the body. Algy suggests that the killer could have been someone from outside the house who came across the fields, murdered his father, then ran away again. It's an absurd suggestion, of course, but you restrict yourself to pointing out that the only tracks are between the body and the front door of the house. Elsewhere, it's deep virgin snow, and none has fallen since Hurley was killed. 'I have to inform you all,' you say eventually, 'that one of us is a killer.'

'My God!' exclaims Algy.

There's an uproar, with Tun-Hurley trying to take charge, Gervaise telling him to shut up, Mina sobbing and Algy flapping about uselessly.

'Hold on, is there something there?' Gervaise says, peering at a spot in the snow a few yards off. You take a few careful steps, doing your best to leave as few tracks as possible. It's not hard to realize what you're looking at: a large hammer, covered in blood. Oh yes, this is the murder weapon all right. And right beside it is a pair of grey gardener's gloves. There's no point checking for fingerprints.

Turn to 97

118

A minute later, Mina enters the room. Something has been taken from her – a little bit of her vivacity. She sits, hesitantly, in a chair upholstered with lavender print cloth. She has probably sat in it a thousand times, but never when such a pall of suspicion has fallen upon the house.

'What would you like to ask me?' she asks, unprompted.

'I would like to ask you about your husband.'

'Of course. Harrison and I had a … marriage.' She pauses. 'I was going to say "a happy marriage", but it wasn't especially happy and there's no point in hiding the fact.'

'No.' She is right. It's easy to tell when a marriage is happy and when it isn't.

'He could be very cold. Oh, I don't mean to say he was a bad man. He wasn't. But he was obsessed with the family name and honour. Their funny little traditions. And not so much with his actual family.'

'Gervaise for one doesn't seem to have enjoyed having him as a father.'

She sighs quietly. 'I've never been able to work out what's going on in Gervaise's mind. He's always been so in control of himself, he just never lets anything slip. He's very good at biding his time.'

'What do you mean by that?'

She pauses for a second and thinks. 'Do you know the Ghost Orchid?' she asks.

'I don't.'

'It's very rare. *Epipogium aphyllum* is from South America. I think it's quite beautiful. It has delicate white flowers that look like little ballerinas. But it only blooms every few years and quite unpredictably. So you never know. You could wait decades, and then suddenly, there it is. I think that's a little like Gervaise. Unpredictable.'

You file her opinion away to consider, along with its implications, later.

'And what about Algy?'

'Algernon has always been quite the opposite. I suppose that's natural, really; boys want to stake out their own characters, not to be like their brothers, don't they? Yes, he's always been an open book. Quite guileless.'

'And what about his relationship with his father?'

'Oh, he tried harder than Gervaise to please Harrison, but it never got him very far. In fact, I think it made it worse. Harrison always called him a fawning coward. Told him he needed a bit of Bloody Thomas in him.'

Did he now? Well, well, well.

'As you know, Algy asked me down here to investigate the poison-pen letters that you have all been receiving.'

'Yes,' she says, clearly a little worried by the prospect.

'What did they say?'

'Different things. Always accusing without actually specifying what we were being accused of. So it would be things like "I know your nasty little secret" and "Prepare for everyone to find out". Quite horrid.'

'Did you suspect anyone of sending them?'

'How could I? They were anonymous. Probably a child's prank.'

You doubt that. 'So the ones that you personally received were just like the others. Vague. No specific allegation?'

'Yes, just very vague.'

She tries to look convincing, but you can see through it. Yes, a specific accusation was levelled at Mina Hurley.

You ask her a few more questions about the household and its staff, but what she tells you is of little consequence and after a while you dismiss her, which leaves you alone to think. But it's not easy exercising your brain while you're being stared down upon by Bloody Thomas Hurley.

You have a few moments before Finney enters and informs you that the police are here already and have ordered that everyone gather in the drawing room. This is an irritation. Your opinion of Scotland Yard has not always been the highest, so you have little confidence in the provincial forces.

'Before we join them, Finney, a quick word.'

'Of course, Dr Tenor.'

'The butler knows all the family secrets, am I right?' He smiles thinly. 'What secrets does this one hold?'

'And a butler is always discreet.'

'Indeed. Given the circumstances, however, it is very important that you tell me if any member of the household has also been keeping secrets.'

He stops and purses his lips. He moves close to you and

lowers his voice. 'If you were to ask me if Mr Algernon had been, shall we say, distracted, of late, I would not be in a position to dispute that.'

'Indeed?' Algy has always been so open with you. It's a surprise to hear that he has hidden depths. 'And do you have a suspicion as to what is distracting him?'

'I do not.' He pauses. 'But I believe his diary might be an *aide memoire*.'

'His diary, you say?' He makes no sign of having heard you. 'Where might I find such a thing?'

'I expect most people tend to keep them hidden in their bedrooms.'

You are both distracted by one of the maids scampering in and informing you that the policeman wants to speak to you.

Turn to 5

119

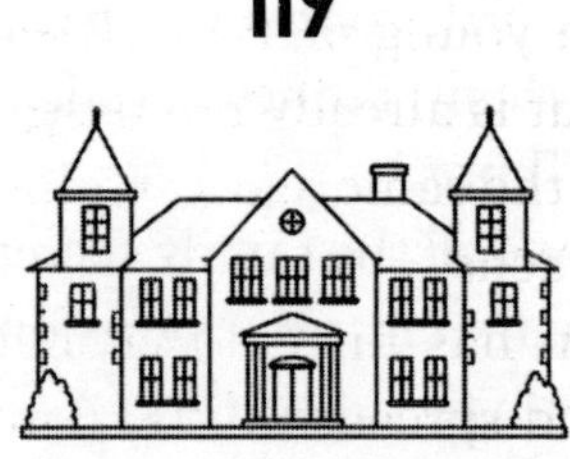

Now you have to return to the drawing room. If Gervaise will be back in twenty minutes with an officer, you will have to work quickly before the police take over. You probably won't even have time to speak to everyone in the room. Stepping back in, you scan the faces. Yes, you can probably question half of those here in the time you have left. So you have to decide which ones.

If you speak to Algy, Mina and Finney, turn to 106

If you question the maids, Leaner and Tun-Hurley, turn to 35

120

There are two people at the table whom you don't recognize. The first is a young man in his early twenties with soft blond hair that is already receding. The second is an older chap, about the same age as Colonel Hurley, with a toothbrush moustache.

The young man has fingers that move quickly as he butters a scone and spreads a little jam around the edge in an odd little ritual.

'Kinn, meet William Leaner,' Algy says affably.

The young man looks up and holds out his hand. You shake it. 'William Leaner,' he says, 'journalist.'

'One of mine,' Gervaise explains. 'Got him down here to stop him being idle on the Northern crimes desk. Not enough happening there and I thought it would be a good idea to run some profiles of military heroes. You know, "how I escaped the Boer and saved a nun", that sort of thing. Our readers like a bit of drum-thumping. Thought I would start with the Guv'nor here.' He jerks his thumb in the direction of his father, who looks up, then goes back to the financial page of his newspaper, grumbling about something being down tuppence. 'Dad's got some old stories that will make the hairs on the back of your neck stand up – just wait until you hear about him and the major taking on a platoon of church-robbing Huns. If it proves popular, I'm thinking of starting a monthly special edition. I've already got a couple of old soldiers and a rear admiral lined up.'

'Pleased to meet you,' you say to Leaner.

'I once wrote a story about you, Dr Tenor,' he replies. He has a quiet, considered way about him, which contrasts with his boss.

'Oh, yes?'

'It was that business down in Poole. Old woman bludgeoned by her neighbour.' You remember the case well. Nasty one about an inheritance. 'I thought you were very impressive in court.'

'Thank you.'

'In a way, we're in the same line of work: bringing crimes to light.'

'I suppose we are. Do you enjoy it?'

'Oh, I do, yes. I can't say the long hours and the constant

travelling up and down the country are to my liking, but it seems like quite an important job to do, doesn't it? I think a free and fair press is the single most important organ in a nation.' You can't help but think he might overestimate the social mission of the *Messenger*.

'It is important, yes. My cases can be morally complicated, though. I wish I always had the moral certainty that it sounds like you have.'

'Moral certainty?' He mulls it for a second. 'I've never thought about it like that. But yes, I think people overthink these things sometimes. There really are such things as good and evil; and I know which one I favour.'

He really seems committed, and that's often in short supply in the circles that you mix in. The coppers tend to be the most cynical sorts you ever meet, so someone who believes in justice – even if his paper spends more words on which married woman has been seen in the company of which disreputable fellow than on exposing frauds and thieves – is welcome as far as you're concerned.

'Well, I look forward to chatting more about the stories you've worked on.'

At that, Algy introduces you to the other man at the table. 'Major Wilfred Tun-Hurley, my father's cousin.'

Major Tun-Hurley stands stiffly, winces in pain and sits again. 'Apologies. Shrapnel in the leg,' he says. 'Tun-Hurley. Coldstream Guards. Retired.' He shoves a hand out and shakes yours firmly. He doesn't need to say another word and you know him through and through: solid, dependable, not a man to make a mountain out of a molehill, not a man to complain. You've met a score like him and you've liked every one of them. They showed you how a life of service to one's country makes a man less self-absorbed, more social – even if that sociability is of the quietest and most reserved kind.

'Major. I think if Mr Leaner has some stories to tell, I suspect you have a book's worth.'

He chortles gently. 'You're right about that. I've seen some things, Dr Tenor. Some are good memories, some not. But I've always done my duty.' Where Algy's father is gruff to the point of blustering, Major Tun-Hurley is solid as a rock. You make a mental note to find an evening to spend in his company, to listen to tales of his adventures.

The maid appears with a silver tray, which she hands to Finney. You can see a number of letters in yellow envelopes neatly stacked on it. Their appearance creates a tremor around the room.

'Oh no, more of them!' Algy says.

'Damn and blast!' Colonel Hurley exclaims, throwing down his napkin. 'Right, hand them out, Finney.'

The butler does as he is told. One is placed in front of the colonel, one in front of Algy, who looks downcast. One is for Gervaise, who looks amused. 'Ah, my favourite correspondent,' he announces. 'Oh, none for you today, Mother?'

'No,' Mina confirms. She is nervously fingering a spoon and trying not to look at the envelope that her elder son is ripping open.

'Well, well,' he announces to the table. '"Your secret is no secret. Soon everyone will know it." That's nice, isn't it?' Something catches his eye. 'Oh, look, you have one too this time, Major.'

Tun-Hurley has torn open an identical envelope. 'Yes, the same as yours. What's this all about, then?'

Yes, what's this all about? You look at Algy. This is what he wanted you to come down to look into.

'We've been getting these for a few weeks. Sometimes the messages are the same for all of us, sometimes they're different.' He blinks, confused.

'I want to know what this is all about,' Tun-Hurley repeats. 'Don't like it when a man says he's watching me and I can't see him.'

'I don't suppose you do,' you say.

'Kinn's a top-notch police investigator,' Algy informs everyone.

'Are you?' Colonel Hurley exclaims.

'I sometimes aid them with their enquiries, but I am, in fact, a pathologist.'

'Extraordinary.' He sounds a little suspicious.

'So will you look into this for us?' Algy asks.

'Oh, yes, what we really need is someone putting us under the microscope,' his brother lobs into the conversation.

'I'll do what I can,' you inform them all, taking a cup of tea.

'Oh, good show. Now, you're in for a treat tonight, because it's time for the Hurley Oath of Fealty.'

An odd name. 'And what might that be?'

'Yes, glad you asked, old stick. It's something that the eldest son – that's Gervaise – has to go through when he reaches the age of twenty-five. Been around for centuries, the old ritual. Always done on Christmas Eve. Father went through it, his father, his father and so on.'

'Don't bore Dr Tenor with the details, darling,' Mina admonishes him.

'Sorry, sorry,' Algy says. 'Look, let's head to The Plough for a couple of hours and we can chew the fat.'

If you go to the pub, turn to 53

If you insist on hearing the explanation of the family Oath of Fealty, turn to 20

121

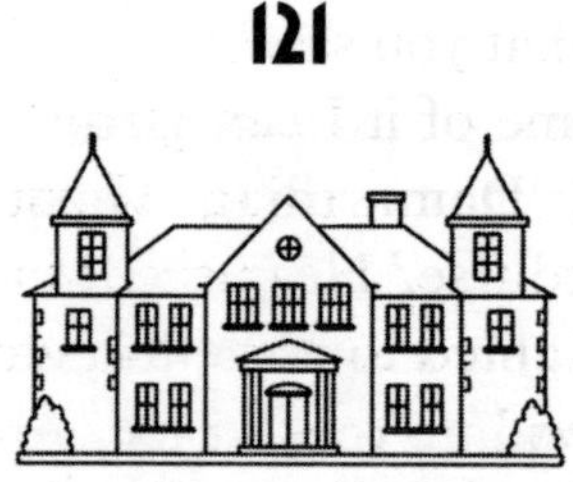

Leaner sees a little storage hut and goes to examine it. You take the opportunity to talk to the major.

'You say you've seen some tough acts in your time, Major.'

'Certainly have. Tough men.'

'There must have been trying times too.'

'There were. That's when you see men at their best and their worst. I've seen heroism. I've seen brutality. Both leave their mark on you.'

'I can't imagine.'

He seems to focus on a scene far away. 'No. No one who has been spared battle can, but at least you understand that, Doctor. There are many armchair generals who think they can tell us what we should or should not have done. Pen-pushers who would run a mile if called on to act.'

You chuckle. 'I'm sure that's right. Was it always going to be the army for you?'

He sits on a felled tree trunk and stretches out his troublesome leg. 'Wanted to be a farmer like my father before me, since you ask. But the farm wasn't doing so well, and he pushed me to take the King's shilling. Glad I did, though. Never looked back. Saw the world.'

'Did you like what you saw?'

'Some of it. Some of it I can gladly leave behind me.' He flexes his leg. 'Damn thing. Worst souvenir. Ended things for me, of course.' He pushes himself up. 'Not that I wouldn't have wanted to come out soon enough. Civvy Street has its draws.'

'What would they be?'

'Peace at night top of the list. Even in peacetime there's always a coming and going, banging and shouting, when you're in the barracks. Damn tricky to get your head down for a good night's sleep. Now it's quiet and dark as can be. And I appreciate that, I can tell you.' You have never really thought about how much old soldiers must yearn for a bit of peace and quiet.

Leaner returns empty-handed. 'Nothing there,' he says. Your search has turned up nothing.

Did you set a trap by leaving the newspaper cutting in the hallway?

If you did, turn to 90

If you didn't, turn to 63

122

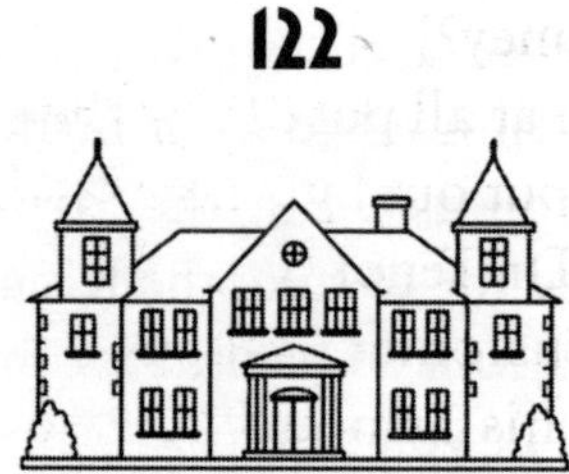

On your way up to your bed chamber you hear hushed voices from the kitchen. Whoever they are, they are keeping their conversation to themselves, and that always piques your interest. You stealthily approach the doorway.

'. . . in your dreams,' you make out a female voice muttering. A moment later, one of the maids strides out. She catches sight of you and bobs a perfunctory curtsey before walking quickly away. You haven't spoken to her before, but she looks about twenty years old and has a pleasant round face.

So to whom was she speaking? You peer inside the unlit kitchen and see Finney lighting a cigarette.

'May I be of service, Dr Tenor?' he asks, surprised but as smooth as ever, pinching off his cigarette.

'Who was that maid?'

'That was Rebecca.' You try to discern from his tone what might have unfolded before you came in.

'She seemed unhappy with something.' His face is a blank canvas. You could read anything into it. 'What was she exercised about?'

'Domestic arrangements. She was unhappy that she will be required to work on her usual afternoon out, due to the weather.'

'Is that true, Finney?'

He doesn't seem at all put out by the question. But then he wouldn't seem put out by a fight to the death, you suspect. 'Quite true, Dr Tenor.'

He's a cool customer, Finney. You wonder how best to penetrate his armour. 'Are you happy working here?'

'Very happy.'

'Do you intend to stay here?'

'As long as I can be of service.'

'I'm sure your service is second to none.'

'Very kind of you to say that.'

'Of course, in every position, there are downsides.' You wait, but he doesn't comment. 'What would you say the downsides are here, Finney? I won't breathe a word to anyone.'

He waits a while, sizing up your promise of discretion. In time, he seems to take it at face value. 'Undoubtedly, Colonel Hurley can be rather exacting.'

'Undoubtedly. And unpredictable at times, I expect. Rather – shall we say – volcanic?'

'I'm sure we could say that.'

'And what of the others?'

He slowly glances towards the empty hallway, assuring himself that there are no eavesdroppers. 'Mr Gervaise's caprices can be difficult to work around. The colonel's other son,' you note a tone of mild contempt, 'requires a lot of *looking after*.'

'Rather like a child,' you suggest.

'If you wish to use those words, Dr Tenor, it wouldn't be my place to contradict you.'

Yes, he's a sharp one, Finney. Sharp, sharp, sharp.

There is a sound from the floor above. Someone walking about, reminding you that you are not entirely private. It's probably time you went to bed.

Turn to 21

123

On your way to the Minster you spot your original quarry: Julia. She is poking through some glass trinkets on a costermonger's cart without too much interest.

'Julia, precious!' Melissa calls. Her old friend looks around and smiles nervously when she sees it is you.

'Oh, hello,' she says. 'I was just looking at these things. Isn't the ballerina pretty?'

It's utter tat, and you and Melissa exchange a glance that tells you that you are of one mind on that score.

'We've just bumped into your hubby,' Melissa informs her.

'Oh, yes?' Julia says, making a poor attempt at sounding light. Whatever he's up to, she knows about it and she isn't over the moon about it.

Melissa softens her voice. 'Julia, darling, you know that you can tell me anything. Have you got mixed up in something?'

'Mixed up?' She says it as if not having the faintest idea what the phrase means.

'Julia. We're old, old friends.'

Julia bites her lip in a childish sort of way and looks downcast. Yes, she has something on her mind that she doesn't want to share. 'I always wanted to . . . be good to people,' she says. 'Good to you, to Constantinos.'

'I know, darling.'

'But I've been wavering. I haven't been committed enough.' She nods her head, as if telling herself off for bad behaviour. Loyalty should have its limits, and you wonder if hers has been pushed beyond them.

'What do you mean by that?' Melissa sounds concerned.

'I should have been more ready for what he needed from me.'

This is starting to sound alarming.

'Who?' Melissa demands.

For a second, it looks like Julia is about to confess to something. She opens her mouth, forming words, but then someone behind her drops one of the glass figurines, the breaking glass makes Julia jump and her resolve – whatever it was – falters. 'I'm sorry,' she mumbles, and she scuttles away without looking back.

'What on earth was that about?' Melissa says, half to herself, half to you.

'I couldn't say. But I think sooner or later we will find out.'

There's nothing for it but to continue on your path to find Nanny Tiggy.

Turn to 16

124

As you walk through the arched stone doorway you feel his eyes burning into your back.

Inside, you find all those who have passed before you gathered in a circle in front of the altar. Their torches provide the only light, rippling across the walls, through the choir seats that are carved with faces and strange animals and over the windows depicting the suffering of Christ on the cross and his eventual resurrection. Murals on the walls depict the same story. The red glow flickers over everyone's faces now, turning them from pilgrims and penitents to demons incarnate. They could be emissaries of the devil who have stolen into the church to rob and destroy it. When you look at Mina her eyes are closed, but then they flick open and meet yours. On the floor, silver chalices filled to the brim with dark red wine surround a steel bowl of water. As you take your place in the circle your face is reflected in it, gently shimmering and shaking.

The last of the servants enter, followed by the colonel. And then the door slams shut. The colonel walks towards you, with the dagger held high once more.

He makes his way into the centre of the circle, which closes up behind him. His voice booms and echoes in the empty church, reflecting off the hard, cold stone walls. 'In the name of our master, we come together to pledge fealty,' he announces.

'Fealty, fealty, fealty,' you all chant.

'Gervaise, speak.'

Gervaise looks uncharacteristically nervous, you think to yourself. He attempts speech, but his first words are no more than a croak. He shakes his head and tries again. 'I stand here, before my ancestors and my God, to pledge my fealty to the one true family.'

'Will you suffer pain?'

'I will suffer pain.'

'Will you pledge your life?'

'I will pledge my life.'

'Then drink.' And Hurley stoops, collects a chalice of wine, holds it to Gervaise's mouth and pours, until it spills down his lips and streams to the stone floor. 'When will our time come again?'

'When the master decrees it.'

'Then drink.' He pours wine into his son's mouth once more. Led by Mina, you all begin to process in a circle around them both, the flames from your torches twisting and bending with your movement. A spinning circle of fire that could be a gateway to hell.

'When the hour comes, what will this be?'

'This will be the blood of those who spilled ours.'

'Then drink.' And this time there's a deep menace to Colonel Hurley's words and the wine is drained from the cup. Gervaise grabs the chalice and holds it above his head, empty now. 'Your time will come.'

'My time will come!'

And all – all but you – repeat his words. 'My time will come.'

It's at that very moment that the cogs begin to turn in your mind. The faith, the family that has been at Hurley Court since Tudor times, through the Civil War, the Napoleonic Wars, the Great War. And, above all, the Religious Wars. And murals of the crucifixion on the walls of an Anglican church that somehow escaped the Reformation?

Of course! The Hurleys are Catholic recusants! Practising their faith in secret when the punishment for pledging their fealty to the Pope and the old rites was to be burned at the stake. And yet, it is strange how the ritual of secret faith has been robbed of its meaning over the centuries, leaving it now just a relic.

At a signal from the colonel, you all cast your torches into the bowl of water, extinguishing them.

The darkness is perfect. You could have been blinded. But in your mind's eye, you still see the circle of fire spinning.

For a long while the only sound is breath. In the silence, no one moves. Your ears attune and you begin to pick out the faintest noises: distant creatures calling, the wind winding around the church, the movement of clothing.

And then, suddenly, it all changes. There's a gasp, a muffled voice, chaotic footsteps on the stones. And what's that? The sound of a struggle! A shout of 'No!' A cry of fear.

'What's happening?' you hear Mina yell out.

'He's got it!' It's the colonel's voice, full of fury. 'Give it to . . .'

'Who's . . .'

Then a shout of pain, a man's pain. 'My God! Help me!'

'Where are you?' a male voice calls out.

There's a spark. A lighter! Someone is attempting to throw some light on the scene. A tiny flame flickers. But then something thuds past you and a hand knocks the lighter flying. You hear it rattle and skid on the floor. Instantly you drop to the flagstones and feel for it. The voice calls out for help again.

If you rush for the voice that has cried out for help, turn to 45

If you try to find the lighter, turn to 30

125

York's museum is a real treasure trove, with a rich collection that begins with Bronze Age tools and artefacts, stretches through the Roman period when the town hummed to the sound of legionary footsteps and encompasses the era when the Vikings made it their home in England.

Tim is standing with his hands clasped before him, a boyish look of wonder on his face as he peers into a case of Roman coins. He jumps when you call his name.

'Oh, hello,' he says, flustered. 'I didn't know you would be coming.'

'I do like digging up the deeds of the past,' you say.

He looks alarmed. 'What do you mean by . . .'

That's a curious over-reaction. 'I don't mean anything by it, Tim. Other than that it's my profession. As a pathologist.'

He pulls himself together. 'Oh, right, yes, of course.'

Melissa and you exchange glances. You try to put Tim at his ease. 'Have you found much of interest?'

'It's an excellent museum, really. I loved reading about the Romans when I was a boy, and here they are, in all their glory.'

Yes, you can see Tim as a ten-year-old poring over books about legionaries fighting the Celtic hordes.

'I remember learning about them at school. Escaping into their world,' you say.

'Yes. Escaping. I needed that.'

You get a sense that his school days weren't a bed of roses for him. 'Childhood isn't always the happiest time.'

He meets your gaze. 'No. It wasn't. So I liked stories and history.' He looks back to the coins, a little bit sadly.

'Your parents?'

He speaks without looking at you. 'Father was very demanding. He had no time for stories. I had to follow in his footsteps.' He pulls a rueful smile.

You can see it's a painful subject and you've heard enough. 'Where next?' you ask.

He brightens up. 'Oh, I did want a cream bun.'

'You always do, Tim,' Melissa laughs. 'No self-control, that's your problem.'

He looks sheepish at this dig. More than you would have expected – maybe it's what his father would have said. 'I'm sorry,' he says, looking at his feet. 'I'll do better.'

'Oh, it's all right, you goose. Have a cream bun if it makes you feel better.'

'Actually, I don't really want one now. Look, if it's all the same, I'll just head off and see the Viking rooms.'

He shambles away, cutting a bit of a sad figure. 'Whatever did I say?' Melissa asks.

'He found that comment about a lack of self-control quite hurtful,' you tell her.

'Was it so very strong?'

'No,' you say. 'That's what's interesting about it. Now, let's go and find your old nanny.'

Turn to 123

126

You leave the shop, chatting, bidding another beadle a good morning, then head out onto the busy pavement of Piccadilly. Omnibuses emblazoned with adverts for Pears soap and Bovril roll along as a knot of urchins charges through the gentlefolk, and everyone looks cheery for the festive season. A break in the motor traffic allows you to step into the road towards the brightly decorated window of Hatchards bookshop. Your pal Alicky – named, exotically, after the Russian crown princess Alexandra – has a new volume out on the ruins of Pompeii, and you want to buy a copy. 'Do you mind if . . . *look out!*' you cry, wrenching Melissa out of the path of a speeding car. Its brass wing mirror glances off her hip, knocking her over, but the vehicle doesn't slow one bit. Melissa falls, but you catch her and you both stumble back to the pavement. A policeman who has witnessed what happened furiously blows his whistle at the car. But you can only watch it turn up Regent Street and disappear. If anything, it is accelerating as it goes. And, suspiciously, the registration number is covered in mud so as to make it unreadable.

'Are you all right, madam?' the officer asks Melissa.

'Quite all right, thank you,' she insists, standing and dusting herself down. She turns to you. 'I'll have a hell of a bruise here in the morning,' she says, rubbing her side. 'Now, did you see?'

'I did,' you say. 'A blue car. A man wrapped up in a muffler.' There's no doubt about it. 'I think I had better come with you to Harrogate after all.'

'Wonderful. Be at King's Cross at eleven thirty.'

Turn to 64

127

'Sorry, Mrs Thresh, so sorry!' calls a white-haired woman running towards you. 'I got caught up in the traffic and the young man driving the cab, well, he didn't know how to get here, and I said, "How can you be a cabbie and not know how to get to King's Cross station?" and he answered back to me with some cheek about only just having become a cabbie and it's in his blood, but he really wanted to be a circus performer.'

You all agree that this young man should certainly be reported to the relevant authority.

'Poor old Nanny Tiggy, you have been through the wars, haven't you?' says Melissa with a discreet wink in your direction.

'Now, Mrs Thresh, I did so enjoy being your nanny when you were little, but I don't think it's right that you should call me so, not now, not at my time of life – why, I'm all of seve . . . sixty, and with arthritis and all.'

'Quite right, Miss Tiggworth. I shall make certain to address you more formally in future.'

'Well, I'm not sure that . . .'

'No,' Melissa says, holding up a hand. 'No more shall

you be "Nanny Tiggy", no more shall you be "silly old bear". From now on, it's formality all the way.'

'Oh.' The old servant looks a little crestfallen.

'Of course,' says Melissa, softening, 'that doesn't mean that we can't have tea and crumpets together most nights.'

'Oh.' And a smile breaks across her face.

'I shall never abandon you. Not like you abandoned me when I was ten.'

'Now, Mrs Thresh, you know full well that I wasn't very well for a while. And your father arranged a very suitable replacement.'

'A dreadful old witch who used to wash my mouth out with soap and water if I used language unbecoming of a young lady, as she described it,' Melissa tells you as an aside.

Tiggy looks rather upset. 'It was not a happy time,' she says, her eyes watering a little.

'Now, now, let's not dwell on the past. Why don't you get settled. We have a long journey ahead of us.'

'That we have,' Nanny Tiggy replies, gamely jumping up into the carriage.

'See that she's comfortable, Freddie.'

'If I must,' he replies, clambering up.

'Ah, and here are Pererin and Simon Yarrow.' A strikingly pretty fair-haired girl in her mid-twenties and her husband, who looks about a decade older than her, with black hair slicked back and neatly parted down the middle, are coming towards you. Her clothes are not exactly cheap, but anything would look dowdy next to the outlandish costume flaunted by Melissa. The husband is grinning widely at you all. 'She's Tim's secretary. Her hubby there used to play association football for a famous team, I'm told. Not that it's really my cup of tea, you understand.'

'Mine neither, I must confess,' you reply.

'He works as a driver for us from time to time now. Tim invited them along. I thought, why not? The more the merrier.'

'Good afternoon, Mrs Thresh,' the girl says, drifting doe-like eyes from her husband to her employer.

'Hello, Pererin. And Simon, nice to see you here.'

'Wouldn't miss it for the world, Mrs Thresh. Got me costume all ready. I'm comin' as a footie player.'

'Right,' Melissa says. 'So, as yourself, really.'

'That's right, that's right.'

'Who did you play for?' you ask.

He looks delighted by your enquiry. 'Arsenal. You follow the game?'

'Not all that much,' you admit.

'Well, Arsenal's the best team there is. There was one match against Sheffield Wednesday, and I scored from a corner. Bent it right in! The crowd just 'bout lost their 'eads!' He gets a faraway look in his eyes as he remembers past glories. 'And let me tell you about the Shield final. We'd—'

'Not again, Simon,' his wife says, clearly bored by his tales. That she doesn't even try to sugar the pill tells you she has been here more than once. 'I'll tell the story myself later. I know it word for word. Let's just get in.' You feel a bit sorry for Simon. He was clearly in his element, regaling groups with stories of old matches. He just had the wrong audience.

'All right, all right. Up 'ere, is it?' He jerks his thumb towards the carriage.

'Up there, yes.'

'Cor, you do pick the nice fings in life, don'tcha? Right, up y'go, girl.' And he follows his wife up into the train.

At the front, grey smoke begins to drift up from the stack. 'They're getting ready,' Melissa says. 'Julia and Constantinos had better arrive soon or they'll be chasing us on foot. They're late already.'

'And they are?'

'The Georgious. Old chums of mine. He's all right, but he'll talk your ear off about how awful the new Greek republic is. I was at school with Julia. Her father was ambassador to Greece, which is how they met.'

'Fancy.'

'Ah, talk of the devil.' A couple are marching along the platform. She is a short and wide thing with excitement animating her face, and he is shorter and wider still. 'Come on, hurry up, you two!'

The Georgious pick up the pace. Melissa introduces you and they seem friendly, though Constantinos's accent makes it a little tricky to hear any nuances.

'How do you know Melissa and Freddie?' he asks.

'We are all members of the same birdwatching society,' you inform him. In your experience, the odder the explanation, the more people take it at face value. You see Melissa force down a smile.

'Oh! It's not something I ever knew she enjoyed,' blurts out Julia. She has a high and piping voice.

'Oh, yes, always up for a good watch. That's me,' Melissa tells her.

'So what are those?' Julia asks, pointing to some birds perched on one of the steel rafters.

'Pigeons.'

'Oh, yes, I suppose they are.'

'Do you have your costumes?'

'Yes, we have,' replies Constantinos, beckoning a porter, who is red-faced and sweaty, carrying an enormous trunk on his shoulder. 'We shall appear as George the First of Greece and his queen, Olga. I have a photograph of them.' He reaches into his pocket and pulls out a carefully folded print. 'Do you know my country?'

'I have visited some of the archaeological sites in your islands.'

'I can tell you that you have not seen one twentieth of my country's historical riches.'

'Is that so?' There's pride in one's nation, but the light of zeal is shining in his eyes. 'I shall have to return.'

'I hope I can one day show you them myself.'

'All right, you two, enough gossiping, up you get,' Melissa orders us.

And you all climb up into the coach. It's beautifully appointed inside, with a curtained-off luggage section at the back that is already stuffed with everyone's bags, and a rather comfortable lounge area, complete with fully stocked bar, at the other end. The seats line the sides, facing in, and the floor is carpeted, so that the whole effect is of a mid-ranking club.

Freddie is already making use of the bar. He knocks back a glass of amber liquid and offers to pour one for anyone else who wants to wet their throat.

'Let me,' says Simon Yarrow. 'I grew up in me grandad's pub. Now. Port 'n' lemon for the ladies.' He mixes drinks for his wife, for Julia, for your hostess Melissa and even for old Nanny Tiggy, who takes a gentle sip and then knocks back the rest in a single gulp. 'Crikey, slow down, old girl,' Simon says under his breath.

'It's medicinal. For the arthritis,' the old retainer explains. 'Perhaps another.' She holds out her glass.

'All right.' He looks dubious, and you notice that he puts less port and more lemon in this time before handing it over.

'What a wonderful time we have ahead of us,' Melissa announces. 'Now, Constantinos, be a dear and tell the guard that we're ready to roll away.'

He salutes gamely and sticks his head out of the door. 'We're ready to depart,' he informs the man, who lifts his green flag and blows his whistle. The whistle is answered by a deeper one from the locomotive, and five seconds later you feel the engine begin to chug and the wheels begin to turn. You're off!

Turn to 95

Discover more from *Sunday Times* bestseller Gareth Rubin . . .

The TURNGLASS

'Vivid, resonant, melancholy and beautiful' JANICE HALLETT

1880s England

On the bleak island of Ray, off the Essex coast, an idealistic young doctor, Simeon Lee, is called from London to treat his cousin, Parson Oliver Hawes, who is dying. Parson Hawes, who lives on the only house on the island – Turnglass House – believes he is being poisoned. And he points the finger at his sister-in-law, Florence. Florence was declared insane after killing Oliver's brother in a jealous rage and is now kept in a glass-walled apartment in Oliver's library. And the secret to how she came to be there can be found in Oliver's tête-bêche journal, where one side tells a very different story from the other.

1930s California

Celebrated author Oliver Tooke, the son of the state governor, is found dead in his writing hut behind the family residence, Turnglass House. His friend Ken Kourian doesn't believe that Oliver would take his own life. His investigations lead him to the mysterious kidnapping of Oliver's brother when they were children, and the subsequent secret incarceration of his mother, Florence, in an asylum. But to discover the truth, Ken must decipher clues hidden in Oliver's final book, a tête-bêche novel – which is about a young doctor called Simeon Lee . . .

'A stunning, ingenious, truly immersive mystery.
***The Turnglass* is a thrilling delight'**
CHRIS WHITAKER

Available in paperback, eBook and audio

HOLMES AND MORIARTY

A new Sherlock Holmes novel, endorsed by the Conan Doyle Estate.

Two adversaries. One deadly alliance.
Together, can they unlock the truth?

Sherlock Holmes and his faithful friend, Dr John Watson, have been hired by actor George Reynolds to help him solve a puzzle. George wants them to find out why the audience who comes to see him perform every night are the same people, only wearing disguises. Is something sinister going on and, if so, what?

Meanwhile, Holmes' arch-enemy, Professor Moriarty, is in danger. Implicated in the murder of a gang leader, Moriarty and his second, Colonel Moran, must go on the run from the police in order to find out who is behind the set-up.

But their investigation puts them in the way of Holmes and Watson, and it's not long before all four realise that they are being targeted by the same person. With countless lives on the line, including their own, they must form an uneasy alliance in order to unmask the true villain. The trail leads them to a hotel in Switzerland and a conspiracy far greater than any of them expected, who can be trusted – and will any one of them survive?

'Beautifully written and perfectly capturing the Holmesian spirit. And, yes, sometimes I side with Prof. Moriarty, and I don't care who knows it. Love an evil genius . . .'
VASEEM KHAN

Available in paperback, eBook and audio

SIMON &
SCHUSTER